USA TODAY BESTSELLING AUTHOR

J.D. HOLLYFIELD

To my readers. May you always feel worth it.

To my family. Thanks for requiring dinner every night and making this book take forever. Next book ya'll are getting chicken nuggies.

And so the lion fell in love with the lamb.
-Edward Cullen

Chapter One

Chase

UN-FUCKING-BELIEVABLE.

I chug my beer and jump off the barstool to grab another, tossing my empty bottle into the garbage next to Levi, one of my best-friends-turned-lame-ass, on the way.

"What's got your panties in a bunch, man?" Kipley, who hasn't seen his balls since he got married and had a baby, leans against the counter, sipping on... *Jesus, what is that? A spritzer?*

I stare him down, appalled he doesn't know why I'm appalled. My best friends have turned into a bunch of vaginas —that's what's wrong.

"First you, now *him*? I mean, you're seriously gonna let him go through with this? He banged your sister. You should kick his ass. Prevent this snuggle fest bullshit." I mean, who allows their best friend to defile their little sister and live to talk about it?

Kip, apparently, since he just laughs. "I already kicked his ass, and I'm fine with it. He loves her, man."

"So! I love lots of things. I don't turn crazy and buy a ring and set off to marry them all!" I can't believe Levi is

1

going to hand in his man card over a chick and propose. I scoff to myself and throw the fridge door open. Snatching a bottle, I twist the cap, needing the long pull of cold beer to calm me.

"Dude, why do you care so much? Relax."

I stare Kip down. How is it not obvious? "I care because our guys' nights have turned into tea parties. What happened to sports night, strip clubs, the casino?"

"We grew up—"

"*Exactly!* Ever since these chicks tied you down, it's like you have no balls. You never want to go out. I heard you talking to Ben about goddamn diaper rash, and Levi just suggested we watch a fucking movie!"

Kip laughs again, irritating me further. "With the tantrum you're having, maybe you could use some diaper rash cream." He ducks as I whip my bottle cap at his head. "Come on, chill out. One day, you'll find a girl who sweeps you off your pretty feet, and you'll be here, laughing at this moment, suggesting we watch *The Notebook*."

If I could throw my beer at him, I would. Instead, I drain it. "Fuck no."

"What're we talking about?" Levi walks in from taking a call from Hannah, Kip's little sister, who's having her own girls' night with Stacey, Kip's ball and chain. May as well throw *anchor* in there since he's plummeting deep into whipped status.

"Chase is having another moment," Kip answers.

Levi eyes me. "Dude, again? He's *completely* okay with Hannah and me."

I shrug my shoulders. "Are you sure? I mean, you banged his sister. Baby Hannah. He should kick your ass."

"He already kicked my ass." He chuckles, then goes to the fridge for a beer.

I slam my empty beer bottle on the counter. "Whatever. These chicks, man. They have you all brainwashed. Even Ben.

Look at his sorry ass sitting on the couch texting like a girl!" We all look over, finding Ben, a cheeky grin on his face.

"Hey, don't hate the playa. These Tinder chicks love me. I'm a swipe right commodity."

I shake my head. "We should have taken my suggestion."

"Sorry, bro, can't do strip clubs."

"Or the casino."

"Yeah, I got super sick after that night you tried slipping me ecstasy," Ben chimes in, barely lifting his nose from his phone.

"Fine," I grumble, pushing off the counter and grabbing my jacket. "You girls have fun knitting ball sac holders for your girlfriends and wives. I'm outta here." The room full of laughing jerks is silenced as I throw the door shut behind me.

I warned them all. Chicks require commitment. And with commitment comes a jail sentence. They insist on stealing your livelihood and demanding you spend every waking minute with them, ditching all your old ways—all of which were just fine before *they* came and ruined everything. I never once heard Ben complain on a strip club night. Or Levi when we went on long trips for football games and tailgating. Even Kipley, who's been tied to his girl since high school, didn't make a peep when we had our three-day golf outings and got so plastered he woke up missing his pants, only to find them up in a tree outside our rental house.

Traitors.

I step outside and search for an Uber, putting in the Wild Horse bar as my destination. I always get lucky there. Tons of chicks with no expectations. Thank God. One minute away. I raise my head to the sky and breathe in the crisp night air, contemplating finding new friends. The Uber pulls up, and I throw myself into the backseat, shoving my hands through my impeccable sandy-blond hair. All the good times, the fun we had…it's all come to a halt. Fun isn't even in their vocabulary. One by one, they're getting neutered. Those chicks must have magical vaginas. There's no other way to explain how they're doing it.

"S'up, man?" the driver says. "See you're headed to the Wild Horse. Hope you're single. I just dropped off my third carload of chicks there. Seems to be the place tonight if you're looking for a good time."

Now he's speaking my language. I sit forward. "Oh yeah? Do tell."

"Think you're the one who's gonna have to tell *me*. Wish I wasn't on the clock. Otherwise, I'd make a stop there myself."

Hells yeah! Chicks. Tons of them. My kind of night. "Well, let's get a move on, my man." I lean back, feeling a little less uptight and more intrigued by the night to come.

∼

The driver drops me off, handing me his card if I need a ride home. I thank him and make my way into the bar. The place is packed. Nineties music blares from the speakers along the packed dancefloor. He wasn't lying. Chicks are everywhere. There has to be a solid eight-to-two ratio.

I brush my palms together. "Gotta love wedding season." Every female within a hundred-mile radius celebrating their bestie, cousin, sister's last outing of singlehood. Bridesmaids are my specialty. And the single ones are the easiest to spot. Always dressed in outfits that would make their grannies keel over.

Little things set each bridesmaid apart. The married ones always have their tits on full display, though they still wear their family locket with their kids and husband around their neck. The ones who have boyfriends love to flash all aspects of their body and offer themselves on the dancefloor, knowing their friends will pull them away before anything goes too far. And then there are the single ones—the ones thirsty for attention and waiting for someone like me to swoop in, charm their panties off, and offer them a night to remember.

My single lady radar is off the charts. Like a hungry lion who just walked into a den full of prey, my Cheshire smile almost hurts as I head over to the bar. I need a drink or two before I choose my main course for the night.

"What can I get ya, bud?" the bartender asks as I slide onto an open stool.

"Double tequila soda." I slap a twenty onto the bar and rotate in my stool to get a full view of the menu. Brunette? Redhead? Maybe a blonde—?

Sniffling from my right steals my attention. I twist on the stool to check out the poor sap next to me, not sure how anyone can strike out when there's enough to go around.

"Hey...uh, you okay?" I ask, shocked to find a petite blonde. Blondes aren't typically my first pick—especially not crying ones. My comfort level dips. The girl doesn't answer me as another tear slides down her cheek.

I tap my foot on my chair and look over to the bartender, hoping he hurries up with my drink so I can move on. Consoling crying chicks is more Ben's department.

"Sorry, I've just...my...my..."

Ahhh...let me guess. The breakup cry. I've been the saving grace for a few of those. No better way to get over one than to get under another. Looks like this may be my department after all.

"...dad. He just passed away."

Way off. Shame I don't do mourning chicks. They require lots of cuddling afterward—not my area of expertise. She turns toward me as I let her down gently. "Yeah, sorry but —*sweet Jesus*..." I choke as she removes her hands from her face and I catch my first sight of her. I swear, an angel just fell from heaven and landed next to me. Words escape me. I stutter out some, but it's all gibberish. Shit. I blink. My dick pokes at my jeans, wanting a peek for himself.

"Are…are *you* okay?" Her voice is as magical as the mouth it's coming from. *Mmm, mouth. Pink, plump—*

"Hello?"

Who? What?

I shake my head. "Uh…yeah. Fine." Just confused how anyone can be so painstakingly beautiful—say *what?* I need to rip my eyes away and search out the pussy who just used the words *painstakingly beautiful.* Tears stain her rosy cheeks. Her skin practically sparkles. Not like my favorite vampire movie, which is fucking awesome—*keeping that one to myself*—but damn, is this chick flawless. I take in her eyes, a deep set of silver sparkling with flecks of blue, sucking me into a trance. I feel like a damn bug flying into the blue light.

Shit, what's wrong with me?

It has to be her eyes. I've never seen anything like them. And her lips. Soft. Pillowy. I'm suddenly willing to give up my right testicle to know what they taste like. *What the hell is happening?* Am I having an existential crisis? Nervous breakdown? This chick is no angel, more like the devil trying to get me to change my ways. And she seems to be winning. All I can think about is holding her, talking to her, taking her out.

"*Jesus, who are you?*" The words come blurting out. I place the back of my hand against my forehead. Do I have a fever? The bartender places my drink on the bar, and I take an impressive pull.

"Excuse me?" Her voice is soft and angelic, the sound of innocence banging on my door of damnation. "Are you *sure* you're okay?" She eyes me warily—a look I'm not used to receiving from an attractive girl…or any female. I flip through my mental Rolodex for lines to smooth this over, so she doesn't think I'm a complete freak, but everything that comes out is wrong.

"Yeah, just feel funny—no, I mean, I'm hungry—I mean…yeah, I'm hungry, but that's not why—have you seen

Twilight? Maybe we could go out sometime and watch—*Jesus!*"
I grab my glass and drain it. That confirms it. She's been sent
straight from the devil to break me. I, Chase Steinberg, will
not be broken by a chick.

A smile creeps across her face, revealing two dimples, and
I fall farther under her spell.

She bites on her lower lip. "I've actually never seen it."

I spit my drink out all over the bar. "What? Impossible!
Everyone's seen—" *What the fuck am I doing?* "I mean…I just
thought all chicks were into that kind of shit." I need to get
out of here before she sucks away my soul…amongst other
things. Shit, my best friend down below twitches at the
thought. Those lips. Those innocent demon eyes—

"Bartender! I'll take another. Actually—make it two." I
need to drown out these foreign sensations jostling inside my
chest. Even her clothes are doing weird things to me, and she's
not even done up like she's at a bachelorette party in dire need
of my services. She's dressed more casually in a pair of tight
jeans, the two rips at her knees giving me a tease of her
creamy skin, and a black tank top revealing her small, perky
chest.

"Well, I'm not like other chicks. Anyway, sorry to bother
you with my problems. I was just hoping—"

"I will." The words shoot off my tongue before my brain
cares to hear the rest of her question. When you have two
heads thinking for you, one always comes through before the
other.

"You will?" She looks surprised, but those lips—pure, soft
lips—curl into a smile made from heaven, and I fall down the
rabbit hole of all things her.

I sit straighter in my chair, brushing away the nonexistent
wrinkles from my shirt. I have no idea why. "Yeah, sure.
Whatever you want. We can just sit here and talk if you
want." *What the goddamn hell just came out of my mouth?*

The bartender finally brings over my drinks. I snatch one

glass and chug it, wincing at the burning in my throat, wondering who's taken control of my mind and body. I've never in my life offered to just talk to a girl. At least not this kind of talking. And I just offered to listen!

I turn back to her. "Are you the devil?" Shit, that was rude. But also vital.

Her laugh is anything but evil, tickling every nerve-ending in my body. "I don't think so. I've been known to disobey my God a time or two, but I'm definitely no devil." Her teeth are white and perfect. I bet she brushes three times a day, up, down, left to right, just like that dental hygienist told me the night she was sucking—*shit, focus.* "Are *you* the devil?" she throws back, her curious eyes and tender smile telling me to shut the hell up and stop ruining this.

"Well, that depends. What kind of company are you looking for tonight?" *There I am!* Finally, laying down the first Chase Steinberg pick-up line. Phew. I was getting nervous there for a second.

Her eyes flutter as she leans forward, her knees brushing against mine. "I'm hoping for you to keep me company *all* night. If that's something you can manage, I say we get out of here. If not, I'll understand and be on my way."

On her way? As in, she would walk out of this bar *alone*? Ditch her mission? Part of me wants nothing to do with just being her company. The big guy down below and I have rules. This one seems different. She deserves more than *that* type of company. But if I don't say yes, what will she do? I can't let her down. She looks so…*lonely.*

Nice excuse, asshole.

"So, what's it going to be? I've had a long day and have an even longer one tomorrow."

"Lead the way, Angel." *Someone seriously kick my ass after this.*

She reaches around, digs in her purse, tosses a few bucks on the bar, and stands, putting the purse strap over her shoulder. I throw another twenty on the bar and, like a dog obeying his master, follow her out of the bar. We're both quiet as we walk through the parking lot to a red Volkswagen Beetle. "I'm staying just a few blocks up at the Sheraton…unless you're not into this."

For the first time since our strange encounter, she appears nervous. I need my flirtatious charm to kick in and smooth things over so she doesn't back out. Her car keys jitter in her hand as she waits for my response.

I eliminate the few feet separating us and do what I do best: finesse my way into her personal space, leaving her no option but to press back against her car. Leaning into her, I grant myself the feel of her lush body against mine. She shivers the moment we make contact, and I love every second of it. I dip my head. Our lips are close, only a breath away, but I don't go in for the kill. I wait it out, curious if she'll accept my advance or turn away. An unfamiliar emotion swarms inside my chest at the thought of her denying me. I've been rejected plenty, but not by someone like her.

"Seriously, I'm in. For whatever. I told you, if you just want to talk, that's fine too." Someone cut my balls off right the fuck now! I don't do sweet, innocent talking. Why am I so damn insistent on it? I need to cut it out. No talking! Unless it's the dirty kind. Filthy! I should kiss her. Hard and stern, so she knows I mean business. I'm all man and ready to keep every single finger-licking part of her body company tonight.

"Why do you keep asking that? Do *you* just want to talk? I didn't peg you as…you're not, like, a virgin or something, are you?"

Never in my life—*ever*—has someone mistaken me as inexperienced. I'm a stallion. Highly rated by all females— even those who'd like to see me dead. Virgin? Oh, screw this—

A sexy little squeal falls from her pretty pink lips as I throw my hand around her neck and crush my lips against hers. I wondered what her lips would taste like. *Cherries.* And what

9

they would feel like. *Goddamn heaven*. Her warm flesh under my palm is as smooth as silk. I press harder into her, breaching her soft lips, getting a full taste of her against my tongue. She's slow to react, probably shocked by my bold move. Good. She needs to know who's in charge here. I motherfuckin' am.

My confidence returns as a purring melody spills from her mouth, her moan just as enticing as her plump lips. My hips brush against her, just light enough for her navel to graze my hard-on. Her small hand grabs my shirt, gripping it for dear life. I reach behind her, cup her ass cheeks, and raise her up against her car. I deepen our kiss, not leaving a single inch of her mouth untouched.

By the time I pull back, I almost expect the sun to be up. God, I could suffocate on her. When I drop her feet back to the ground, her eyes are still closed, allowing me to get a good look at her. The streetlight shines in the distance, illuminating her flushed cheeks and pink lips, now swollen from our incredible kiss. Shit, I want to go back for more. Nibble on her bottom lip. I bask in the beauty of her cute little nose, the lining of her neck, the dip in her tank top revealing what's in store. *Damn, what I wouldn't give to get a peepshow of this every day.*

"Still trying to decide if I'm the devil?"

I bring my eyes up to meet hers. Silvery orbs peer back at me, and I get lost in the beauty of her uniqueness. Never have I met a girl with such mysterious eyes.

"No. I'm realizing you may be an angel."

Her lips curve into a sexy smile. I raise my hand to her chin, grazing up the side of her cheek with my knuckles. "What's it gonna be, Angel?" That little taste isn't nearly enough. I need to get her naked and feast on the full meal. A slight shiver rolls through her. She masks her nerves with a smile that threatens to take me out by my knees and have my big buddy below burst through my favorite pair of jeans.

"Prefer less talking and more company. You good with that?"

This chick. "Completely."

"Then let's go have some fun."

I'm as quiet as a mouse, obeying her strict orders of no talking while we make the short drive to her hotel and even shorter walk up to her room. The second the door is unlocked, she's on me. Her boldness startles me, but I'm totally down. I kick the door shut as my hands cup her tight ass and bring her little frame against me. And damn, let me be the first to admit there's no better feeling than having this tiny woman wrapped around me.

Unlike our last kiss, she takes the lead on this one. I walk us farther into her hotel room, savoring her smell: cherries and vanilla and all things that spike my appetite. She's frantic, pressing her lips firmly against mine. The sensitive side of me that's been out of commission for a while wants to tell her to slow down because I want to enjoy this. But my dick tells me to keep this movin'.

My growl of approval matches hers when her tongue connects with mine. I snap, losing focus on who's really in control. Her hands linger in my hairline, pulling at the base of my scalp. I throw us onto the bed, grinding into her. She shows no mercy, tugging so hard, I think she pulls out a chunk of my hair.

I do love an aggressive girl, but this one's different. There's desperation in her force. She needs something from me, and damn straight, I'm going to give it to her. I tear my lips from hers, leaning up and stealing a glance before doing what I've been dying to do since we met. I reach for her tank top and slide it up her stomach, her porcelain skin now on display.

Goosebumps sprout in my wake. I bend down, pressing my warm lips right above her belly button. Just like every other part of her, she tastes divine. My tongue skates up her firm belly until I'm gifted with her tits. My hands stop and admire what God gave her, squeezing them in my hands. Her back is off the mattress the second I pinch her tiny nipples through her lace bra. Freeing one of her breasts, I cover her nipple with my mouth.

"Jesus," she moans, taking out more of my hair.

"Not Jesus, but I'll take the compliment." I smile against her nipple and bite down. Another arch of her taut little body. I can't help but tighten my hold as she pebbles in my mouth. *Goddamn, put a fork in me—I'm done. I can die happy.* But what fun would that be? Releasing her, I offer the same attention to her other breast, loving the way she bucks under me, which gives me a high like no other. I ache for another hit. She's about to turn me into an addict. I release her from my mouth with a pop and continue my happy journey of removing her top. When it's gone and tossed to the floor, my view is glorified perfection. Hot pink is definitely my new favorite color. Bright lace covers her breasts, leaving the enticing appeal of pale flesh and pink nipples.

"You sure are a sight for sore eyes," I praise, my hands brushing up her sides. My mouth waters at the thought of my lips around her entire breast, licking up her neck and kissing her deeply. I'm so needy, so desperate, I can't sort out which to attack first. "Fuck it," I say out loud, bending forward and taking her mouth. Her sweet moan is like dessert before dinner. I kiss her hard, demanding more contact, appreciating how responsive she is when she kisses me back.

I should slow down, make this last. This night hasn't even started, and I never want it to end. Her hips push off the bed, rubbing against my hard-on. I almost bite her tongue as I groan out. So much for going slow. I inch back, grinding against her. The connection almost blinds me as I repeat the action, sending us both into a whirlwind of bliss. This is some high school, dry-humping stuff, but holy shit, it's the best dry-humping I've ever had.

I force myself to pull away, regretting it before my lips even leave hers.

"What? What's wrong?"

Nothing. Everything. I don't even know this chick's name and she's about to bring me to my knees. Every single thing I've learned and mastered over the years has gone out the window. I feel like a teenager trying not to prematurely ejaculate in my pants before I can get either of ours off.

"Absolutely nothing. Just thought this would be a bit more fun if we didn't have clothes between us." I wink at her, thanking myself for pulling it together. Nerves return, flooding her face, and I debate pulling back. Clothes are fine. I've never minded a nice, dry…

Before I finish my thought, she presses off the mattress. I throw my leg off the side so I'm no longer on top of her. Before I can assess her next move, her bra is unhooked and falling to the ground. She pauses, waiting for me to take the lead. I'm frozen, unable to pull my eyes away from her perky tits. Her hands are stalled at her jeans. I snap out of it, kicking into overdrive. I tear at my own jeans, my eyes never leaving hers. My pants get stuck at my ankle, and I tug hard, losing my balance. She tries to reach for me as I fall backwards right off the bed.

"Oh my God, are you okay?" She leans over as I pop up, still working on my damn jeans.

"Perfect." There! Off they go. I bring my focus back to her and notice she's already naked. "Jesus fucking Christ." I wipe my hands down my face, needing to wake up. She truly is an angel. She's on her knees, her back slightly arched, like my very own submissive. Her small hands rest on her creamy thighs, giving me a glimpse between them. Smooth, shaved, mine…

I mentally smack myself out of whatever haze I'm lost in and make a move. One foot in front of the other, I climb back on the bed, her eyes dipping down to my waist. They go wide, and I smirk. He *is* my best asset. I reach out for her, but she jolts back, grabbing my hands before I touch her.

"Wait. Before we…let me…" The bedsheets are in a knot under her tight grip.

I remain still, worried she wants to pull the plug on this. Maybe I should be the one to. She bites at the inside of her cheek, her knuckles turning white. Maybe this isn't what she—

I almost lose my balance when she jumps off the bed. My first thought is she's on the run. I twist to get a better look as she rounds the corner, positioning herself at the end of the bed. My eyebrows dip, trying to figure out what she's doing, when two hands thrust forward, throwing me against the mattress.

"What the—?"

She climbs on top of me, her legs straddling mine. As I lift my head, I watch hers bend forward. "Oh, Jesus," I moan, almost swallowing my tongue as she wraps her mouth around my dick. From uncertain to a bold little firecracker, she takes my cock in, sliding her tongue down my shaft and pulling back.

"Fuck." My head falls back, eyes rolling as she wets the tip of my cock, her tongue doing a little dance before taking me fully. My body jolts as my dick hits the back of her throat. Her hands tighten at the base, and she strokes me up and down, her head bobbing on the tip. I'm in heaven. Complete heaven. Her hair is like silk as I thrust my fingers through the softness. She doesn't need any assistance. She's doing a stellar job on her own, but I can't help the savage in me as I grip her hair tightly, guiding her to take me deeper.

"Yeah, like an angel," I moan, working my hips, feeling my balls tighten. Shit, I'm gonna come soon. I loosen my hold on her, offering her a chance to pull back or slow down. I don't want this to end sooner than it has to, but she doesn't take the bait. Dammit, she speeds up. "Fuck, Angel. I'm gonna…I'm gonna…"

I try to warn her, but she only takes me deeper. My hips thrust up once, twice, and I groan, practically choking on my own breath. She doesn't pull away, working every inch of me, until my body collapses back onto the bed. Jesus, that might have been the best blowjob I've ever had. I don't even know if my legs work anymore.

Shaking off the remaining buzzing sensation, I sit up, startling her.

"Where are you—?"

I flip her on her back, and the cute sound that leaves her lips puts a smile on my face as I tug her hips down and spread her pretty thighs. "Oh, you don't need to—*ohhh!*" She gasps as I cover her sweet cunt with my mouth. If it were possible so soon, I'd probably blow a load again at the mere taste of her. My tongue jolts forward, licking her, enjoying the way her thighs tremble against my head. With every swipe, her thighs tighten until I go for the gold, thrusting inside her pussy.

Her hips shoot off the bed, and my hands grab at her ass to hold her in place as she fights me. In and out, I tongue-fuck her, loving the way her body vibrates against me. With each lick, suck, and nibble, she falls apart around me, her pants and moans feeding the beast inside me. I can't hold back and thrust harder, faster, my fingers digging into her skin. Hell, maybe I *can* come again this soon. I'm hard as steel. My balls clench.

Her legs begin to death squeeze my face as she hits her peak. A scream, almost silent, breaks through, and her tight walls clench around my tongue as her cunt spasms. I lap at her juices like they're icing on a cake, feeling so high, I can't imagine having to stop.

All it takes is the mere thought of being inside her for me to pull away from the prettiest place on earth. "You're seriously God's most perfect creation," I praise, wiping at my chin. I jump off the bed, searching for my jeans to grab a condom from my wallet. When I look back at her, she's sitting up against the headboard, face flushed from her orgasm. "Hope you're prepared for a long night. I'm nowhere near done getting my fill of you." I prowl onto the bed, ripping the wrapper with my teeth and sliding the condom on. Reaching for her legs, I place her perfectly under me, then nudge them nice and wide, placing myself at her glistening center. My eyes travel up her taut belly, past her perfect tits, making my way to her silvery gaze.

I pause at the fleeting glimpse of unease. "You good?" I ask, worry suddenly swimming in her eyes. "Hey, if you don't—"

"No, I do," she quickly answers, grabbing for my neck and pulling me down. Our lips connect, and I dive right in, loving the way we fit together. I press the tip of my cock at her warmth, teasing her. Her body shivers beneath me, and I drive forward.

A low gasp breaks through the air between us as I growl in confusion, my eyes searching hers. "Jesus, Angel…are you…?"

Fuck. What did I just do?

The whole time—the nerves—it was because she was—

"Does it matter?"

Does it matter? Yeah. I'm not into taking a girl's virginity, and *yeah*, it fucking matters! *Would knowing have stopped you?* Fuck. That damn sensitive side says yes, but the asshole side— the side I'm more in tune with—says not a chance. After that first taste, she could have confessed she used to be a man and I wouldn't have given it a second thought.

I shake my head, not needing that kind of image blurring my mind. "No, but you could have warned me. I would have done things…taken things slower."

Her eyes fill with guilt. I grab at her chin, making her stay focused on me. "Listen, forget it. Did I hurt you? Do you want me to stop—?"

"No, please. I want this." She bites down on her bottom lip. I'm suddenly hyper aware of her heart beating against mine. I hold her eyes, searching for any signs that I should stop. Last thing I need is her changing her mind halfway through. "I'm good. Please." She takes me by surprise again, grabbing the back of my neck and claiming my mouth as she thrusts her hips up. I can't even fight off the groan at the way she feels around me. Her grip tightens, and a ripple of pleasure shoots down to my balls. The tension around her eyes warns me the pain has yet to subside, so I grab at her hips to keep her still.

"Easy there, Angel." I slowly pull out and wait to make sure she's okay before easing back in. Each time I enter her, I fight not to moan. She's so damn tight around me. "You okay?" I ask, my voice hoarse, full of pleasure.

"Yes, yes, please...more," she pants, her hands reaching forward and scratching down my back. I use a bit more force, thrusting into her. Her lips part, and a flutter of soft moans parade from her mouth. I pull back and thrust forward, over and over. A mist of sweat builds along my forehead as I work harder than I ever have to please this girl. My cock has never been happier. My hands caress every inch of her skin.

I. Can't. Get. Enough.

"You're like heaven. Does this feel good for you, Angel?"

"Yes, please, yes," she begs, finding the courage and meeting me thrust for thrust. She wraps her legs around my waist, giving me a deeper advantage, and I almost black out. Her pants become frantic. Her head thrashes from side to side. I grunt and hold my breath as her nails dig into my ass, fighting away my orgasm. No way do I want this to end.

Her breathing turns to quick whimpers. She's nearing the finish line. "Oh, God, I'm going to...Jesus, I'm going to —ahhh!"

The way her beautiful little cunt clenches around me as she falls over the edge of ecstasy...there's not a chance in hell I can hold on any longer. I drive into her two more times. My head arches back, and my eyesight shorts out as my own orgasm takes over. I heave forward, falling on top of her.

She holds me tight, her eyes never leaving mine. My lips

find hers, and I kiss her until her body relaxes. I take her lower lip into my mouth and nibble ever so gently, wondering why all lips aren't as addictive as hers. I've been around the block, and not a single girl has turned me into the mush I feel right now. Pulling back, I slide out of her, making sure not to hurt her.

"Hold on. Be right back." I walk into the bathroom, discard the condom, grab a hand towel, and soak it under the warm water before heading back to the bedroom.

"Oh, God, you don't have to—"

"It's Jesus, and I want to. Lay back." I smirk at her as she rolls her eyes, then press the warm compress between her thighs. I sneak a peek at her. Her eyes are now closed. Her cheeks are still flushed, looking like she just got the best ride of her life. I finish cleaning her up and stand, tossing the towel in the corner. "If you're tired, we can put on a movie and—"

This time, I'm the one who squeals. She catches me off guard, pouncing on me. "I'm not much for watching TV," she says, then slams her lips to mine. We almost tumble off the bed, but I find my balance and flip us, bringing her on top of me. "What are you into?" My lips tip up in a playful smile.

"Do you have any more condoms?"

Is the Pope Catholic? "I do."

"Then I say we make the most of our time together." She's back on me, her mouth on mine, her pussy grinding against my cock. My only thought is to pray this night never ends.

Chapter
Two

Chase

I'M COMPLETELY SPENT. SORE. BUT I'VE NEVER FELT BETTER. I stretch my arms out, basking in the sun against my face from the open hotel blinds. I flip over, ready to eat my angel for breakfast, but she's gone.

Sitting up, I peer around the room. Her clothes are no longer scattered around the floor. There's no trace of her. The only thing left that tells me she was even real is the faint scent of cherries.

I fall back against the bed, a smile so fucking huge spreading across my face. "Jesus…" I laugh at her nickname. What a pair we were. And what a pleasant surprise she turned out to be. Her being a virgin was unexpected, but her eagerness blew me away. She was a spitfire. And a bit of a masochist if the tattoo of her nails down my back is any indication.

"Shit…" I laugh again, shaking my head and throwing my legs off the bed. I walk into the bathroom and take a piss. She was so wild. Like an innocent bird finally let out of her cage, using her wings for the first time. Curious. Adventurous. Shy. Bold. Absolutely amazing.

A frown mars my lips as disappointment sets in. She left without saying goodbye. I want to tie her up and spend the rest of eternity pleasuring every single part of her.

My phone dings. I head back to the bedroom and pull it out of my jeans.

Benny: Where you at? Need me to pick you up for the party?

Party? What party? Who has a party this early in the— "Oh shit!" The Matthews' barbecue. Levi is proposing. Fuck. I scan the clock. It's almost ten. The party starts at eleven. Shit, how did I sleep this late? *Well...where should we start?* Forget it. I text Ben back, telling him to suck my dick and I'll drive myself.

I gather my shit and take off, pulling up my app to request an Uber. When I get home, I shower, letting out a mixture of hissing and laughing as the water stings my back, only to find more scratches on my ass cheeks. *Damn, that girl was a minx.*

I dress in my Sunday best, jump in my truck, and head over to the Matthews'. A smile on my face, I turn on the radio. As luck would have it, the perfect song comes on. "Wild Angels" by Martina McBride blares through my speakers as I swerve through traffic, trying to remember the last time I felt so...rejuvenated. I beat my fist on the steering wheel, belting the chorus as I pull into the Matthews' residence.

Mrs. Bealson, their ancient neighbor, glares at me from her front yard. I wave, offering her a wink, and blow her a kiss. Light on my feet, I skip up the walkway, pushing the doorbell. Man, while those pussy-whipped losers probably sat around holding hands while watching chick flicks, I had a night I can't wait to brag about.

I go to hit the doorbell again, seeing a silhouette coming to my rescue. As the door opens, I put my best smile on, ready to greet Mrs. Matthews and charm her off her feet so she gives me the first slice of her famous apple pie—

"What the *fuck*?"

"What are *you* doing here? Are you *following* me?"

"Following *you*?" I gawk back at Angel standing in the doorway. What the actual *fuck*?

"Seriously, you need to leave—"

"Hey, nice of you to show. Glad you stopped pouting." Kip leans over her shoulder, addressing me, but I'm too busy picking my chin up off the ground.

"What...who...she..." I've been rendered stupid.

"Huh? You okay, man? Rough night?" Kip laughs.

"Her." I just point. What the hell is going on? "Her... dad...dead..."

"Who, Bridget? She's my little cousin. Remember my dad's younger brother? The pastor?" *No, I certainly fucking do not.* She stands there, looking just as confused, making no move to tell her *cousin* we already know each other.

"Bridge, this is my best friend, Chase. Chase, Bridge. Oh, and, Chase, don't even think about it. Again, my uncle is a pastor who's very much alive. Poor Bridget isn't even allowed to hold a dude's hand until she's twenty-one."

He pats his *cousin* on the shoulder while *I* choke on my own breath. "*She's how—how—?*"

"Dude, don't barf on my front step. Come in or not. I gotta find Stace. The baby pooped again." Kip prepares to turn away from us before coming back to me. "Oh, and Chase? Even wink at her and you're dead. Hear me?"

No winking. Got it. How about taking her virginity? Before I can even reply, he walks away.

Seems like my angel is the devil in disguise after all.

And I'm on the fast track straight to hell.

Chapter
Three

Bridget

KIPLEY TURNS TO WALK AWAY, AND I SLAM THE DOOR IN *HIS* face. The face I never, in a billion years, thought I would see again. My heart hammers against my ribcage, and I wipe my clammy palms down my white cotton summer dress. This can't be happening. The almighty Lord has officially had it with my shenanigans. This is him punishing me for my unholiness. My father is finally going to follow through on his threats to send me off to a convent where he thinks a bunch of nuns will cleanse my black soul.

A round of banging resonates from the other side of the door.

Crap. *Crap!* What do I do?

Well, for one, don't stick around to confront your latest sin.

I turn on my heel and take off down the hallway. The front door bursts open, and a chill skates down my back. I pick up my pace, my lips strained upward as I smile at Aunt Getty.

"My dear, you are looking just lovely—"

"You too, Aunt Getty. Thanks!" I wave and hurry past her, making an escape out the sliding glass door into the backyard.

The sun blinds me as I step outside. I cup my hand over my eyes. The pounding of angry footsteps echo from inside, and I throw myself into the sea of relatives and friends, hoping to find a hole to hide in until the ghost of my bad choices is gone. Problem is, he's not a ghost at all. I haven't been able to stop thinking about the stunt I pulled last night. The fight with my father that had me acting so irrationally. God, I was so angry. All of it finally boiled over, and I stopped thinking clearly. Thinking at all. It pushed me so far, I believed going through with such a crazy plan would fix things.

Fix me.

My cheeks flush at the memory of last night. The boldness that took over when I propositioned a complete stranger and let him touch me in a way only one other person ever has. Then I allowed him to take something I'd been foolishly holding on to for a dead person. A naïve belief that you save your virtue for the one you marry. The one you give your heart to. Well, I'd been doing that for three years and that person was taken away from me. I just wanted the pain to go away. The hurt and emptiness to fade. I wanted to stop feeling so alone. *And how did giving up your virginity to someone you don't even know work out?* Not good, since he's no longer a stranger.

I shake my head in disbelief. I've done some crazy things. Rebelled over the years. But this one takes the cake. "Jesus, what was I thinking?" *Actually, don't answer that, Jesus.*

I make the mistake of looking over my shoulder, and there he is, standing in the doorway. I grip my biceps. He's even more attractive than he was in the low-lit bar. More breathtaking than when he was naked and blanketed over me. I watch as he scans the backyard, the crease around his eyes becoming tight as he makes eye contact with— "Oh, shoot." I whip around to take off, barreling right into someone.

"Oh boy!" Hannah, my cousin, squeals as we both attempt to steady one another.

"Oh my god, I'm so sorry. I was just—I was just…uh—"

"Dodging your dad?"

When am I not dodging him? "Uh…yeah, him."

She gazes at me with sympathetic eyes. "Are you two not seeing eye to eye again?"

"Not seeing eye to eye? I'm not sure that's the right phrase. More like a battle zone and we're on opposite sides."

Hannah lays her hand on my shoulder. "It can't be that bad. I thought you two were starting to get along. I thought he was starting to understand—"

I let out a harsh laugh. "Understand? The only thing he understands is his way of life is the only way. That we all need to follow the scripture of the almighty Jesus Christ who saves, but when I needed my *God* most, he was nowhere to be found. I won't be part of what he preaches. Just another devoted follower who believes in a higher power. I'm done falling for that."

I fight back the tears, the angry waves of emotion that flow through me day and night. Ever since the night I lost the one person who owned my heart. An accident took Jax, and my *God* ignored my pleas while I begged him to save him.

"Bridge, I'm so sorry. These past two years couldn't have been easy for you."

Shaking my head, I rid myself of the memories. The fight between Jax and my father. His constant disapproval. Jax's willingness to let me go if it meant me not losing the love and support of my father. The last night I saw him. The last time he told me he loved me.

"You can't do this. I don't care what my father says, I love you."

"And I love you, baby girl, but it would forever be us against them. They're your family—"

"You're my family! I don't care what he thinks. You show me more love than he ever has. I won't survive if you leave me. You told me we were forever."

His large hand cups my cheek. "We are. Just not the way we

24

planned. I would never leave you, but I have to step back and let your dad calm down. He needs time. Maybe this was too soon—"

"Too soon? How long do two people who are in love have to wait to get engaged? It's been three years. And I'm an adult. He has no say in what I do."

His eyes become sullen. Pain in my stomach explodes. "I know, babe, but without his approval, I won't go through with it. I have too much respect for him."

I slap his hand away. "Then you know we'll never be together. Because he'll never agree." He reaches back to catch the tears that flow, but I step away. "You leave here tonight, you can take this with you." I snatch off the diamond ring he placed on my finger days before and toss it at him. "You know what? Just leave."

"Bridge—"

"No, I get it. You're not willing to fight for us. For me—"

"Dammit, you know that's not true. I've fought for you ever since the day you landed in my life. Every single day. And I'll continue to fight until there's nothing left inside me. But this? I need to do this the right way. I want to scoop you up in my arms and give you your happily ever after. Make you mine in ways I've been dreaming of since the first day I laid eyes on you. But I don't want there ever to be doubts."

"There wouldn't."

"There would. They're your parents."

Tears fall in violent waves down my face. He bends down to pick up the ring and attempts to hand it back to me, but I turn away. "Bridge, I love you. Just give him time. We have our entire lives." I don't budge at his words. Eventually, he gives up and hops on his motorcycle. With one final gaze, his eyes memorizing every part of me, he nods and takes off down my street.

I never saw Jax again.

"It doesn't matter. My dad got his way. No bad boy troubled kid from the wrong side of the tracks stealing his daughter's virtue and kidnapping her to live in the woods like a bunch of hoodlums." Hannah's eyes crease at the harshness of my reply. "Shoot, I'm sorry. I'm just having a hard time—"

"Stop. You don't need to explain to me. I may never know the pain you're going through, but I'm here for you. For anything. I know our parents rarely see each other, but that doesn't mean we can't. Call me. Anytime."

She wraps her arms around me. Hannah has always been such a light in our family. "I wish my dad was more like yours."

Hannah chuckles and pulls away. "What do you mean? You wish your dad was ridiculously overprotective of his grill and won't let anyone help in fear they may steal his master status?" We both burst out in laughter. "I have no idea what the future holds, but I have faith it *will* get better. Your happily ever after is out there."

My happily ever after died in a car wreck two years ago.

I offer her a smile to help ease some of her concern. "Yeah, maybe."

"Now, let's go have some fun. Oh! Speaking of fun..." Her eyes dart over my shoulder. "Bridge, have you met my brother's best friend, Chase? Not sure if you two met at Kip's wedding—oh wait, you were sick."

Nerves explode inside me. *Please don't let him be behind me.* There's a chance Kip has more than one friend named—

"S'up, Hannah Banana." Nope. *That's him.* "No, actually I haven't, but I'd *love* to meet your cousin." Crap. His tone is less seductive than I remember. Possibly a bit of anger in there.

"You having a bad day? Geez. Put the fangs away. Chase, this is my cousin, Bridget. I'm not sure if you two have met."

Oh, we have. In a lot of ways.

I suck in a breath and turn around. "Nice to meet you." I start to turn back around, but he reaches out, captures my hand, and shakes it. And by shaking, I think he's trying to dislocate my arm.

"Oh no, it's nice to meet *you*. Do tell, who exactly are you again?"

Chase and I hold one another's heated glare. Unlike last night, when our gazes were filled with passion, this one is loaded with anger, confusion, and a tiny bit of I'm in deep trouble. The last one is mainly coming from me. We're in a stand off until Hannah speaks up, reminding me she's been witnessing our strange interaction.

"Chase, chill out. I know you lack in manners, but maybe show a tiny bit." We don't budge. "Yeah, okay…so, you can probably let go of her—shoot, Levi's waiving me over. You two get to know one another. I'll be back." Hannah scurries off across the lawn to Levi's side without another word. We, on the other hand, don't move a muscle.

"So, *Angel*, ready to confess? Or are you going to admit what I already know? You're exactly what I thought—the devil."

I hiss, snatching my hand back. "Oh, give me a break." Rolling my eyes, I turn on my heel to put as much space between us as possible. Preferably an entire planet. He captures my bicep, stopping me.

"I don't think so. We're not done talking. You're going to explain to me why you tricked me. How'd you even get into that bar last night? You're not even—"

"It's called a fake ID. And please, tricked you? There wasn't anything that happened you weren't on board with. Well…except our lack of *talking*."

He hisses back at me. "I didn't want to talk."

"Really? You only offered a million times. And for the record, I'm not in the market for a bestie, so if you're wanting to make friendship bracelets, curl each other's hair, and talk until I slice my ears off, you can buzz off."

His eyes widen to the size of saucers. "You—I've never—"

"Met me? I know, because I've never met you either. Glad we're on the same page. Now, if you don't mind, I'm going to look for better company." His lips part in shock. He drops my hand, and I take the opportunity to race as far as I can from a man who has awoken every single nerve-ending in my body... and maybe my dormant heart.

Chapter
Four

Chase

I'M NOT A TALKER. I'M NOT A FUCKING TALKER! "AND I DON'T listen," I mutter to myself as I chug my beer, my eyes darting directly across the pool to my new nemesis. Legs that go on for days. Hair that feels velvety smooth wrapped around my fist. Those little pouty lips I can still feel buzzing around my cock. No good, lying, sexy little minx. And I swear, if Ben doesn't stop flirting with her, I'm going to go knock him out.

"Dude, what's up with the scowl? You still in a pissy mood?" I turn to Levi and take another pull of my beer. "I've told you a million times, Kip doesn't care."

I shrug. "Well, he should. How do you know she even likes you? Gonna put a ring on her finger? Let her take all your money? Next, she's gonna make you talk and listen all the time. Chicks do that."

Levi chuckles next to me. "Well, for one, I enjoy listening to her. And I'm pretty sure she's just as in love with me as I am with her."

I shrug again. Another gulp. "Whatever. Your funeral." Did Ben just touch her shoulder? Cocksucker!

"You know, maybe if you stopped being so against love and tried it out, you might find yourself enjoying it. There's more to chicks than just sex, man."

Yeah. Lying. Deceiving. The devil in an angel suit. "Whatever you say." I finish my beer and fight not to whip it across the pool at Ben's big ass nose. "Just don't say I didn't warn you." I walk away, leaving Levi and his annoying smirk to seek out one of Mr. Matthews' burgers. If anything will make me feel better, it's his damn good grilling.

∽

Bridget

I can't stop wiping away at my tears. That may have been the most beautiful proposal I've ever witnessed. It was nothing compared to the simple moment when Jax proposed to me. Us laying in the valley like we did most nights because I didn't want to go home, staring up at the stars, sharing dreams. He held my hand and bolted up, straddling me. His grin was so infectious, I couldn't fathom how lucky I had been knowing I got to spend the rest of eternity staring at that smile. My smile.

"Stop looking so happy."

He tries to hide his smile, but it's impossible. "I can't. I am happy. I'm always happy with you." His lips dip and press against mine. "Do you see yourself happy for a long time?"

My brow raises, intrigued by his question. "In my story, I live happily ever after. So, I would say a long, long time."

"Hmmm." He makes a curious sound, debating my answer.

I slap him on the side. "What? It's true. My happiness is defined by the way my heart feels. And when I'm with you, it feels whole. Content. Loved. That's how I want to feel forever."

Emotion spreads across his beautiful face. He bites down on his lower lip and takes in a slow breath. His hand disappears inside the front pocket of his jeans, retrieving a small diamond ring. "Good, because my forever is you, and I want to make that shit official."

I take a tissue and dab under my eyes. I can't believe my beautiful cousin is getting married. A memory of us as kids resurfaces. During holidays when our parents would gather for after-dinner drinks and we would hide in her closet, flipping through the pages of her wedding album. Crazy to think after all these years of seeing Levi's name written all over her notebooks, she's finally getting her happily ever after.

"Crying because you feel bad you tricked me is a bit dramatic, don't you think?"

I turn to Chase, who's still wearing his scowl. "Do you ever stop thinking about yourself? Your best friend just got engaged. Maybe you should spend less time sulking and more time celebrating his happiness."

His hands prop against his hips as his lips open and close. "I am *not* sulking. I don't sulk. I'm a man." My eyes fall to his hips as he taps his foot like a diva. "Oh, for the love!" I yelp as he snatches up my arm and pulls me behind a big oak tree without making a scene. "I swear to god, woman, if you refer to me as anything but a fierce, attractive, unbelievably sexy, manly man who didn't talk and made you moan my name in three different languages, I'm going to have to remind you who I am."

His head is dipped so low, the warmth of his breath skates across my cheeks. My body trembles under his hold. His grip becomes heated against my skin. Flashes of last night assault my brain. His mouth devouring mine. His tongue inside me. The way he held me close, molding my body to fit perfectly around him.

My lips part. My eyes become heavy. It would be reckless, but the urge to have his lips on me again is outweighing the risk. He made me feel alive, and I ache to feel it again. Lust pumps through my veins. Excitement for the unknown.

"That's right, Angel. Remember what these lips feel like all over your body." His head dips even lower. I can almost taste the beer on his breath. It makes me famished for it. For him. I raise my chin to close the gap between us.

"Bridget, are you back here?"

My spine becomes rigid at the sound of my father's voice. The same way I'd done a million times with Jax, I push out of his hold just as my father appears from around the large tree. "Oh, there you are. I've been trying to find you." His eyes pull away from me to Chase. "Mr. Steinberg. Nice to see you again. Chase, correct?" My father sticks out his hand, and Chase accepts it.

"Yes, Reverend—I mean, sir. I mean…Mr. Matthews." *Jesus, why doesn't he just come out and say we were about to give each other sexual favors?*

"Dad, did you need something?"

His attention comes back to me. "I wanted to speak with you. What are you two doing out here"—he looks around, eyeing the distance from the party and us—"so far away from everyone?"

I open my mouth to say I was about to fall to my knees and offer him fellatio to really piss him off, but Chase beats me to it, sputtering out, "We were…we wanted to surprise the lovebirds. And were practicing. Levi, that silly guy, loves karaoke. We're going to sing to him—right, Bridge?"

He stares at me, begging me to go along with him so my pastor father doesn't strike him down into damnation.

"Yeah, it's gonna be magical. If you'll excuse us, Dad, we really want to get it right."

My father's gaze settles on me, trying to break me down until I give in and expose all my sins. Little does he know, the past two years have hardened me. My walls are up so high, the only thing he'll see is my growing hatred toward him.

"Well, all right then. But please hurry. I would like to spend some time with you before you venture off again." His message is clear: he's not happy I took off in the middle of our argument yesterday and didn't show until today at the party. Too bad. I have nothing to say to him. Now that I think about it, I have even less to say to Chase.

"You know what? We're good. Think we got it. I'm gonna go back to the party. Hannah needed me." Before either has a chance to comment, I push past them both.

Chapter
Five

Chase

SHE JUST FUCKING LEFT.

She didn't even stick around for our karaoke solo. Well, fake solo. But still. I wasn't done with her. She still had a lot of explaining to do. First off, why she lied about who she was. Or how her dead father was not dead at all. And a pastor at that.

I was so mad she blew me off, I left. My prissy friends laughed and blamed it on my jealousy. Who the hell was jealous of men who had forfeited their livelihoods?

My pussy-whipped friends were the least of my worries. The fact that she left without allowing me to get her contact information is the thorn in my side. *As if she wants to talk to you.* Not my problem. She has to. Lots of questions. Like if her dad hadn't interrupted us, would she have let me steal her breath and kiss the hell out of her?

I slap myself. "You sound like a pussy." I hit Kip's speed dial and tap my foot on the tile of my kitchen, waiting for him to answer. *Stick to the script. Act normal. Fish for answers. Don't sound desperate.*

"Yo, dude."

"Kip, my man!"

"Whatever it is, no. You know Stacey is not down with weekend getaways anymore. Throwing my phone out of the car at the beginning of our last trip so I couldn't call home really put the nail in the coffin for you, buddy." Whatever. I did him a favor. No chicks on guys' trips.

"Whatever. Not calling about that."

"Oh, okay, what has you sounding all sketchy?" Dammit. Act cool.

"Nothing, bro. Just calling to see what's up. Great party the other day. Man, it's been a long time since the whole family's been together. Remind me about your cousin again?"

It sounds innocent. No red flags. Just a simple inquiry—

"Don't even think about it. She's a good kid. Plus, she's been through a lot the past couple years. She doesn't need some playboy messing with her. Not to mention, my uncle would put a stop to it."

Never say never. "Well, I wouldn't dare think of it. But I mean...she seems more mature than a kid. Probably old enough to date guys of all ages. Who knows, maybe even a guy my age—"

"Chase, no. Whatever it is you're thinking, don't. Ain't gonna happen. Hey, I gotta go, Stacey's waiting for me. Was there something you wanted to—"

"Sorry, the food I ordered just got here. Gotta go." I hang up and toss my phone across my small kitchen table.

Prick.

Why the hell is he so concerned? I don't plan on dating her. I just want answers. Once I get the answers, I'll leave her alone. Simple as that.

Going with plan B, I hit my next speed dial. "Hannah Banana, it's your favorite person!"

~

Bridget

Once upon a time, I had a dream. Plans. A future. College. Marriage. Kids. A husband who would keep me safe and warm until we were old and gray. All that went down the drain the night Jax died. Because of my father. He took it all away. I didn't want to go away to college and live out my plan without him. How was I supposed to continue on this path alone? I refused to believe my father when he told me there'd been an accident. He was lying to me, so I would let Jax go. It wasn't until I saw the report in the paper. The photo splattered across the front page. Too many bent and broken pieces for anyone to walk away from.

College was a dream of the past. I found work instead, picking up shifts at the library during the days and at a local diner at night. Dead on my feet, I would trek home, only to sleep for a few hours and start all over the next day. This was my life. This was my punishment for allowing him to leave that night. Maybe if I hadn't been such a bitch or gotten upset over something that would have otherwise been honorable, he wouldn't have left. Or maybe I would have left with him. At least then we would have been together.

I wave to Helen, the head librarian, and make my way to the information desk. Taking a seat, I bend forward to place my purse in the desk drawer.

"Hey, Bridget?" Helen calls. "Someone in the nonfiction section is asking for assistance. Think you can help them out?"

I lock my purse in the drawer and stand. "Sure thing." I head down the aisle until I hit the nonfiction section. I turn the corner and stall in my step. "I doubt this is a coincidence." My lips downturn at Chase standing in the aisle, holding a book on teenage periods.

"Oh, wait, you work here? I was in town and—"

"Give me a break. Why are you here? How did you know where I—?"

"Why didn't you tell me you were a virgin?"

A gasp sounds from the aisle over. "Shhh! Are you kidding me?"

"No. I want to know."

I take two angry steps toward him, my voice low, angry. "You came all the way here, to my work, to ask me why I didn't tell you I was a virgin?"

He nods, as if it's the most reasonable thing to ask a person, waiting for my answer—one I don't have and won't give. "It's none of your business. Unless you're going to check out *The Beginners Guide to a Girl's Menstrual Cycle*, then please leave." I twist on my heel, and he grabs at my arm.

"Wait." I tug on my arm, but he doesn't budge. "Please." I turn around on his plea. "Just give me a chance. I'm not a bad guy."

"What do you want, Chase? We had a night together. We were never meant to see each other again. We should keep it that way."

"And I agree. Clingy girls aren't my thing—shit!" he hisses as I kick him in the shin. "I take it back. I'm not into violent chicks. Shit, that hurt."

I pull on my arm, and he lets go. "Good, so we're done here."

"Hell no, we're not done!" He raises his voice, garnering attention from Sue, our other librarian.

"Bridget, everything okay over there?"

"Yep. He's looking for an erectile dysfunction guide. I told him it's in the next aisle over. Mind helping him? I have to get back to the desk."

Sue smiles, trying to hide her humor at the book request, while Chase turns red with anger. "Have a great day, sir. Hope that book helps."

I walk off, a smug smile on my lips, the lingering thought of those sexy, sinful eyes creating a tingle down below.

~

The diner is crazy busy tonight. Every time I think I'm about to get some downtime, a rush of people come in.

"Bridget! You got an angry customer at table seven! Says he's been waiting on service for over fifteen minutes. Get your ass out there!" Hank, the manager, yells over the counter. What the heck? I've been diligent with every customer.

"Sorry. I'm on it." I hurry out, placing four plated burgers and two milkshakes on a table and rush over to—

"You've got to be kidding me." Chase is sitting at table seven, like the booth has been reserved just for him, reading an erectile dysfunction book.

"Finally." He doesn't take his eyes off his stupid book. "I'd like a double cheeseburger and fries, extra cheese—oh, wait. My handy book just told me fatty foods is a cause of my erectile disfunction. Cancel that. I'll go with the chicken salad and a water with lemon."

I roll my eyes, a sigh leaving my lips. "Are you serious?"

"I'd say as a heart attack, but since I'm changing my eating habits—hey! You're not allowed to assault customers," he gripes when I throw a towel at him.

I shake my head and walk off, putting his order in. I may have added that he wanted the cheeseburger after all and requested it to be burnt. Once his food is up, I can't decide if he eats it to prove a point or he was really that hungry. He sits there for the rest of my shift, ordering random side dishes and water. And still, I ignore him. He has to get tired of this little game and leave sooner or later.

"Hey, Bridge, who's the hunk at table seven who can't keep his eyes off you?" Carol, the other server, asks.

I finish ringing up a bill and look up at Chase as he quickly diverts his attention to the ketchup label. "He's just a guy who was in the wrong place at the wrong time."

A guy I should have never gotten involved in my messed-up life.

"Well, lucky for you, he's a looker. I'd be all over that if I were you."

In another life, so would I. One where I wasn't emotionally broken. "Well, you can have him. Just make sure he pays his tab. I'm heading home. See ya tomorrow."

I stuff my apron in my purse and slide out the back door. Heading up the alley, I take a turn down Hamilton Street.

"You always walk home at night alone?"

I practically jump out of my sneakers. "Jesus! How'd you get out here so fast?" I turn to confront him.

"Your friend inside gave me a heads up you were trying to bail on me. Now, she's my friend, 'cause I just tipped her my entire wallet for the information."

I roll my eyes. "Sorry you wasted all your money. Have a good night."

His voice stops me again. "I don't know what your problem is. *You're* the one who propositioned me, so why are you being such a bitch?"

I spin around so fast, I almost give myself whiplash. I'm in his face within seconds. "How dare you? You know nothing about me."

"You're right. I don't. What I do know is I keep trying to and you keep blowing me off."

"Maybe you should get the hint."

"Maybe you should stop being so stubborn and get to know me."

"Oh, geez, there's that needy guy shit again."

He scoffs. "Needy?"

"Yeah, needy! What do you want from me? I turn you down at every angle and you still just pop up like a stalker—"

He wraps his hand around my neck and pulls me into him, his mouth claiming mine. I want to pull away. I should pull away. But his touch is everything I've been craving since I lost

Jax. My heart speeds up. My hands wrap around his neck. His tongue pushes past the barrier of my lips, and I allow it. We explore one another until our kiss turns desperate. His grip tightens, bringing me against his massive chest.

Flashes of Friday night filter through my mind. My fingers dig into the back of his neck. I forget we're standing on a sidewalk in the center of town—a small town where everyone knows my father. If he got word I was openly making out with a stranger, it would be his final straw. Just a little bit longer, I'll have enough money to afford my own place, move out, and never look back. Until then…

I rip out of Chase's hold, hating the absence of his touch. His eyes are fogged with the same emotion swirling through my veins. Need. Desire.

"What? Why'd you stop?"

Because you're not in my plan.

Because you're not him.

Because for a split second, I wanted it.

"Because it wasn't doing anything for me, and I'm not into kissing for charity."

His eyes, a mix of light brown and green, pop open. "Charity?"

"It's the nicest word I could think of."

He scoffs. "You were melting in my arms, Angel."

"More like dying. That was painful."

"*Painful?*"

"I mean, I've had worse, but it's second runner up." He looks ready to blow. I get the feeling he's never been told he's not good at something. If I wasn't lying to get myself out of this situation, I would be right there with his fan club, holding up my five-star banner. "Look, I bet you're a nice guy, you're just not for me. Let's simply call it what it is: a dud. No sparks. Not gonna happen." He looks as shocked as my body feels. My lips are still tingling. My skin is on fire. My words aren't matching the way my sex pulsates at the sight of him. I need to get away from him.

"Maybe we should try it again."

God, he doesn't give up. "No."

"Yes."

"Not gonna happen."

"Well, it *should* happen."

Why is he making this so hard? "Seriously, do you obsess over everyone you have sex with?"

"I am not obsessed."

A sarcastic snicker falls from my lips. "You just normally show up at people's jobs?"

"Yes. I mean, no. I mean—I was in town. I needed a book and was hungry. Complete coincidence you happened to work at both. Maybe you're the one stalking me."

I let out a full laugh. "*I'm* the stalker?"

He shrugs. "Yeah. The nail marks on my neck are a clear indication you want me. Bad. Practically attacked me."

"Give me a break," I scoff.

"You know what? I will. You seem like a nice girl. We'll chalk this up as a misunderstanding. Now, if you'll excuse me, I have a library book to return." He doesn't even allow me time for a rebuttal before he turns on his heel and casually walks off down the sidewalk.

Chapter
Six

Chase

THE ENTIRE DRIVE OVER TO LEVI'S IS TORTUROUS. My Spotify playlist has gone to hell. Every song is like a universal sign playing through my speakers that Bridget is right. Maybe I am an obsessed stalker. Morrissey's "The More You Ignore Me, the Closer I Get" blares through my speakers, which agitates me, so I skip it. The Police's "Every Breath You Take" is another no. I'm not watching her every move. I skip it again and Death Cab for Cutie blares, "I Will Possess Your Heart". When Sarah McLachlan comes on, I snap.

"What the hell!" I slap the stereo off to get the damn song off as Levi opens my passenger side door and hops in my car.

"You all right? Did you want me to give you and your stereo another minute to finish your argument?"

"Fuck you, man."

"Whoa, chill. Just saying. I've been standing outside your window watching you for the past minute and a half."

"Well, music stations are shit nowadays. What kind of crap are they playing? What happened to songs about sex, drugs, and gangster rap?"

"As opposed to what?" Levi snickers.

"I don't fucking know. All this love drama bullshit."

Levi's brows shoot up, and I instantly regret the words that just came out of my mouth. "What did you just say?"

"Nothing. I don't know."

"No way, man. Spill. I don't think I've ever heard you say that word. Has a—oh my God! Has a girl actually gotten to you?"

"No! Yes! I mean—I don't know…"

Levi slaps his palm against his thigh. "This is going to be good. Why don't you tell me now and then replay it when we get to Kip's—"

"No! Kip can't know about this."

"So, there *is* a girl?"

"No. There's not a girl… Okay, *hypothetically*, there's a girl. More like a situation I can't figure out." I turn to Levi and ask the question I've never had to ask before, "How do you know when a chick really doesn't like you?"

Of course, this asshole laughs.

"It's not obvious? Hypothetically, of course."

"I don't know. It might be obvious. But there's no way she can't *not* like me. There's this thing about her. This *weird* vibey thing. I don't even know what it is. I think I… maybe it's because I haven't gotten laid in so long." *Translation: I got laid by the most angelic girl and now I'm broken.*

"As in you like her?"

Jesus, where's he going with this? "No, I don't like her! Okay, *hypothetically*, I like her. But she doesn't seem to like me—and I don't understand why. I mean, look at me. I'm every girl's wet dream."

Levi chuckles. "I think your Tinder rating says otherwise."

"Dude, get your apps straight. Tinder doesn't allow people to rate. Which would be a fantastic score if they did… and for those other sites, if you read past all the girls who are mad because I forgot their number—which was not my fault—I'm a stellar catch."

"Okay, fine. Why do you think she doesn't like you?"

I sit and ponder all of our encounters. "She told me."

"Then there's your answer. What's the problem?"

"The problem is there's no way she doesn't like me!"

"I hate to be the one to break it to you, but not every girl wants to fall at your feet."

"Pffft." I flick my hand at him. "Lies, but I'm not talking about every girl. I'm talking about *this* one. She's different. I'm not looking for her to fall at my feet. I'm looking for her to… to…" *Talk to me.* I swipe my hands down my face. "Fuck me."

"I'll pass."

"No, asshole. Not talking about you. Her. Maybe she's right. Maybe I *am* obsessed with her."

Levi's obnoxious laughter is not helping right now. "Wait, she said you were obsessed with her? Oh man, I've got to meet this chick. She sounds like a keeper."

She is a keeper.

"Don't plan on it. I'm not into chasing chicks. If she wants to deny herself this sexy piece of meat, her loss. She'll come running, and I'll have already moved on to the next toy." I throw my car into drive and speed down the road, cutting off this conversation. "If she's not into me, then I'm just as not into her."

"Are you sure about that?"

"Chase Steinberg doesn't chase chicks. They chase me." I turn to Levi, offering him my notorious playboy wink.

~

Three days later

It's only because I have to return the book. I've got a clean record and won't ruin it with a late fee at the library. I could not care less about seeing her. In fact, I hope she's not working today, and I don't have to.

"Good afternoon, sir. Can I help you?"

"Yeah, I was wondering if Bridget Matthews is working today?" *Yep. Obsessed.*

"She is. Did you want me to call her up?"

"No but thank you. I'll just go find her." I start to walk away when she calls after me.

"She's in the mystery section. I can take that book if you're returning it."

I look down, forgetting the book in my hands. "Oh—yeah. I need to return this."

Her lips twitch. "Certainly. Thank you."

Dammit, Angel.

"It was for my roommate. Poor guy. It's probably hard for him to live with such a stallion." At that, I walk away, seeking out the mystery section. I find her kneeling down, placing a book on the shelf.

She's dressed in a flowered tank top and shorts, and her hair is up in a messy bun. I take a few seconds to admire her sexy little frame. Of course, I can't help but notice how her top is nice and snug around her tits. I force myself to blink, willing away my half chub.

"Fancy seeing you here. It must be fate."

Her head whips up at my voice. Her eyes dilate, and the way her full lips part only encourages my growing boner. In the next second, she masks her surprise with an adorable little frown.

"You seriously *are* stalking me. You know this is becoming creepy, right?"

"I agree. Maybe we should exchange information so we know where each other is going to be. Otherwise, it's probably gonna keep happening."

She rolls her eyes and takes another book off the cart, placing it on the shelf. "Nice try, but no."

"Okay. I guess we'll keep seeing each other. I'm huge into reading nowadays, and man, that burnt burger really hit the spot."

"Chase, really?"

"Have you ever had a burger so crisp, you chipped a tooth? Delicious."

I don't know whether I hate myself for the torture or love the fact that I just earned the sexiest little giggle off her lips. I take that as my in and walk toward her. "Maybe if you have some time, you can recommend another book."

She stands and starts pushing her cart down the aisle. "Yeah, criminal law section. I'm sure you'll find some books on stalkers."

I follow her like a lost puppy. "No thanks. I'm pretty educated on that one."

"Okay, how about the relationship section? There's a book called *He's Just Not That Into You*. You could probably use some pointers from that one."

"Yeah, probably not that one either. I'm pretty sure he *is* into her." My dick twitches at the flush in her cheeks.

"Okay, fine. The self-help section has a really great book on accepting defeat."

"Strike three for you. I *definitely* haven't been defeated. Looks like you owe me lunch now."

Her lips part, and I fight not to wrap my arm around her neck and kiss away her cute little stupor.

"How exactly do I owe you lunch now?"

"You just failed at recommending a book to me. The only way to make up for it is to let me take you to lunch."

"Chase, I don't think—"

"It's just lunch, Angel. Simple meal. Simple conversation. We may even enjoy each other's company. Then we go our separate ways. I'll even consider turning in my library card."

Her eyes glimmer with humor. She's contemplating my offer. Inside, I'm a little girl, jumping up and down in a candy store, begging her to *please say yes, please say yes, please say yes.*

"I'll even let you pay so you don't get any ideas."

She rolls her eyes. "How chivalrous of you." She exhales a deep breath. "Fine. *Just* lunch. After, it's bye-bye, no more showing up at either of my jobs."

"Done." I slide my palms together and sway back and forth on my heels, a winning smile across my face.

"You look creepy again."

I remove my smile. "Got it."

"I get off in twenty minutes. There's a little café a block away. They serve quick food. It would be perfect."

Not if I order everything on the menu. "Sounds great. I'll just be in the next aisle over reading." She shakes her head and gives me her back without another word as she rolls her cart down another aisle and out of view.

I feel good. The best I have since the last time I saw her and got a taste of her sweet little cherry lips. I snag a book off the shelf and find a table. Sitting down, I contemplate how our conversation will go. I don't want to ask any deep questions and scare her off. But I'm dying to know what her intentions were that night. I've been with a lot of chicks, but I've never been with one who shows up at a bar with intentions of taking home a stranger to lose their virginity. Looking back, I feel like an asshole for going through with it, but I also wouldn't change it. Everything about her was perfect. From her subtle moans to her curious wild side. She was just as much beauty as she was sass. I don't know how she was a virgin, let alone not scooped up by some guy and wearing a gigantic ring.

"God, I sound like a pussy. Maybe I *am* a pussy—"

"Shhh..."

I turn to my right where a mom and little girl are reading a book.

"Shit, sorry—I mean, shoot. I'll just read my book quietly

over here." I hold up my book and wave it at her, and her look of disgust deepens.

Then I look at the cover.

Self Help: Life after Prison.

Goddammit!

I throw the book on the table and get up and wait for her outside.

Leaning against the building, I practice some simple lines. *What brings you to these parts?* No. *What beautiful eyes you have, are they natural?* Dude, no. *Your teeth are exquisite. Do you floss?* What the hell's wrong with me? "Get your shit together." Don't say anything stupid. Maybe I just shouldn't talk. I check the time. Shit, it's been longer than twenty minutes. She wouldn't... She totally snuck out the back door and is halfway home by now. The main door opens, and to my surprise, she walks out. *Phew.* "Thought you were going to ditch me there for a second."

"And have this continue? I'd rather take the lunch and get it over with."

I smile to myself. She's cute when she's annoyed.

∿

Bridget

We don't speak the entire walk to the café, and it suits me just fine. I have no idea why I agreed to this. *Because you're curious. And attracted to him. Let's not forget that.* Whenever he's near, my body buzzes. I sneak a peek at him. He's...*whistling?*

"This it?" he asks, stopping at the corner café. I nod, and he steps forward, holding the door open. I walk in and examine the bulletin board, seeing if anyone has put any new jobs up since the last time I ate here.

"Looking to change jobs?" he asks as I finish scanning the

normal listings. "Don't you already have two? You work a lot already."

I have no plans of answering that question. "Hello." I wave at the girl pushing up her fake boobs. "We'd like a table please."

She flutters her eyelashes and smiles. "Sure. How many?" Her eyes never leave Chase's.

"Just two. It's a pity lunch. His boyfriend just broke up with him." Disappointment spreads across her snooty face. I lean in closer. "About that table…?"

Sighing, she picks up her dry erase marker and crosses off a square on her seating chart. "Shame. Follow me." She drops the menus on the table and tells us to enjoy our meal. When we're both seated, the awkwardness settles in. Maybe this was a bad idea.

"Hey, guys, I'll be back to take your orders." A waitress drops off two waters. I grab my glass as a distraction and take a sip.

"So, what's good here? I'm not really feeling like dick today." Chase pretends to scan the menu as I spit my water right back out.

"Oh god." I cover my mouth. "I'm so sorry. I—" Why did I say that? I grab my napkin and hand it to him so he can wipe his face.

"No problem. In some cultures, being spit on is a sign of respect."

"It is?"

"No idea. So, how are you? What's your favorite color? Food? Do you like pets?" His fingers tap against the table in a nervous rhythm.

God, he's strange, unpredictable, and extremely cute when he's nervous. "What's up with the weird ice-breaker questions?"

He takes a sip of his own water. "I don't want to cross any

lines or scare you off. Figure if I stick to the basics, you won't run and might even possibly consider a second date—"

"This isn't a date."

"Oh, right. Hell no. Good call. Please don't go running and telling your friends this was a date. Anywho, what's good here? Please don't say the tuna melt." He lifts the menu to hide the twitch in his lips.

"Actually, I hate tuna, so I wouldn't know. If you're willing to be adventurous, try the muffuletta sandwich. It may be too many calories for you."

He pulls the menu down. "Why would it be too many calories?"

I shrug. "I don't know. I assume someone like you watches their calories. All muscle, no fat kind of guy. You probably run a gym or something." *A gym? Really, Bridget?*

His lips curl into a smug smile. I just gave him a compliment—and he knows it. *Shoot.*

"Thanks for noticing." He flexes, and I can't help but laugh.

"Please stop."

His arms go down immediately. "Shit, sorry. Yeah, no gym. I actually work in construction, so I do a lot of heavy lifting."

Explains the perfectly tanned skin. The waitress returns, her notepad and pen ready. "What can I get you two?"

Chase nods for me to go first. "I'll have the chicken salad, please."

"And for you, darlin'?" she asks, scribbling down my order.

"I'll have the muffuletta sandwich." He looks up at me and winks. My chest tightens. A shiver runs down my spine. *It was just a wink, Bridget. Calm down.*

"Got it. It'll be right up." She walks off, and I'm half tempted to grab her and beg her to sit with us so it doesn't feel so awkward. Like a date. If I'm honest, it wouldn't be the worst thing if it was.

I'd have to be crazy to turn down someone who looks like that. Plus, he's actually funny and not horrible to be around. I'm certifiable if I add in how amazing he is in bed. Not that I have any experience, but if I never have sex again, I'd still be fulfilled.

"I'm not going to bite, you know. You can stop looking so worried." I snap out of my haze. He seems to have kicked his nervousness, looking more content than I feel. I need to pull it together.

"Well, now that we got that out of the way, I can finally relax." My lame reply cuts the tension, and we both share in a silly laugh. Feeling less nervous, I take the lead. "How did you find me?"

He stalls before answering. "I can't really disclose my—"

I raise my hand. "Check—"

"Hannah! It was Hannah. She folded like a cheap suit."

My brow rises in surprise. I assumed it would have been Kipley. "Interesting."

"Please don't be mad. I didn't make it easy on her, and I may...well, I may have told a little lie in order to get your information."

Now, I'm even more intrigued. "Do tell."

"Shit. Okay. Promise not to take off?"

I tap my fingers on the table, enjoying his discomfort. "I'm waiting."

"So...I may have told her I was thinking about changing my life around and wanted to ask you for spiritual guidance— don't leave!" He reaches over the table and grabs my hand, his large palm blanketing over mine. "I had good intentions. I swear."

"And were those intentions to get another round with me? Is that what this—?"

"Jesus, no! I mean, if you wanted—God, shut up, Chase." He takes a deep breath. "Let me start over. I lied because I knew Hannah wouldn't give any information otherwise. If I told her I was interested in you, she would have shut me down immediately."

"Why?" He has yet to let my hand go, and I'm kind of enjoying his warmth against my skin.

"Long story. Look, I'm sucking at this, I know. We met on...strange terms—*great* terms— but those aren't my intentions now. I like you. Like, convince-you-to-let-me-take-you-out-on-a-date like you. If you don't like me, then I retract my statement and friends it is. I'm super busy with my modeling career, and... fuck, I'm not a model. I'm babbling. You make me nervous." Releasing my hand, he grabs for his water and chugs it.

I, on the other hand, burst into a fit of laughter.

"I know. I'm blowing this."

I shake my head as another round of giggles takes over.

"Okay, it's not that bad."

I try to inhale a breath to relax but snort out in another fit of laughter.

"Okay, it is that bad. Shit."

"No, no. It's..." I take a few deep breaths. "It's honestly been such a long time since I've been around someone— someone like you. I have to admit, I'm enjoying it."

"Considering I'm botching this non-date lunch, I'm not sure if your comment is a good thing or bad."

I wipe away the tear at my eye and sigh. "It's actually a good thing. I haven't laughed in a long time. It feels good."

His nervous smile morphs into satisfaction. He adjusts himself taller in his seat. "Well...good. I have more where that came from. Jokes for days—"

"Let's not get ahead of yourself here."

"Yep. Yes. Good point."

I bite the inside of my cheek to hold back my unrestrained laughter. I can't seem to read him, but I sense he'll be fun to discover. I sit back in my chair, enjoying his quirky smile and the way his V-neck shirt offers a nice little peek of his tanned, muscular chest. I stare too long and get caught. Thankfully, our food arrives, and I dodge that bullet.

"If you need anything, let me know. Enjoy, kids." The waitress is gone again.

The smell of the food hits my nose, and my stomach growls. I can't remember the last time I ate a full meal. Between both jobs and heading straight to my room to avoid my parents, I haven't taken time to think about food.

My stomach growls again.

"Um, is there a gremlin in your purse?"

I chuckle and pick up my fork. "No, more like in my stomach. I'm starving." I take a bite of my chicken salad and moan in delight. God, this tastes like heaven. With each bite, another moan falls off my lips. I look over at Chase. His brows are pinched. "Oh no, what's wrong? Do you not like it?"

"Oh, I like it…"

I look down at his sandwich. He hasn't even taken a bite yet. "How? You haven't…"

Oh… Oh! "Oh my god, I'm sorry."

"No. Don't be." He adjusts himself under the table, and my cheeks turn to hot coals. I grab my water and take a sip because I'm suddenly feeling incredibly hot. When I peer over my glass at Chase, a large silhouette behind him grabs my attention. A man in a dark, pristine suit is posting an ad to the bulletin board.

"Excuse me. I'll be right back." I leave Chase and his discomfort and walk up to the front of the café.

Nanny Wanted
Looking for a full-time nanny.
Will supply vehicle and housing.
Experience preferred. Certifications preferred.
Full compensation. Includes insurance and benefits.
Jonathon Brooks (309) 555-3244

"Interested in the job?"

I pull back to address the man. "I'm always interested, but sadly, I don't have the credentials you're asking for. I've never watched kids before."

The man turns to me, the glare from the window shining off his diamond watch. "Do you enjoy children, Miss…"

"Oh, Bridget. And yes. I used to work in the daycare at my church, but it was nothing compared to this. I hope you find someone." I turn to walk away, and his deep voice calls out to me.

"Tell me more about your daycare skills?" I turn back. His smile is gentle. Friendly. "I'm desperate and short on time. If you're familiar with children, I would love to try you out. I pay well. A competitive salary. Full benefits. I even have a guesthouse if housing is an issue."

He pulls out his wallet and hands me a business card. I accept it, reading the text. *Jonathon Brooks. CEO. Brooks Industries, LLC.*

"You can Google me and make sure I'm not a serial killer. I have a six-year-old daughter named Anna. Her current nanny left abruptly and I'm in a major bind. If you're at all interested, please come to my home and meet her. If you two hit it off, I would love to hire you. If not, I'll continue my search."

A full-time job? Salary? *Benefits?* This all sounds too good to be true. At the pace I'm at, I'm close to being able to escape the claws of my father and move out. But this may be my opportunity to do it even sooner.

"May I ask about salary?"

"Assuming you can work a normal work week schedule, some weekends, and some late nights when I travel, I'm offering forty-five thousand a year to start. It's always negotiable if you require more."

I sway to the side, and Jonathon reaches out to catch me. "Whoa, are you okay?"

"Yes, sorry. I…I'd like to think about it if that's okay?"

He nods. "Of course."

I thank him and stroll back to the table so I don't pass out, the salary amount doing double flips in my head.

When I sit down, Chase is staring at me. "You didn't find a new date while you were up there, did you?"

If I'm not mistaken, there's a bit of jealousy in his tone. I find it cute and reply with a playful smile. "Well, maybe. He did just offer me a job." I waggle my brows.

His own go up. "Oh, is that how we proposition beautiful girls nowadays? Looks like I've been going about this all wrong."

I laugh and show him his card. "No, I'm serious. He just offered me a job. A nanny position. To be honest, it seems too good to be true."

He reaches forward and snatches the business card out of my hand. "Let me see that." He inspects it for all of two seconds. "Yeah, not a good idea. That suit looked like a knock-off. Very serial killer-ish if you ask me."

I laugh and try to grab the card back, but he pulls away. "Come on now."

"I'm serious! I know this kind of stuff. Here, let me help you out."

He startles me when he gets up. "Wait, where are you going?"

Chase walks over to the hostess stand and whispers something to her. The trampy little smile that spreads across her face irks me. Leaning forward, she hands him a piece of paper. Chase scribbles something on it, then walks over to the bulletin board and pins up the piece of paper.

What the heck is he doing? He comes back and sits down.

"What did you just do?"

"I have a job too. I'm looking for someone to hire. Thought I'd give it a chance." Rolling my eyes, I stand up and make my way back over to the bulletin board, reading the piece of paper he pinned. I hold my stomach as a fit of laughter takes over.

"Are you serious?" I ask as I reclaim my seat.

"What? It worked for that guy. Thought I'd take a chance."

"Yeah, but *he's* offering a salary."

"A date with me is priceless."

I can't stop giggling at how ridiculous he's being. A girl standing at the bulletin board reading Chase's ad steals my attention. "Looks like I might have some competition." He twists in his chair and looks over.

We both watch as she unpins it and puts it in her purse. "Wow, this place *is* a hotspot. You're about to have a date for hire," I lean over, laughing.

"Shit." He jumps out of his seat and races toward the front entrance. I hurry after him, but I can barely move fast enough I'm laughing so hard. He gets stuck behind a family, allowing me to catch up. Grabbing his bicep, I lean into him, trying to catch my breath.

"What are you doing? You're going to crush that poor girl's dreams."

"Well, that dream was meant for you."

I'm still laughing. "You're gonna have to tell me if she calls." His lips purse into the cutest pout. "Who knows? Maybe she'll turn out to be the woman of your dreams." I have to bite my lip to hold in my laughter.

"This is your fault," he grumbles.

"My fault? I didn't tell you to pimp yourself out."

"Ugh...you're going to get it."

"Hmmm...we'll see."

We find ourselves staring at one another, our banter morphing into something deeper. Something more intense. His eyes fall to my mouth, and I can't help but bite at my bottom lip.

"Don't do that," he grumbles.

"Do what?" I ask, knowing exactly what he's talking about. I do it again.

"That, dammit. Don't do that."

"What? This?" I do it again, and his eyes blaze.

"Seriously, I'm a weak man. I can only hold back so much."

"So scared."

"You should be." His mouth captures mine, catching me off guard. I stumble, and his hands wrap around my hips as he kisses me with fervor. It's hard and fast and over too soon.

"Um, excuse me?" The hostess comes up to us. "No offense, but I thought you told me he was gay?"

Chase pulls me tightly into him. "I'm not gay, sweetheart. Just ask my sister here."

Bastard.

Chapter
Seven

Chase

"Oh, come on! How did you not catch that?"

"Because he sucks. How he hasn't been demoted to the minors blows my mind," I gripe to Ben. He has the worst taste in baseball teams.

"Seriously, bro? His batting average is top ten in the entire MLB."

I wave him off and take a swig of my beer. "Whatever you say, man. Guy's a waste."

Ben scoots off Levi's couch, throwing his hands up. "What the hell are you talking about? He's—"

"What are you two arguing about now?" Levi walks back into his living room.

"When are these two *not* griping like a bunch of girls?" Kip adds, and I flick a bottle cap at him.

"I'm not griping, asshole. The guy sucks—"

"You kidding me? That was probably the first time all season he dropped a ball! Since when do you not know your baseball? What's up your ass, bro? You're crabbier than normal. That chlamydia taking longer than usual to heal?"

"Fuck you."

"Whoa, you *are* crabby," Levi jumps in. "Thought you were gettin' some. What happened to that girl you were all bent out of shape about?"

"Wait, you got a girl?" Kip sits up.

"I don't have a girl," I blurt. *Thanks a lot, Levi.* I cut him a look, and he laughs.

"Yeah, you do. The one who doesn't like you. I think our boy here is in love."

I'm going to kill him.

"Who is she? Do we know her?" Kip asks.

The last thing I'm going to do is spill the beans on my newest little obsession. Yeah, it's come to that. All I can think about is her cute as hell smile, her laugh, and the little jokes I find funny as hell. Everything about her is perfect, and for some damn reason, I can't get enough of her. Angel or devil, I want her.

The problem is she's playing hard to get. Or she doesn't like me. I don't know which has me more on edge.

It's been three days since I've seen her. I got offered overtime at work and couldn't turn it down. When I showed up at the library this morning, they told me she'd quit. When I showed up at the diner, they told me the same thing. Who just quits without telling people?

She does.

I almost stooped to a whole new pathetic level and drove past her house, but reined myself in. Now, I'm sitting at Levi's, unable to enjoy a usually fun day of watching sports and drinking with the guys.

"You gonna tell us who she is or sit there and growl some more?"

"Fuck you, I'm not growling. And she's no one."

Levi shakes his head. "Whatever you say, man. If you ask me, that's the face of a man who's in denial."

"For real," Kip says. "I remember when Stace used to play

hard to get. Damn, I did some dumb stuff to get her attention."

Like stalking? How'd that go? Asking for a friend.

I take a deep pull of my beer. "Look at you now, neutered with a curfew."

Kip leans back in the lounge chair and raises his hands to lock his fingers together behind his head. "Best decision I've ever made. My woman can cook, is a lioness in bed, and the best damn mom—"

"Jesus, enough. Keep your misery to yourself—"

"Who's miserable?" Hannah appears, holding a bunch of shopping bags. Levi hops up and greets her, taking the bags as he kisses her.

"Dude, get a room," I gripe, turning back to the TV.

"Wow, someone's extra lovely today." Hannah walks by and ruffles my perfect hair. Levi takes his seat, and she sits on his lap.

"Don't mind him, babe. He's in love."

Goddammit!

"Wait, with who?"

Great. The last thing I need is for Hannah to ask questions.

"That's what we're trying to find out."

Hannah eyes me suspiciously. Shit. "Wait, is this why you asked me for—"

I'm out of my seat and pulling her off Levi's lap before she has the chance to finish that sentence. "Hannah, I could use your help. Lawyer question."

"Dude, I'm the lawyer, ask me," Levi chimes in.

"Uh...no. I need a female perspective. Come on. Let me get you something to drink."

"Did Chase just offer to get someone a drink?" Ben asks. I flip him off as I drag Hannah away.

"Seriously, what's wrong with you?"

I stop once we hit the kitchen, release her arm, and turn the water on so the guys can't hear.

"Does this have anything to do with Bridget—?"

"Shhh…they can hear you."

"This *is* about Bridget—"

"No! I mean, yes. Maybe. Listen, you can't say anything. Especially to Kip."

"Chase, he's my brother. I don't lie to him."

I scoff at her. "Says the one who had an affair with his best friend for months. How could you? He's still not over it."

Hannah rolls her eyes. "That's different. And for the last time, he's fine with it. You're the only one who's still bent out of shape about it. Are *you* secretly in love with me? Jealous?"

"Ew, no." *Hannah Banana? No way.*

A humorous smile explodes across her face. "Oh my God, I'm messing with you. You're for real weirding me out."

"Listen, I'm not asking you to lie to him. Just don't mention it. I don't even know what's going on. We just had this really great lunch date, not that it was a date, but it kind of felt like one, but…she's great, and I like her, and she loves books and eats pie in the littlest bites, and got me to love burnt burgers, and she won't give me her number or act like she likes me, but I think she does, and I just want to—"

Hannah slaps me.

I stare at her in shock.

"Sorry. You were really freaking me out."

I agree.

I nod. "Thanks. It's just…I like her."

She stares at me for a second longer. "Hmmm…"

That doesn't sound like a good *hmmm*. "I also need your help. Maybe give me her number? If you help me, I promise not to stand up at the wedding when the priest asks if anyone objects."

She rolls her shoulders while crossing her arms over her chest. "You'd have to be invited to do that."

"Yeah right. As if I don't already know I'm invited. I'm a damn groomsman. Right? Wait, did he already ask the guys? Am I not invited?"

"Oh my god, I'm joking. This is bad." She has no idea. "Okay, listen. I'll consider keeping your secret—under one condition."

"Anything."

"You never call me Hannah Banana again."

"Oh, come on. You're asking the impossible!"

"Then no deal."

"How about just on holidays or Tuesdays—" She pulls away. "Fine! Done."

"One slip and I tell my brother."

"Hannah Banana is in the past."

She sticks her hand out, and we shake. "Okay. We have a deal." She turns around to walk back into the living room when I call for her. "Wait, where are you going? You said you'd help me."

"I did. She called me this morning and gave me the same weird run around about saving your soul and I gave her *your* number. You're welcome." Hannah smirks and walks off.

She asked about me.

She has my number.

I just sacrificed the best nickname for nothing.

"Dammit."

~

How damn long does it take a chick to call, man? *How long does it take for my balls to shrivel up?* What's happening to me? Maybe my phone's broken. I shoot off a text to Levi.

Me: Call me real quick.

Levi: Why?

Me: Just do it, asshole.

My phone buzzes, and I answer.

"What do you need, man?" That worked. I hang up.

Two hours pass.

Me: Call me again.

Levi: So you can hang up on me again? No.

Me: *inserts middle finger emoji*

Me: Call me

Benny: Busy

Me: Stop letting your mom blow you and call me. It's important.

My phone rings. "Bro, too far with the mom comment. Judy is a wonderful woman."

What the fuck! I hang up. My phone works just fine. Why isn't she calling—?

My phone buzzes in my hand. I go to hit the ignore button, but an unknown number floats across my screen.

Shit.

It's her.

Or the fifth goddamn extended car warranty caller today.

Screw it, I'm answering. "Extended car warranty service."

A soft breath floats across the line, and I fist pump in excitement. "Oh, sorry, wrong number—"

"No, no. Right number. Chase speaking." *Seriously, loser?*

"Hey...it's, um...Bridget."

"Hey, how's it going? Good? You been good?" *RIP. Here lies Chase's chill.*

There's a brief pause, and I worry she's hung up on my pathetic ass. "Good. Great, actually. I quit my two jobs to take on that nanny position."

"I know—I mean...wow, that's awesome." Why don't you just come out and tell her you're a creep? "Maybe we should go celebrate?"

Say yes. Say yes. Say—

"That would be great. But I was hoping you could help me out first?"

I take in a slow breath so I don't offer myself on a platter

63

too quickly. "Yeah, sure. I'm pretty free." *Missing: my swagger. Please return immediately if found.*

"So, I was wondering, since you have such a big truck, could you help me move?"

Chapter
Eight

Bridget

"I won't stand for this." I shove another shirt into my suitcase as my father hovers behind me. "What will people think, you moving in with an older, single man with his reputation?"

"That he's wealthy, widowed, and in need of a nanny," I argue for what seems like the millionth time since I told my parents I took the job.

"This is a small town. People talk. There was speculation his wife did not die of natural causes. He was questioned. But wealthy men like him, they don't think the law pertains to them."

"That's ridiculous."

"A member at church caught whispers that his nanny didn't leave willingly either. Some say she's missing. He's probably done something terrible to her. I refuse to let you work for him."

Packing up my toiletries, I zip my suitcase and tug it off the bed, forcing my father to step back. "It's not your decision." I turn to face him. "I'm not a child anymore."

"You're acting like one. Making these rash decisions. What do you think this is doing to your poor mother—?"

"I don't know, she would have to actually speak to me to know." Pain stabs at my heart. I can't remember the last time my mother looked at me without disgust. She allowed a petty rumor from her church group that her innocent daughter was sinning with an outsider taint her views of me. She never accepted Jax. She couldn't get past the shame I brought to her circle. I didn't make things easier after he died. But at that point, she had written me off. I was done trying to prove to my own mother I was still worthy of her love.

The doorbell rings.

"That's my ride. I gotta go."

My father trails behind me. "Good. I can meet the man unsuitable to house a child—"

"And as I've told you a million times, I haven't been a child in years."

"In the eyes of the Lord—"

I halt, spinning around. "Don't you say it. Don't label me as one of *His* children. He is nothing to me."

"Bridget—"

"No! I'm sick and tired of you throwing his words at me. A God who preaches about salvation and peace. I don't feel or see any of it. He's supposed to save his children. Where was he when a man sideswiped the one person I was supposed to spend the rest of my life with? Where was he when Jax was taking his last breath? He doesn't save. And you're just a pawn preaching words that mean nothing."

I know I went too far. The hurt that flashes across his face proves it. I shake my head. "I can't keep doing this with you."

"Then stop acting like a martyr. You say you're not a child, then do the right thing. Tell this man you won't take this job. Go to college. Find peace in your future instead of running from it."

My breathing hitches, and I rub at the sharp pain in my chest. "That future doesn't exist. You made sure of it."

"Bridget, how many times do I have to tell you, the accident was not my—"

"It *was* your fault! He would have never been on the road that night if you hadn't turned your back on us. We truly loved each other. What was so wrong with that? He wanted to give me a future. He wanted college for me. A great job. A beautiful house with children. He wanted to give all of that to me. But you—you refused us, just like you're refusing this now."

"You were too young. And he wasn't in a place to provide—"

"He loved me! He would've done anything for me. We had a plan. You took that from me. Your selfish *God* took that away."

I wipe at my angry tears. I'm done having the same argument. It will never bring him back. "I'm done fighting with you. You told me so long as I lived under your roof, I had to obey your rules. This is me choosing to make my own rules. Accept it or not, it doesn't change my decision." I give him my back and run down the remainder of the stairs.

"Bridget, stop. We're not done—what is *that boy* doing here?" Chase's face peers through the paneled glass.

Without answering, I whip open the door.

"Hi, sorry I'm kind of late. Traffic. Hey—shit, are you okay?"

"Yeah, we've got to go." I want to push him out the door, but he steps forward, concern in his eyes.

"You've been crying?" He lifts his hand, using his thumb to wipe away the wetness on my cheek. "Angel—"

"It's fine. Can we just go—?"

"Chase. My nephew's friend. I didn't realize you and my daughter were this acquainted."

Chase looks over my shoulder at my father, the color

draining from his face. "Oh, hello, Mr.—Pastor Matthews. Nice to see you again. Beautiful day. Sorry I was late getting your daughter. I wasn't speeding, though. Super safe driver. Lovely home you have—geesh," he grunts as I shove my palms into his chest and push him off my front step.

"I expect you to leave the contact information and address of this employer," my father says.

"I'll text it." Chase practically trips backwards as I push him again. "Can we please go?"

"Yeah, sure. Um…nice seeing you again, Pastor Matthews." He waves and catches his balance as he turns forward, glancing down at the small suitcase in my hand. "What about your things?"

"I'll get the rest later."

His eyes drift to my father, then land back on me. It doesn't take a genius to see we were fighting. "Got it. Let's go." Bending down, he grabs the suitcase from my hand, then escorts me to his monster truck.

"Here, let me help you up." He opens the door and holds my hand as I climb up. He doesn't say anything as he climbs in and pulls away. A few minutes pass before I break the silence—anything to deter him from asking questions I don't want to answer.

"You know, if I didn't already know, I'd think you were trying to compensate with this huge truck."

He turns to me, already wearing that devilish grin. "Let me know if you need a reminder."

I offer him a disgusted scoff even as warmth enters my belly. My stomach tightens at the thought. "Nope. I'm good."

His goofy smile is hot as hell. His deep-set hazel eyes draw me in. The anger and hurt from the fight with my father fades. God, he's so handsome. Chiseled cheekbones. Lips—

"That's not the look of someone who isn't interested."

I clear my throat. "I'm not. Trust me."

Chase chuckles, bringing his eyes back to the road. "Okay then. Want to talk about what happened back there?"

"No."

"In case I didn't already mention it, I can be a good listener."

I angle my body toward him, cocking my head. It's impossible to keep my growing smirk hidden. "Only a million times."

"Hey, it wasn't that many. Like twice, maybe."

"Whatever you say, Steinberg."

"What was that, Matthews? I didn't hear you because I wasn't listening—*ouch*. Your violent streak only turns me on more—*okay*! I surrender." I bite my lip, holding back my giggle. "How about we stick to the basics? Want to give me an address? Or is this a ploy to get me to take you back to my place?"

"You wish, playboy. Just the ride will suffice." I give him the address for the Brooks' Estate, and Chase enters it into his GPS.

"Hmmm…I know where this is. Really sketchy part."

He's unbelievable. "It's the nicest part of town."

"Define nicest? Did you do a background check on him? Call his references?"

"Chase." He cocks his head my way. "I'm taking the job. If you don't want to help me, that's fine. Just drop me off and I'll get—"

"Okay, okay, I get it. Keep my mouth shut. I'm just a pretty face with a huge truck…amongst other things. Just know the offer still stands."

"What offer?"

"Taking you back to my place and—" His phone rings, cutting him off. "Shit. It's work. Hold that thought. Hey, Craig…"

I leave him to his work call and stare out the window. A part of me wishes—no, begs for him to do just that. Take me back to his place and relive every single moment from the hotel. It might turn my mind off. Shut off all the voices. The doubt. The worry. Let him have his way with me and forget that my life is a goddamn rollercoaster destined to crash at any moment.

Chase ends his call as we pull into the long driveway of Jonathon Brooks' home.

"Sketchy part of town, huh?"

Chase has his nose to the windshield, taking in the enormity of it all. "I mean...I've seen bigger."

We pull up in front of the house and Chase parks. Mr. Brooks walks outside to greet us. Before Chase goes on another lecture about this not being a good idea, I hop out of his truck.

"Bridget, I'm excited to welcome you into my home. Anna has been running around the house just as eager."

I reach out and shake his hand. Chase walks around the front of his truck, and I pretend I don't see him rolling his eyes. "Thanks. Me too."

Mr. Brooks takes notice of Chase and releases my hand. "I told you I would have sent over a service to gather your things."

"I know. It's fine—"

"She has me, no need. Chase." Chase sticks his hand out. Mr. Brooks eyes him suspiciously but returns the gesture.

"Jonathon." Chase stares him down, but Mr. Brooks dismisses him, pulling his hand away. "Let me show you where you'll be staying. Can I have someone grab your things?"

"Again, I got it," Chase interrupts. I beat him down with my evil stare, silently telling him to back off. The last thing I need is to get fired before I even start.

"I guess your friend has it covered—"

"Boyfriend," Chase blurts out. His arm suddenly wraps around my shoulders, tucking me tightly against him. I try to look up at him, wondering what the heck he's up to, but he has me pinned to his side. "I've always got an eye on my little angel here."

Jonathon observes us both, unable to hide his annoyance. His lips lift into a subtle smile. "I'm glad. She definitely seems like a wonderful young woman. Let me show you where you'll be staying." He gestures for me to follow him, and we walk a few yards before the guesthouse comes into view. "This is the guesthouse. It's fully equipped with everything you'll need. If there's something you require, just let me know and I'll have it brought in. You're welcome to anything in the main house. If this doesn't suit you, there are guest rooms in the main house."

Chase scrunches his nose at the idea. I can practically see the wheels of his argument spinning. His mouth opens, but I beat him to it. "Thank you. This is just fine. Wonderful, actually."

Chase's eyes narrow, and I nudge him in the gut with my elbow.

Mr. Brooks pleasantly smiles. "I'm glad you approve. The slightest inconvenience, let me know and I will accommodate."

"I'm super handy, so there'll probably be no need. She can call me."

I'm going to murder him! What is he doing? Pulling out of his grip, I follow Jonathon into the guesthouse. He opens the door, and my mouth almost drops at how homey it is. I instantly fall in love with the kitchen, which is tucked in the corner and gives off a chic cottage feel. The back wall is lined with gorgeously painted robin egg blue cabinets and a gigantic pearly white granite-covered island with bar stools sits in front. The living room area is fully furnished with luxurious leather couches and a hanging television the size of all my TVs at home put together. There is a spacious hallway, which I assume leads to the bathroom and bedroom. "Wow, this is beautiful."

"And all yours. Let me know if you'd prefer different décor. Please provide a list of your food requirements. I can have our chef fill your fridge as soon as possible. Also, there's full security, so you should always feel safe. I'm notified every time anyone enters the property." Mr. Brooks glances at Chase, and they silently standoff in a pissing contest.

"Mr. Brooks, thank you for everything. I'll get that list to you soon."

He goes to place the keys on the kitchen island, and I turn to Chase, mouthing, "Knock it off." Not only does he not listen, he wraps his arm around my neck, tugging me to his side. Before I can punch him in the gut, Mr. Brooks turns back. I slap a smile back on my face.

"Please, call me Jonathon." Chase squeezes me tighter. "Well, if you'll excuse me, I have some work to attend to. Again, I'm grateful to have found you. Please settle in and let me know if you need anything. Dinner is served every night at six. Anna would love it if you joined us." I nod, my smile strained. Chase is practically choking me.

Jonathon disappears back to the main house, and Chase finally releases his death grip.

"What the heck was that all about?" I snap. "Boyfriend? Really?"

"What? I was doing you a favor. Did you see the way he was looking at you?"

"Like an employer looking at his employee?" I argue, annoyed. I haven't even started and Jonathon is probably already second guessing his decision.

"Yeah, right. He was eating you alive. I did you a favor."

I scoff. "A favor? How so? By already putting me in an awkward position with my new boss?"

He crosses his arms over his chest. "No, by making him think you're taken. Now he won't try to pursue you. I've read —I mean, *heard* girls talk—about that *Fifty Shades* book stuff. Older rich men. Cute, innocent girls falling for their sicko antics. Before you know it, you're going to be chained up in his basement exchanging safe words. You're welcome for that."

I stare at him a beat before placing my hands on my hips. "And what if I like being chained and gagged?"

His jaw almost hits the ground. "Wait, you—"

"Yeah, I enjoy some spanking and hair pulling. The thought of a whip slashing against my cheeky ass. Silk ropes around my neck. God, all the bondage and toys." Chase's pupils dilate to saucers and his pants tent.

"You—you're serious?"

"*God* yes." I drag my fingertips up the center of my stomach, between my breasts, then smooth them around my neck.

"Christ all mighty," he hisses.

"Wanna know what else?" I purr.

His head bounces up and down, and I bite down on my lower lip. "I think it's pretty hot you watch romance movies. Also, I'm *totally* messing with you. Jesus, are you always this gullible?" I push past him, biting back my laughter, and walk down the hallway to check out the bedroom.

"Dammit!" He hustles behind me. "For the record, I've never seen that movie. Nor do I care what happens. That stuff you mentioned did nothing for me. I'm a wholesome guy—"

My amusement slices through my lips, and I explode into a fit of laughter. Dropping my suitcase, I turn around. "Says the guy who tied me up with his belt a few weeks ago? Or was that all for show? I do remember you being really into—"

"Don't you even say it."

"Say what?" I raise a brow.

He huffs, running his hands through his thick hair. "Christ, I didn't really want to talk, can we just stop bringing that up?"

I cover my mouth in an attempt to hold in another fit of giggles.

"Bring what up?"

He comes at me, and I jump back, laughter bursting from my lips. "You know damn well what I'm talking about." Gripping my bicep, he tugs me forward. "When I have something to talk about, I'll let you know. But when I'm with you, that's the last thing I'm thinking about doing." His head dips low, his lips hovering just above mine. My intake of breath gives me away. "Now, unless *you* have something *you* want to talk about, I'm going to kiss you now. Being my *girlfriend* and all."

I don't bother correcting him. I don't argue when his eyes bore down on me. I certainly don't stop him when his warm lips press against mine.

When we finally break for air, I worry I've lost all feeling in my legs. Thankfully, he keeps hold of me before I melt into a puddle at his feet. My brain struggles to work properly. I inhale a shaky breath, trying to pull myself together.

"Well, that was a sure way of avoiding—"

A little knock against the door gains my attention. Pulling away, I adjust myself and walk down the hall and open the door, finding Anna.

"Hey, there."

"Hi. Do you want to see my doll collection?"

I bend down to Anna, putting myself on her level. She's cradling the same doll she had with her the first time I met her during my interview. "Of course. I'm just getting settled and I'll be right up."

Anna cocks her little head over my shoulder. "Was he in your suitcase?"

I steal a peek at Chase. "Him? No, that's my friend, Chase. He's helping me unpack. He's leaving, though." I smirk at him and turn back to Anna. "Lucky for you, I'm all done. Why don't we say goodbye to my friend and you can show me your collection?"

Chapter
Nine

Chase

CAN THESE GUYS PLAY ANY SLOWER? I LOOK AT MY WATCH FOR the fifth time. Only three goddamn minutes have passed.

"You going to hit the ball or tell us the whole story of how you fed your balls to your girlfriend?"

Levi flicks me off and readies himself to take his shot. "For the record, she's my fiancée, and I thought you two came to a truce?"

Truce schmuce.

"No idea what you're talking about. Just hit the ball." Jesus, when did I start not enjoying golf? *When you started making plans with your obsession right after.*

Kip slaps me on the shoulder. "You good? You've seriously been on edge lately. Ever since the girl Levi mentioned. Sure she isn't just a fling?"

Fling? You mean no sleep, all I think about, fixation?

"Fling is putting it strongly. Not my type, man." *I wish she would chain me to her so she could never leave my sight.* I can't stop thinking about her. Everything about her keeps me on edge. Her soft, cherry-tasting lips. Her subtle little moans when I steal kisses. The way she secretly looks at me when she thinks I'm not paying attention. The sadness I see in her eyes when she thinks I'm not watching. She's an itch I can't scratch. A challenge I can't conquer. A possession I want to claim.

I shake my head.

Never again, Steinberg.

I told myself never to fall down this path again. There's a reason I avoid sentiment. The whole hearts and flowers bullshit. *Just because she did a number on you doesn't mean every other chick will.* Shoving down memories of Caroline, I push off Kip's hand. "Don't worry about me, man. I'm all good. Juggling bitches like a champ. You all wish you were me." Levi takes his shot and makes it onto the green. I step up and drop my ball. An image of Bridget and the way she looked that night, her mouth doing all those amazing things, has me clenching my eyes shut. I take a deep breath and swing hard.

And just like my efforts to get her to like me, my ball fails to hit the green and lands in the sand.

∾

Drilling vibrates in my ears as I lift the auger and grind it into the ground. My name rings out from behind me, and I pause, swiping at the sweat on my forehead.

"Steinberg, I need you over by sector three."

I shut down the drill and pull off my gloves. Waving at my foreman, I walk past the site office. My phone buzzes in my pocket, and I pull it out, almost falling over my feet. Bridget's calling. *Okay, man. Play it cool. Don't act as excited as you are. Be a man.* I clear my throat and, for some reason, deepen my voice. "S'up?"

"Chase, please, I need help."

∾

I can't remember the last time I broke every traffic law—okay, maybe it was the other night, but still. Shoving my truck into park, I throw myself out and race toward the guesthouse. The door opens and a frazzled Bridget fills the open space. Her cheeks are flushed. Her hair is a mess and she's wearing glasses. Damn, she is incredibly gorgeous.

"Oh my god, I need you!"

Okay, I wasn't expecting this kind of approach.

"I can't get the faucet to stop spraying!" Grabbing my shirt, she pulls me inside, stopping in front of the geyser shooting out of her sink. I rush over and fiddle with the knob, soaking my shirt.

"Shit." I kneel in a puddle of water and open the cabinet under the sink. Leaning in, I reach for the valve and twist it to the right, shutting off the water line.

"Oh my god, thank you. I was trying to wash my coffee mugs and it just started shooting water at me. I couldn't get it to stop." I sit up as she inspects the flooded room. "Oh God, I'm so fired."

I wouldn't lose sleep if she was. I don't like the way her boss looks at her, and I definitely don't like the way he looks at me with eyes that scream with possessiveness. He has another thing coming.

"Nah, it's fine. Gives the place character. Not that he couldn't afford an indoor pool."

"How am I going to fix this? The rugs are ruined. The furniture—"

"He's rich. He can fix it. Why are you staying in a place that has faulty equipment?" Standing up, I wring out my shirt. "Good thing you called me, being your boyfriend and all." I wink, easing some of her worry.

"*Fake* boyfriend. I don't do those."

"Good. I don't do girlfriends. This is working out just fine."

She eyes me, curious. "Good. We're both on the same page then. This isn't a relationship or anything. Just—"

"Wingman status. Besties who kiss. Water drowning savior."

Her laugh is so damn cute.

"I'm not sure I would have drowned, but thank you for saving me."

I bow. "You're welcome. I'll take a lunch date as my prize."

"Lunch date?"

"That's correct. Saving you worked up an appetite. It's the least you can do, *girlfriend*."

Her brow raises, and I fight not to grab her and kiss the hell out of her. "What do you say? The diner down the road? I'm in the mood for something…meaty."

She laughs, adjusting her messy bun. "Look around you. I can't just leave. I have a pool in my kitchen."

"No problem. I have a guy who owes me a favor. I'll have him come over and drain the water and clean up. Now, how about that lunch?"

"Fine. But you're soaking wet."

"I have a change of clothes in my truck." I lift my drenched shirt over my head, loving the hitch in her breath. "Did you want me to stand here a little bit longer, or are you done ogling?"

I love messing with her.

"Yeah, uh…no. Totally done. I can burn my eyes out now. You should probably keep your shirt on. Nothing to see there." This time, it's me who's laughing. I twist up my shirt and whack her in her tight little ass as I walk by and open the door—"Whoa." I stop, before almost slamming into—

"Am I interrupting something?" Her douchebag boss looks over my shoulder, eyeing my girl, then back at me. His gaze blazes with disapproval. I open my mouth to tell him to fuck off, but Bridget beats me to it.

"Oh my god, no. It's not what you think. The faucet. It— well, it just started shooting water, so I called him to help me fix it. I didn't want to bother you. I'm so sorry. I was going to call someone and get this cleaned up—"

"Nonsense." He steps past me. "I'll take care of it. Are you all right?"

If he puts his hands on her, I'm going to snap each finger in half. I open my mouth to tell him off, but Bridget interrupts again.

"Yes, fine. Just embarrassed. I'll pay you for the damages."

"Please, this isn't your fault. I should have had all the plumbing inspected beforehand. Let me make it up to you. You can stay in the main house until I get this—"

"She's staying with me." There. Finally got a word in. And *what* did I just say?

Douchebag and Bridget gawk at me.

"Yeah, I wouldn't want my *girlfriend* to be put out either. Thanks for the offer, but she's gonna stay with me."

"That's not necessary. I have a perfectly suited guest room."

Is this asshole for real? "Yeah, and I—"

"Mr. Brooks, I appreciate your offer, but I don't want to be in your hair. The weekend is coming up. I wouldn't want to impose." Douchebag opens his mouth, but Bridget quickly speaks up. "Again, I'm so sorry for the mess. You can take my first paycheck or…however many it takes to pay for it."

He crosses the line, placing his hand on her shoulder. Red tints my vision. I take a step forward, ready to pounce on this asshole, when Bridget shoots me a *don't you dare* glare.

"I told you, please call me Jonathon. And don't be silly, Bridget. This isn't your fault. If anything, I will compensate you for the inconvenience. You have my word by the time you return, I'll have this cleaned up and as good as new. I assume by the end of the weekend?"

"Of course."

"Good." He pulls back, taking too long to remove his hand, and nods. "I'll leave you to it. Enjoy your weekend." He turns to me, his eyes less courteous. "Both of you."

I don't respond. My glare says enough. *Stay away from my girl, you creepy old fuck.*

"Well, if that wasn't the most awkward sword fight I've ever witnessed."

I pfft and turn around. "You kidding me? What's up with that guy? *Call me Jonathon.* More like creeper. And his hand on your shoulder? You should press charges."

She rolls her eyes at me. "Press charges? For what?"

I stutter over my response. "I don't know—harassment?" Dammit, why does she keep doing that? "He shouldn't touch you. It's against policy."

She folds her arms over her chest, accentuating her perky tits. "And what policy is that?"

"Boyfriend policy. Only I can…uh, put my hand there." When she tells me to beat it, I can only blame myself.

Thankfully, she only shakes her head and laughs. "Has anyone ever told you how ridiculous you are?"

"A time or two. Now, let's go. Make sure you pack your bag."

"For lunch?"

"No. For the weekend. You're staying with me, remember? Boyfriend duties," I say, then head out to my truck before catching that damn sexy eyeroll.

∼

Bridget

Absolutely ridiculous.

If he thinks I'm spending the weekend with him, he's out of his mind. *Says the one who packed that bag…*

Dammit. What am I doing?

Getting attached. Remembering how to smile. The exhilarating feeling of my heart beating again.

My world crashed and burned the night Jax died. And a piece of me died with him. My heart was so broken, there was no way of it ever mending. I blamed my father, but I also blamed myself. I knew my shoulders would always be heavy with the guilt I feel, and my soul would feel the stain from his death.

Until now.

Two years of shutting myself off from the world and refusing any kind of happiness. I'd convinced myself no one would ever come into my life that made me feel the way that Jax did.

Until now.

My heart and mind are in a constant battle. My heart says to let Chase in. I've suffered enough. Maybe he is my salvation. But my mind won't let go of the memories. The fight. The accident. And if I let myself give into this temptation, what does that say for my love for Jax?

I gaze back at Chase as he takes a bite of his club sandwich, snorting out a laugh as a glob of mayonnaise slips down his chin.

Gorgeous. Funny. Strange at times. Spending way too much time on a broken girl. "Okay, spill. What's your deal?" I hand him a napkin as the mayonnaise drips onto his shirt.

"Shit," he grumbles, trying to wipe it off but making it worse. "As in my agenda here? Just a guy who needs to eat. Speaking of, you haven't touched your salad. Do you want me to have them get you—"

"I'm not talking about that. I'm talking about you. Everyone has a story. What's yours?"

He pauses for a moment, setting down his sandwich and leaning back in his chair. "I'm not sure I have one. Just an average guy who met a girl in a bar and wants to get to know her."

My eyes narrow as I fold my arms over my chest. "Yeah, yeah, yeah—same song and dance. If you want to bullshit me, that's fine." I grab my napkin off my lap and place it on the table. "But after this lunch, these strange encounters are done. I can always stay with—"

"Fine! You win. What do you want to know?"

"Why don't you date?"

"Why don't *you* date?"

"I asked first. You said you don't do girlfriends, why?"

He shrugs. "I'm a busy man. I don't have time for all the hearts and flowers. I'm a highly sought-after man. I need to keep my options open—"

I start to stand, and his arm shoots out, stopping me. "Okay, okay! I had a relationship turn sour and promised myself never to be in that position again."

Finally, some truth. "Explain."

He stalls, then blows out a harsh breath. "Not much to tell. We were good, then we weren't."

I start to stand again. "Okay! Jesus. I was in love with her. I thought she was the one. Turned out, I was only one of many. She'd been cheating on me for years. I saved money, bought a ring, and caught her with one of her college professors. There. Happy?"

No.

"Chase…I'm so sorry, I didn't—"

"Nope. You don't get to do that. My turn. What's your story? Why no boyfriend?"

Great. Why did I pry? "Just not my thing."

"Wrong answer. I'd threaten to get up and walk away, but I'm not going anywhere, so spill, Angel."

Damn him for throwing my own antics back at me.

"I'm waiting."

"I had a boyfriend. We were in love. He asked me to marry him. That same night, he died in a motorcycle accident." He inhales sharply, sympathy dancing in his eyes.

Exactly what I didn't want. "We're not playing that card, are we? I don't need any of that. It was a long time ago. And I promised I would never put myself in a vulnerable position to get hurt the way I did. That promise still stands."

He stares at me for a few more beats then nods. "I'm not a fan of your puppy dog eyes either. Let's just make a deal that there's no need to feel sorry for one another. I'll stop looking at you like I want to hug you, and you can stop looking at me like you want to rip my clothes off and make me feel all better."

Oh my god. "Okay, buddy. Whatever you say. But you've got a deal. I don't feel sorry for you at all, so don't feel sorry for me."

He sticks his hand out. I do the same, and we shake on it.

Chapter
Ten

Chase

REMIND ME AGAIN WHY I OFFERED TO HAVE HER STAY with me?

Because you don't want to let her out of your sight. Correct. Also, there was no way I was allowing her to be any closer to her creeper boss. The problem is, I failed to mention I lived in a complete bachelor pad. And the maid is off this weekend. She also doesn't exist.

Unlocking my door, I hurry inside, snatching a pair of socks hanging over my couch and an empty beer bottle on the end table. "Um…yeah, so, it's a bit messy. I was going to clean but…yeah…"

My eyes bulge, and I practically dive over the couch and shove the Cosmopolitan magazine under my shirt. "Sorry. Not mine. I'll…uh, be right back. Make yourself at home. Gonna —be right back." I snag a few more articles of clothing and some trash and throw myself into the kitchen. "Shit." I dump the empty beer cans and magazine in the garbage. I take a whiff of the socks and decide to toss them too. "Jesus, what was I thinking? Hey, idiot, maybe invite the girl over *after* you've cleaned your place and gotten rid of the beer and chick mags."

"Are you talking to me?" she calls from the living room.

Shit! "Uh…no." *Get ahold of yourself, Steinberg.* "Just getting us some drinks." Drinks. I whip open my fridge. What are the chances she likes beer? Or expired milk? Those are her only options. I go with a beer.

I walk back out, two beers in hand, and find her seated on my couch. She looks at ease, which I fucking love. It helps take away some of my own nerves. I snag a seat next to her.

"Did you want a beer?" I stretch my arm out to hand her one.

"No thanks. I'm good."

I reach back. Shit. Maybe expired milk was the better bet. "Yeah. Me either." I place them on the coffee table. "So, what do you feel like watching?" We both reach for the remote. She makes it before me. As she points it to turn my TV on, a small bead of sweat forms. What was the last thing I watched last night? There's a good chance it's sports. There's also a small chance the last thing I was streaming was porn. Come on! I have this girl on my mind nonstop. A man has needs!

"I don't care. Let's see what's on."

Don't be porn. Don't be porn.

The screen lights up, reminding me exactly what I paused it on just before I fell asleep. Great.

In slow motion, I watch her press play.

"I—I don't know who—"

"Is this…is this *Twilight?*"

I wish I had a different answer. "Yeah…not sure how. Who watches that shit?"

She smirks and turns up the volume. "Sure. You spilled the beans like a little girl the first night I met you. You were for sure watching this. Let me guess…" She goes into my guide. Dammit! "Knew it! Saved to favorites." My childish frown doesn't match her humorous grin. "Man, I have to ask, are you Team Edward or Team Jacob?"

"Thought you haven't seen it?"

"I haven't. But it doesn't take a genius to know the characters. People were obsessed with it for years."

"See! I mean, it was okay—"

A knock has my head snapping toward the door. Who the hell?

"Uh…are you going to get that?"

Hell no. "It's probably the wrong apartment. People get them mixed up all the—"

Another round of banging, followed by the sound of Ben's voice. "You gotta be kidding me."

"What? Who is that?"

My soon to be ex-friend. Why the hell is he here right now? Doesn't he have lives to save or some shit? I check the clock, forgetting I'm normally at work at this time and Ben comes over to crash during his long shifts, since my place is closer to the firehouse. Remind me to revoke that offer.

More knocking.

Not tonight, pal. Maybe if we stay quiet, he'll think I'm not home and leave.

Another round. "Dude, I saw your truck outside. I'd let myself in but don't want to catch you spankin' it."

Oh, come on!

"Sorry, let me get rid of him." I hop off the couch and head toward the door, opening it a crack. "S'up, dude. What do you want?"

"For you to hold me after a long day. What do you think? Open up. Got any beers?"

I jam my foot against the doorframe so he can't nudge it open farther. "No beers. I'll see you later, though."

"Dude, what's your problem? Let me in."

"No."

"Yes."

"No."

"Dude, open up! I've had a shit day." He pushes against the door, and I stumble back, allowing him entry. Dammit! How he's stronger than me, I have no idea. "Dude, are you seriously watching *Twilight* again? Oh…there's a chick on your couch."

"Yeah, asshole. Maybe it's time you leave." He ignores me and walks closer to the couch. There's no way he's leaving quietly. Then it hits me. If Ben recognizes her, I'm dead. "Dude, for real, you've got to—"

"No shit…" He walks around the couch. "I know you."

This is bad. *Really* bad.

Bridget reaches her hand out to him. "Hi. Bridget. We met at my cousin's engagement party."

Recognition sets in, and Ben's eyes light up like the Fourth of fucking July. He steals a peek at me, his smug smile telling me all I need to know. I'm busted.

"That's right. You're Kip's cousin." He takes another glance at me before giving her his full attention. "Fancy meeting you here." He smiles wildly. Instead of getting the hint and leaving, he takes a seat next to her. "What are we watching? Oh, I see, Chase's favorite. Is this the first round or second? Our boy here can't get enough of his vampire romances."

"Fuck off, dude. Time to go."

"Not a chance. I see you already have a beer waiting for me." He snags one of the untouched beers and turns to Bridget. "You don't mind if I stick around and watch with ya, do you?"

Say yes.

Say yes.

"Not at all. We can experience it together. I haven't seen it, but I know Chase loves it. Especially the sparkly part."

What the *hell?*

Ben bursts out laughing. I scowl at them both. "Oh, I like

you." He falls back against the couch, throwing his arm over the back.

His comment pisses me off. He just smiles wider. Bridget, the traitor, seems to find this funny as well. They also know nothing. The glitter scene happens to be one of the best parts of the movie.

"Well, Edward Cullen waits for no one. Shall we get comfy and watch some soft-core vampire porn?"

I'm going to murder him.

Bridget giggles, and I hate that he gets that sweet little sound from her. Those musical giggles belong to me.

"Why the frown, Steinberg? Don't like sharing? Bridget and I can play cards or something while you watch your flick. I know you normally like to be alone when you—"

"Just start the fucking movie." For someone who saves lives for a living, he should see the danger in my glare and shut the hell up before I put an end to his.

Bridget covers her mouth, concealing a snicker, and starts the movie. Ben looks at ease, sipping on *my* beer, next to *my* girl, as the beginning credits play.

They ruin the first movie with all their lame ass jokes.

By the second, they quiet down, and I'm semi able to enjoy it because they become invested. It's hard not to be.

When the third one ends, I steal a glance over to see Bridget has fallen asleep.

Ben stretches out his arms. "Man, great movie."

"Yeah, I'm sure." I roll my eyes.

He looks over at Bridget, then tilts his head and makes stern eye contact with me. "Gotta ask, what are you doing, man?"

"Nothing."

"It doesn't look like nothing. It looks like you have Kip's little cousin at your place. And I've never known you to be a gentleman, so I'm gonna ask again, what are you doing?"

"I don't know," I hiss under my breath. "It's complicated."

"As complicated as Levi and Hannah? Because this sure looks like the same thing, and if I'm not mistaken, you're the one who had the biggest problem with it—"

"My *problem* had nothing to do with them. It had to do with you all ditching our guys' nights for chicks. Selling out to hang out with girls instead of manning up and doing the right thing."

"And that was?"

Not leaving me behind. Not making me regret turning my back on finding someone. Not turning into the pathetic, foolish guy I was with Caroline. "It doesn't matter."

Ben doesn't press. He's been around long enough. We bunked all throughout college. He's well aware of the damage and scars left by her.

"Fine. But I hope you know what you're doing. When Kip gets wind, he's going to murder you."

"Well, he's not going to."

Ben releases a low chuckle, and Bridget stirs. "Can I give you a piece of advice? Don't fuck her over. She seems like a great girl."

Like I don't already know that. I know she's too good for me. And no matter how hard I try, I'm scared to death I'm going to hurt her in the end.

"Thanks for the advice, Romeo, but I'm doing just fine. And I'm not going to hurt her. We're just friends." Ben snickers, and I want to smack the shit out of him. "Will you be quiet? You're gonna wake her."

"Okay. Sorry. Would hate to wake your *friend* up. Give me a break. I've sat here for a whole six hours while you two played googly eyes. Friends my ass."

"You don't know what you're talking about."

"Whatever, bro." He moves to stand. "Lie to me all you want but heed my warning. Kip is not going to take this news lightly. And if you want more advice, I doubt your *friend* is going to approve of you keeping her a secret. You may want to rethink this. Not sure this one is going to end well."

If I wasn't so worried about waking her up, I'd tackle Ben and pummel a few good hits to his pretty face. But he's right. Kip is not going to accept this. I'm living in a fantasyland if I think this is all going to work out in my favor.

"Whatever. Thanks for the tip. Don't you have to go save lives or something?"

He shrugs me off. "My next shift isn't until tomorrow. Gonna head over to the firehouse and snag a bed for a bit. See you for the games."

"Yeah, see you."

Ben heads out, leaving me alone with a sleeping Bridget. An angel who's going to end up sending me straight to hell.

~

Bridget

I feel like I'm floating on clouds as I snuggle into the soft bedding. A familiar smell wraps around me, and I burrow deeper into the feathery pillow. My body is so relaxed, it's as if I just slept for days. I inhale a deep breath, the scent provoking a flashback. I know what it is, but I can't pinpoint why. My body craves it. My heart beats faster for it. I search for answers, but the wheel inside my memory spins and spins. Why do I know this smell? I ache for it. Lust for it. Hurt for it.

The fog in my mind starts to wane. An image faintly appears. A memory. A trigger.

It can't be. I'm dreaming. This is not real.

I shake my head and clench my eyes tighter. He's not here. I haven't smelled him in over two years.

The scent only becomes stronger.

My belly tightens, and I force myself to wake up—to open my eyes so the memory buries itself back down inside the hole in my heart. My vision blurs, and I blink the fog away. The room is familiar from so long ago. *This can't be.* I suck in a ragged breath, slamming my eyes shut. *Breath, Bridget. This isn't real.*

Shifting to my other side, I nestle into the warmth of the blanket. The smell becomes stronger. Fear swells in my throat. *It's not real. It never is. He won't be here when you open your eyes.*

My eyes snap open. Sharpness slices through my gut. My breath is stolen as I attempt a gasp. I fight my eyes to still, afraid if I blink, he'll disappear. My breathing picks up. I reach out to touch his cheek, my hand shaking. I pull back at the feel of his skin.

"You're not real. You're never real," I whisper, shaking off the sight of him.

His eyes open, and the distant memory of his emerald orbs stare back at me. "Hey, baby girl. You're up early."

I don't understand. He's... "How...why are you here?"

His deep laughter sends a ripple of goosebumps down my arms. "Why wouldn't I be?"

Emotions grow thick in my throat. "Because you're not supposed to be. Because you never are. Because you're dead."

His grin, just as I remembered, spreads across his handsome face, his teeth gleaming back at me with his signature smile. "What are you talking about? I would never leave you. Come here." He reaches for me, wrapping his hand around my waist and pulling me into him. "Does this feel like I'm dead?" The heat from his body feels real. The strength of his hand holding me feels real. His head dips. His plump lips, just as soft as always, press against mine. "Do I feel real to you yet, baby girl?" He hums against my mouth, increasing the pressure.

He doesn't make note of the tears starting to rush down my cheeks. "You do. But this is impossible. You left me..." A slight whimper travels up my throat. I wrap my arms around his neck to bring us closer and kiss him harder.

"Does this feel real to you, baby girl?" The echo of his voice skates down my spine. His hand slithers below the waistline of my pajama pants. I moan into his mouth as his thick finger disappears inside me. "Tell me how you really feel?" He pulls out slowly, then inserts two and pumps in and out of me. "That's right, baby. Ride my fingers. I love the way you feel around me. Love listening to your little moans while I get you off. You'll always be mine." My eyelids squeeze shut as I lose myself to his touch. "You're soaking my fingers, baby. I love that I do this to you. I'll always make your body melt for me."

I shake my head back and forth, and my body begins to quake. "Please..." I beg.

"Say my name, baby girl."

I open my mouth to breathe his name, but the words don't come out. *Why can't I say his name?* I make another attempt. Still, I remain silent.

"Say my name, Angel."

The name. It's not right. That's not his nickname for me. His fingers take on a faster rhythm, moving deeply in and out of me. I bite at my lower

lip, mere seconds from orgasming.

"Say my name, Angel. Say my name and I'll give you what you want."

My words finally expel, but it's not the name I'm trying to say, and I cry Chase's name. He's suddenly above me, his fiery hazel eyes staring down into mine. My orgasm ripples through me, and I shoot up, moaning his name. My heart beats erratically. I grab at my chest. My head whips back and forth, searching my surroundings. My hands shake. My sex is still pulsating. Embarrassment flushes through my cheeks at the aftermath of my dream.

"Christ almighty," I groan, pulling the sheet off me. I scan around the room, confused. It takes a moment before I figure out I'm in Chase's bed. That last thing I remember is getting mad that Edward wouldn't change the girl into a vampire. I must have fallen asleep after that, and he put me in his bed.

I brush my hands down my face, the dream still heavy in my mind. My palms skate down my arms, still feeling the tingling sensation of his touch. I was dreaming about Jax. That's who I was giving myself to.

Until I wasn't.

I throw my legs over the bed, planting my feet on the ground. This was a bad idea. Staying here. Thinking this would be an innocent arrangement. Even unconscious, the lines are being crossed. I fall backwards, laying against his bed. Just to torment me more, Chase's cologne tickles my senses, and I groan. I can't do this. I'm not in the right headspace. I never will be. My body hates the fact that I'm rejecting what could be. But I can't go through another heartbreak. I promised myself that much.

I need to nip whatever this is between us in the bud. He's too attractive for his own good—and *way* out of my league, anyway. He would just get bored with me, and I'd be back to square one. I look at my watch. It's only seven in the morning. I need to sneak out and go back to Jonathon's house.

"Good plan." I nod and get up.

The problem is...my things are by the couch—where Chase is most likely sleeping.

"Okay. Slight bump in the plan. Just...be quiet. Grab the bag and leave. He seems like a heavy sleeper." Got it. I can do this. I open his bedroom door and listen for noises. Hearing nothing, I creep down the hallway. The good news is it sounds like he's sleeping. The bad news is when I spot my bag, it's sitting on the coffee table—right in front of the darn couch.

"Heavy sleeper. Grab it and go." Light on my feet, I tiptoe to the couch, holding my breath. As quiet as possible, I reach for my bag. Nice and slow, I pull it away, making the mistake of peeking at Chase in the process and gasp.

"Christ on a cracker..." I whisper, the rest of my sentence

stuck in my throat. Bare butt cheeks are on full display. My core pulsates. I bite the inside of my cheek, taking a deep breath. I need to get the heck out of here. Maybe I should just take a quick photo. Memories and all that. *Turn around, Bridget!* Yep. Right. Got it.

I twist on my heel right at the sound of his voice. "There's room for two if you're interested."

I squeeze my eyes shut. "Uh...no thanks...I'm good." What's *not* good is how dry my mouth is. "Uh...why are you naked?" I fight not to turn back around for another peek.

"Habit of living alone. Sure you don't want to snuggle? It will be a tight squeeze, but you can just lay on top of me."

I turn toward him and curse myself. He's sitting up, the thin sheet barely covering his package. *Deep breaths.* I wet my lips. "No. Hard pass." That didn't even sound believable.

"Sure about that?"

"Yeah. *Sooo* not interested."

Damn him and that sexy smirk.

"Okay then. You don't mind if I just go use the bathroom, do you?"

No. Don't do it. Don't—

Blessed baby Jesus.

I take that back. There is *nothing* baby about his essentials saluting me as the bastard gets up from the couch and stretches. "Beautiful day. Let's go grab some breakfast, yeah?" He walks past me, never dropping that smug smile. I keep my lips thinned and my expression un-readable. Until my eyes slip and I look down.

Holy moly.

I'm in big trouble.

His low chuckle makes me want to smack him. The closest body part is his delicious ass. I clench my hands as he swaggers to the bathroom.

Move your feet and walk away, Bridget. Escape.

"Want to share a shower? It'll be faster and we can get to breakfast sooner."

I struggle to clear my throat. "In your dreams." Darn it! That did *not* sound like I was not interested. More like interested, but *semi-not* interested. As in *shouldn't* be interested but intrigued. "Fudge! What's wrong with me?"

"What was that?" The sound of splashing water tells me he's moved into the shower, the hot spray running down his muscled chest. His hands working up his six pack. Soap. So many suds. *What am I doing? Get ahold of yourself!*

"Nothing. I'm...I'm bored. Just gonna go...somewhere else. Hurry up. Breakfast waits for no one." I twist around like a smart, level-headed, opportunity-missing girl and storm as far away from the bathroom as possible.

～

The cold shower trick must only be a guy thing. The frigid water did nothing for me.

Right after I left the confines of Chase's nudist colony, I grabbed my backpack and locked myself in the guest bathroom, fighting to make all these unfamiliar sensations go away. The intrigue. The curiosity. The want. I couldn't get my body to stop buzzing and almost stomped back into his bathroom and made him set me right.

Just weeks ago, I was this innocent, naïve virgin with no real guidance into the world of sex. I used to have this vision of myself offering that special part of me to the person I'd spend the rest of my life with. It would bond us forever.

Instead, I gave it to a stranger. A man who isn't a stranger to me anymore. One who seems to find himself nesting inside my mind and my heart. Someone who makes me feel so alive, it scares me.

Freshly showered, yet feeling no relief, I slip into a pair of leggings and an off-the-shoulder t-shirt. I check in the mirror, making sure my hair looks decent, and blot my lip gloss so it's a perfect mix of color and shine. "Oh, stop this." I'm acting ridiculous. Like a teenager with googly-eyes for a boy I have a crush on. In reality, he's just a guy I had a one-night stand with. I know nothing about him. He could be a serial killer for all I know. *Well, statistics may confirm zero serial killers are fans of Twilight.*

Still...this is wrong. Messed up.

It's time to come to my senses and get the hell—

"Angel, you ready? I'm starving."

And just like that, his voice has me slipping on my shoes and opening the door. "Did someone say breakfast?"

～

I can't stop tapping my foot against the floor of his hallway as we wait for the elevator.

"Impatient much?"

I turn my head his way, missing his comment. "What?"

"I said impatient. We may fall through the floor with your stomping foot before the elevator makes it."

I slam my foot down. "Nope, just bored. Trying to think about what I'm going to do once I ditch you after breakfast."

He chuckles, a deep, throaty sound. "Good. I was just standing here wondering what I would be forced to do if I was stuck with you all day..."

My eyes dart to his, and I instantly regret it. Everything in the way he looks at me tells me he had plenty of ideas—and they all had to do with me staying.

I try to steady my voice. "Good thing I'm dying to be out of your hair."

"We're on the same page then."

"Yep. We are."

"Good."

Thank God the elevator finally makes its appearance. And

it's full. The thought of waiting for another one has me plastering a smile on my face and pushing past limbs and ignoring the grumbles as everyone shifts for me to fit.

"Excuse me. Sorry. Just gotta get to my girlfriend," Chase calls out as he shoves his way through. So much for him getting the next one and giving me some distance. "Ah, there we go," he says, his eyes locking on mine as we're pressed against each another.

The door shuts, along with a theatrical number of groans. Maybe we should have waited for the next one. But I couldn't stand there a second longer. If I did, I was going to jump him and rip his clothes off. Not that being shoved up against him in the crowded elevator is any better. I try to stay still, but with every little bump, my body brushes against his. I dare to look down and acknowledge my nipples are getting hard. I lift my arms to cross over my chest. We hit another bump, and my hands jerk into his crotch.

I squeeze my eyes shut. *Why is this happening to me?* When I reopen them, I make another mistake and peer up at Chase. His intense gaze turns my knees to jelly. They gleam with challenge. Daring me to fight what's happening between us. I refuse to give in to his little game. I inhale deeply, trying to think about something gross. As soon as the doors open, I'll make my escape, skip breakfast, and change my phone number.

Thirteen. Twelve. Eleven.

The door opens to let a couple out, and I breathe a small sigh of relief at the freed-up space. Anything to get him away—

Two people climb in, pushing us chest to chest.

I divert my attention to the wall, finding the cracks in the paint the most fascinating thing to count—anything to avoid the heated feel of his eyes on me.

"Can you stop brushing up against me? It's giving me the wrong idea."

My eyes snap to his. Smug bastard. "I don't have a choice. If I had room, I'd be on the other side. Trust me."

Why does he have to look so hot and composed when my heart feels like it's about to burst out of my chest? I reposition myself and face forward to avoid his sexy stare that says *I'm undressing you as we speak*, while I reply with *Yeehaw, let's go.* This only creates a bigger problem because with the lack of available space, my butt rubs against his crotch.

Ten, nine, eight...

Seven, six, five...

The elevator suddenly jolts, and everyone jerks to the right. Chase wraps his arms around me, securing me tightly to his chest. He leans forward. "Old building," he murmurs in my ear. My body is going to ignite into flames if we don't get to the lobby soon. I'm seconds away from jumping out of my skin. The places where he's touching me burn. His cologne has taken over my nostrils and my mind...well, my mind is two milliseconds from shoving my hands down his pants and finding treasure.

Breathe, Bridget.

Two, one...

The elevator stalls. *Come on...* I rapidly tap my foot against the floor.

Two... three...

No, no, no, no...

"I hate when the elevator does this... such a faulty system." The girl in front complains as the elevator fails to open on the first floor and starts to trek back up.

A woman leans forward to press the button for the first floor. "Wait!" Chase blurts out, startling everyone. "Actually, I forgot... my wallet." He squeezes through the crowd, reaches out and presses the button for his floor. With each floor that gets closer to Chase's, my heart threatens to explode out of my chest. The doors open, and he drags me out, a barbarian dragging his prey back to his cave.

We stumble through his front door, and he kicks it closed behind us, then turns, pressing me up against the wall. "I'm done playing games. So, unless you're not, I'm ready to get down to business."

He doesn't allow me to answer. The way my body trembles in his arms is the only answer he needs. His mouth crashes over mine, his full lips warm and enticing. Our hands claw at one another. My shirt is ripped off as I fight to get his up and over his head. His cock strains against his jeans. He grinds into me, and my lips curl up at the corners.

"This is a bad idea," I pant, getting his shirt stuck over his head. He steals a glance at me, and there's no hiding the lust he sees staring back. He stifles a smile, and I want to swipe that smug look off his face. No matter how hard I pretend, he knows I want this just as bad.

"You have no idea what a good idea this is going to be." He takes over, tossing his shirt to the side. His mouth is back on mine, his tongue breaking the barrier of my lips. Heat spreads between my thighs, and I open for him willingly. The thickness of his cock presses into me, and my back slides up the wall. A shaky breath escapes me, and my head falls against the surface. His lips pull from mine, grazing down my neck. "So damn sweet," he murmurs, the warmth of his breath skating along my skin. Goosebumps pebble down my arms. "Fuck, I could devour every piece of your milky skin." He pulls back my bra to expose one of my breasts. His mouth covers my nipple, and I hold on for dear life as he nips and sucks. "Tell me what you want, Angel."

My legs clench tighter around his waist. My sex pulsates. I'm drenched between my thighs. "I want you to stop talking."

His chuckle vibrates against my breast. My skin becomes too hot. He bites down on my flesh, and my back arches. "Chase," I moan out his name.

"That's right baby. Beg. Tell me what you want."

I close my eyes and pull at his hair. "I want you to shut up and fuck me." My vulgar words stun me, but if he doesn't touch me soon, I'm going to combust. His hands become ruthless, tearing at my leggings. He shoves them down my ass, growling at the sight of my soaked panties.

"That for me, Angel?" He rubs my clit, and I pull in a tight breath, still fisting his hair.

"It's gonna be for someone else if you don't get the job done." I can't help but grind against his hand, dying for even the smallest amount of friction. He pulls my underwear to the side and plunges a finger into my wet, aching sex. "Chase," I whimper, biting my bottom lip. He pulls out and eases back in, this time offering me two fingers. My hips work back and forth, fucking his hand. I can't take any more of his teasing. "More. Give me more," I demand. My body shakes. My sex becomes deprived of what it really wants. I need more than just his fingers.

He works me harder, faster, until my walls clench around him. "Oh God," I moan out my orgasm.

"The way you look right now." He pulls out, his fingers coated in my juices, and pushes his jeans down past his ass. There's no warning, but I don't need one, before he slams inside me. I cry out in pleasure. "Jesus, you're so tight and wet. Fucking perfect." He thrusts into me, each one bringing me closer and closer to the edge. Another orgasm builds, and I fight to hold back, never wanting this to end. "Still think this is a bad idea?" He pulls out, thrusting deep.

"Please…stop…talking—*ahhh*!" My eyes fall to the back of my head, and I cry out, losing myself to another explosive orgasm.

"Shit," Chase grunts as I squeeze around him. He pistons into me, his cock growing wider, causing another long moan to fall from my lips. "Fuck, I gotta pull out—"

"Don't you dare—pill—keep…going…"

His eyes darken to the deepest shade as he plunges into

me, once, twice, three more times, until he growls out my name as the warmth of his cum fills me.

It takes a solid minute for us to catch our breath. His forehead rests against mine, and I bask in the warmth of his breath. When another minute passes, he leans back and pulls us off the wall.

"Where are we going?"

"Sure as hell not out anymore. All food will be delivered today. You're not leaving my bed until next week. We're doing that about a million more times."

I can't hold in my laughter. He is absolutely ridiculous.

He's also on to something. "Good thing there are apps for that. No talking needed. You already do so much of—ouch!" I cry out in laughter as he slaps my ass.

"Don't worry, my mouth is going to be too occupied sucking your sweet little pussy to do any talking."

So. Amazingly. Ridiculous.

Chapter
Eleven

Chase

THERE'S NOTHING BETTER THAN SLEEPING ALONE. NO ONE TO share the covers with. Fighting for bed space and pillows. I always had a rule. Never bring girls back to my place and never spend the night. After offering them a night they'll never forget, I take myself home to the comfort of my own bed and sleep like the dead.

Until now.

I gaze over at the little bombshell sleeping like the dead in my bed and smile at how perfectly she looks cozied up in *my* sheets, hogging *my* favorite pillow.

She looks absolutely perfect here.

I pull her into me, obsessed with the way her little body fits snuggled up against mine. I can't get enough of her smell, the lingering scent of cherries and vanilla. My lips find my favorite little spot under her earlobe. "Morning, Angel." I nuzzle my nose against her neckline.

She squirms under me, attempting to hide her adorable face in the pillow. "Please. No more. I don't even think my legs work."

I chuckle against her skin, leaving a warm trail of kisses down her neck. "Wasn't offering. You've tapped out on all your free rides. If you're looking for any more, you're going to have to pay up."

She peeks back out, her sleepy gaze peering down at the big guy. "Free rides?"

"Yep. I've been very generous the past two days. Sunday is the day of rest—and to pay up."

"What exactly am I paying up on? Didn't know I landed myself an escort."

I steal a quick kiss. "You haven't. But my fake boyfriend services only go so far. It's time to officially sign up."

She stares at me, trying to process. Yeah, it's a lot. I'm not even sure what I'm asking. *You're asking her to go steady, Casanova.*

"Let me get this straight. The past two days have been my free trial, and if I want back on the horse, I need to pay? And by paying, you mean be your girlfriend?"

She's hot *and* smart. "Correct."

"Why would I want such a thing?" she asks, baffled.

"Because we're good together." Is there any other reason? She only chuckles in reply. "What, do you not agree?"

"Just because you're good in bed doesn't mean we should date for real. Ever."

"Wasn't going to be the first thing I pointed out, but if you're starting there, that's one reason why we damn well should."

She full on laughs. "Why would I even consider such a crazy idea? It doesn't scream bad idea whatsoever."

"Maybe you like being bad," I reply.

"Maybe *you* are insane. Us dating? Insane."

"Are you scared? I thought I pinged you for a girl who likes adventure."

She releases a cute little snicker. "I'm not sure I'd consider dating you an adventure—more like a disaster."

"Oh, you mean delightful. Or is it delicious?" I grab her

hips, and she squeals at my touch. "If we dated, you would have full access to me whenever you want. If you're ever in need of saving, I'll rescue you. You have a full-time breakfast, lunch, and dinner date. Not to mention, not only am I an A-plus in the looks department, I'm super handy. The perfect catch, if you ask me."

The most beautiful laughter falls off her lips. "Oh, in that case, sign me up! Sounds like exactly what I need in my life." She stares at me a beat until her humorous gaze shifts. "Oh my god…wait…you're not serious, are you?"

"Would it be a terrible thing if I was?"

The humor in her gaze fades as she ponders my question. "We've both made our past clear. We're both broken. Two broken people don't work. It just makes a bigger mess."

I've been trying to be patient and understanding, but I'm done. I roll her onto her back, capturing her beneath me. "All I hear are excuses. Sometimes two broken pieces end up fitting perfectly together."

Her plump lips part, but no rebuttal falls off her tongue. "I told you. This has been fun, but I'm done playing games. I get it. You're scared. Hell, I never thought I'd ever be in a situation to care about someone like I'm starting to with you. And yeah, it's been fun playing your boytoy, but I have way more I want to offer you. So, I'm going to give you a second or two—"

"A second or two?"

"Yes, because you lying under me, looking all delicious, the second you agree, we've got some business to attend to. So, go on, have that internal battle where you tell yourself this is a bad idea, then realize it's a great one and agree so we can get on with it. Your two seconds start now—"

Bridget stretches forward and her arms wrap around my neck even before her time is up. Her mouth crashes over mine, and I waste no time in devouring her sweet lips. I break the barrier, wanting all of her mouth. Our tongues clash as we dance around each other.

I suck on her bottom lip. "You taste amazing." I can kiss her forever. Taste her. Devour every single inch of her. "Does this mean you've made your decision?"

Without allowing her to answer, I cover her mouth, then break away. "Say it, Angel."

"You truly are ridiculous."

"And all yours. Just a simple answer—ouch! Jesus!" I howl as she takes her fingers, clamps down on my nipple, and pinches.

"That's for being so bossy. One thing you need to learn about me is I don't take well to demands. I'm always willing to meet in the middle, but this whole caveman, 'you are mine' thing? It's not working on me. Just this once, I will look past your egotistical way of asking if I will be your girlfriend and—"

I crush my lips to her for a swift kiss, then pull back and jump off her.

"Wait—I wasn't done! Where are you going?"

"You just admitted you're my girlfriend. Gotta go update my profile page. Make it official."

By the time I get back, she's climbing off the bed in search of her clothes. Her pouty lips are adorable.

"You seriously just left me to update your profile status? What are we, in high school?"

"Nah, I'll do that later when I post selfies of us kissing and holding hands. Right now, I want to celebrate. And nothing sounds sweeter than decorating you in frosting and licking each delectable bite off you." Her eyes drop to the container of icing I have in my hands.

Yeah. It's celebrating time.

Chapter
Twelve

Bridget

IT'S OFFICIAL. I HAVE TO BE OUT OF MY EVER-LOVING MIND.

I can't fight my smile, thinking about our weekend. How ridiculous Chase is. Persuasive. Amazing. Funny and giving. So, *so* giving. My cheeks blaze crimson. I giggle under my breath as I walk up to Frosted, the small bakery in town, before heading back to the Brooks' estate. I open the door and practically skip inside, hopping into line. My phone buzzes in my back pocket, and I reach for it, my smile bursting when I see Chase's name...or the name he programmed.

Chase your boyfriend: I think you forgot something. You should come back here. I'll make it worth your while. *Inserts winking emoji*

"The line's moving. You should move with it." I pick my head up from my phone and mumble an apology to the guy behind me. I step forward and reply.

Me: Sorry, can't. I took a detour to the donut shop. Thought to sweeten up my boss since I flooded his guesthouse and probably cost him my entire salary to fix it.

Chase your boyfriend: You don't owe him anything. Don't let him make you feel like you do. Should I come get you? He probably can't eat sugar. Old people have tons of health issues and shit. Plus, you know I'm a big fan of frosting.

If my cheeks hadn't already been blazing, they were now. Seconds after giving him the answer he wanted yesterday, he jumped out of bed and left the room. I thought he was serious when he told me he was leaving to update his damn social media status. Instead, he almost put himself into a sugar coma with the amount of frosting he licked off me. I couldn't even make out what I was screaming by the end. And when I came back to earth, because whatever he had just done with his tongue had me flying so high, I knew I wasn't going to regret this new adventure.

Me: Sorry. No can do. But maybe if you're lucky, I'll save one for you.

When it's my turn, I practically sing out my order, adding an extra box for Chase. "Thanks. Have a wonderful day," I chirp. Light on my feet, I head out. My phone buzzes again, and I laugh out loud at the screenshot of his profile page in edit mode. "What a nut—"

"Thought that was you."

Juggling the donut boxes, a hoarse voice pulls me away from my screen. My gaze locks on a woman I haven't seen in two years. Since his funeral. Diane Taylor. Jax's mother. She looks unwell. Her skin is the color of someone losing the battle to alcoholism. The scratches on her face due to addiction. My stomach bottoms out, but I force myself to find my manners.

"M—Mrs. Taylor."

"So glad you remember me. You look well. Alive. Unlike my son." Her words jerk me back a step. I suck in a sharp breath. "Laughing like everything is just peachy in your perfect little world."

"What? I was just—"

107

"Just moving on, as I assumed you would. Girls like you never stay committed."

Jax's mom never liked me. She was shattered by the news of her son's death. Who wouldn't have been? As much as I tried, she refused to speak to me. On many occasions, I attempted to bring her meals, but she ran me off her property. I just wanted to help her. Do what Jax would have wanted me to do. But she wasn't well. One of the main reasons Jax wanted to leave this place. To get away from her. The drinking. The drugs. After a while, I stopped trying.

"Mrs. Taylor, I'm not sure what you're getting at. You know I loved your—"

"No, you loved what he gave you. You knew he was supporting me—and you hated it."

"What? No—"

She takes a quick step forward, jabbing her finger at me. "His father left us with nothing. My Jax worked so hard to make sure there was food for me. Money to pay for my medications."

Her medication came in the form of needles and powder. As much as Jax tried, she abused his kindness, but he couldn't watch her suffer. So, he kept giving her the money in hopes one day she would clean herself up. If anything, for him. "I know. But that money wasn't being used—"

"He died because of you. You took *everything* from me!" Her sharp words are a slap in the face. Guilt burns deep inside me, torching the headway I've made with my acceptance. I shake my head. "No, Mrs. Taylor, I loved him." I would trade places with him if I could.

"You're the devil who stole my son. It should have been you that night. You!" She swings her hand out to slap me, and I use the box of donuts to block her, smashing them along the sidewalk. "I'm going to make you pay. Make you wish it was you that night." She lurches forward and spits in my face.

"Killer." She raises her voice, pulling attention to us. "She's a killer! She killed my son!"

Bystanders walking down the street stop and stare. Panic seizes my lungs as I gasp for air... "I didn't. I'm sorry. I loved —" My voice breaks off. I can't even finish. I give up salvaging any of the donuts and take off running.

Chapter
Thirteen

Chase

HEY, KIP. YOU'RE LOOKING GREAT TODAY. I'M DATING YOUR cousin. Is that a new haircut?

No.

S'up, Kip. Great weather we're having today. I'm sleeping with your cousin.

No. Definitely no.

Kip! My man! I'd do anything for you—like date your cousin behind your back.

"Shit." This isn't going to go over well. *Just walk in. Spill the beans. Take the hit.* Maybe it won't be as bad as I think it will. Levi had it coming. Banging his sister and all. At least I'm coming forward and admitting I'm banging his cousin before he finds out on his own—unless he already knows. "Shit." I look around to see if Ben's car is here. It is. "Great." I'm too good looking to be hit in the face. At least Levi's nose was already fucked up from football. I stall, debating on walking in or making a clean break. Maybe I should just send him a text. Less violent that way. It'll give him the time he needs to calm down so we can talk about—

The door swings open, startling me out of my internal thoughts. I squeal like a fucking girl. "Gah! S'up! This weather, right? Love you, man."

"Dude, are you okay?" Kip stares at me.

"Yes. Of course. Why wouldn't I be?" Unless I'm about to *not* be.

"Uh…maybe because you've been standing outside my front door for almost ten minutes mumbling to yourself. The guys are inside taking bets on what drugs you're on."

"Wait, you can hear me? Like, you've been *listening* to me?" I'm a dead man. I love my nose. It's perfectly shaped. And soon, it's going to be crooked like Levi's. Shit!

"What? No, just get in here. You keep setting off my front door camera and the baby's trying to sleep."

He turns his back to me and heads inside as I fight not to vomit in his front bushes. Jesus, what's wrong with me? *Aside from the fact that you're dating a girl you shouldn't be but won't be un-dating her anytime soon because you've found yourself pussy-whipped and may be in love with her.* "What?"

"Huh?" Kip turns back.

"Oh…nothing." *Just having a mental breakdown.*

I need to pull my shit together. I walk farther into Kip's place, finding the whole crew sitting on the couch, the game on. "S'up, pussies," I say, my throat suddenly dry. Why was that so hard to say? *Not sure, poser.* Shut up.

"You talking to yourself again, Steinberg? Last night still lingering on ya?" Levi laughs as he sips his beer.

I make my way over to an open seat and throw myself into it. "Real funny, jerk-off. Just trying to remind myself why I'm still friends with you girls. Surprised the game's even on and not soap operas."

Levi laughs me off while Ben stares at me with suspicious eyes.

Kip comes up behind me and hands me a beer. "Where

the hell have you been anyway? You blew us off Sunday. Must've been a good weekend."

They have no idea.

I also really need Ben to stop staring at me. I pull my eyes away from him and clear my throat. *Act cool, man.* "Sorry, not gonna let you live vicariously through me. You got yourself into that marriage mess. Deal with it."

I take a deep swig of my beer, hoping they drop it and watch the damn game—

"No way. Normally, we can't get him out of our hair, and now he disappears all week. Did you join some sex colony? Oh! Or has it gotten so bad, you're stalking nunneries, trying to convert the innocent?" Kip and Levi laugh.

Ben does not.

"Listen, assholes, I don't do clingy chicks. You've got the wrong idea."

"Dude, that's *all* you do. It's why so many of them hate you. You just *do them* and leave them high and dry."

Not anymore.

And to answer your questions, I'm reformed and dating your cousin.

"Well, I hate to break it to you, but I had to work all weekend. Some of us aren't baby fed by our wives and fiancées. I've still gotta make a living." Another swig. Another lie I choke down.

I regret doing it, but I steal a glance over at Ben just as he shakes his head and flicks his eyes to the game, dismissing me.

He doesn't have to say it for me to feel it. His disapproval stings. I've never been one to care what others think of me. I'm a live-by-the-seat-of-my-pants kind of guy. But Ben's disappointment bugs me. If he knew our situation, his outlook would be different. He wouldn't just see me as a player messing with an innocent girl...then why can't I come out and admit I found a girl I'm completely lost in and I'd love if they all came to my neutering ceremony.

This girl is my kryptonite. And once people find out, I'm as good as dead.

"Well, speaking of chicks, man, you're never gonna guess who I ran into the other day." I cock my head back at Kip.

Change of subject. Thank God. "Oh, please don't keep me waiting. The suspense is killing me." I take a deep swig of my beer and bring my eyes to the TV.

"Caroline."

I choke on my beer. I twist around. "Where?" That scheming bitch hasn't been back home in years.

"I was at the store getting some diapers and saw her. She looks the same. She asked about you. Told me to tell you hello for her."

I bite the inside of my cheek and fight back the explicit thoughts wanting to spew out of my mouth. "Yeah, sure." I turn back toward the TV, this time not making eye contact with Ben. Ben is the only one who truly knows what happened between us. Only because I threatened his life if he ever made it public knowledge that I'd been played and broken. Not to mention he saw me cry. If it weren't for his support, my life could have taken a darker turn. I started drinking heavily. Not that drinking wasn't already a sport of mine, but I got ugly about it. That little switch in my brain that controlled my empathy and caring for women shut off. The only thing I cared about was getting revenge. By doing that, I slept with every random chick and left them high and dry. Just like she'd done to me. Too bad it never made me feel any better. The pain of her betrayal never lessened. The anger. I swore I would never let another female fool me. It's why I dropped out of school after only two years, came home, found a job in construction to support my "fuck it" lifestyle, and never left.

"What's with the snarl? Thought you two ended on amicable terms?" Levi asks.

Another swig. "We did. A lifetime ago."

"Man, I remember you two. Always hot and heavy

whenever we were all home from college. What'd you really do to mess that one up?" Kip jokes.

I clench my hand so hard around my beer, the glass threatens to shatter.

"Caroline? You two must have been high," Ben chimes in. "That chick had some weird ass fetishes. Like animal fetishes. Thank God he broke it off with her."

Ben looks my way and raises his beer. "Glad that bitch is gone."

I raise mine as a secret thank you.

"Damn, who knew. She's still hot, though. Maybe you two should get together. This day and age, fetishes are the new—"

I shoot up from the couch, startling everyone. "Gotta take a piss. Don't go knitting too many purses while I'm gone." I strut down the hallway, holding in the anger I hide so well when it comes to her. *Why the hell is she back?* It doesn't matter. She knows to stay far away from me.

I pull my phone out, needing the sound of Bridget's voice to calm me. When I dial her number, it rings a few times before I'm sent to voicemail.

Chapter
Fourteen

Bridget

"COME OUT, COME OUT, WHEREVER YOU ARE," I CHANT DOWN the dimly lit hall of the Brooks' estate. More like a fortress. "I'm coming to find you!" I call to Anna as she hides. We've been at it for over an hour, and I'm feeling defeated. Door after door, I jiggle the handle and peek inside. I will never understand the need to have such a large house when only two people live in it.

Another door, another failed attempt at finding her. "Where the heck is she?" I mutter to myself as I make my way down the never-ending hallway. I should have laid down boundaries before I agreed to this. For starters, only hide on the main floor. "Okay, you win. Come out now." It's close to dinner. The last thing I need is for Jonathon to come home and for me to have no idea where his daughter is.

My back pocket buzzes. I pull my phone out to see Chase's name across the screen. I hesitate for a moment, then decline his call.

Ignoring him won't make it go away. I'm not ignoring him. I'm just trying to figure things out. For starters, how not to feel guilty for finding happiness again. I can't get the hateful words from yesterday out of my mind. Seeing Mrs. Taylor rattled up too many old emotions. So much hidden pain. So many broken promises.

Chase made me forget those promises. His own affection filled those empty spaces. His smile and laugh made me believe it was okay to feel again.

Until I saw her.

Every hateful word she spewed was true. It was my fault her son was gone. She's right to blame me for her pain. If Jax was still alive, maybe he would have gotten her the help she needed. While she continues to suffer, here I am moving on and forgetting my promises. Playing coy with a guy I carelessly let inside my heart, allowing him to see a side of me that truly wasn't available. I made a commitment to him I can't keep.

I inhale a deep breath, fighting back tears. Fighting back the hope of bringing light back into my life. I don't deserve it, and Chase doesn't deserve the baggage I come with. *He has baggage too. You can fix each other.* We can't. And I can never let him know I was the reason the only person I've ever loved died. I wouldn't be able to bear the look of disgust—the same look my parents bore on me for being with him—the same destructive look his mother seared me with for what I cost her.

A knot tightens in my stomach, and I slide my phone back into my pocket. "Okay, Anna. Game's over. Time to get ready for dinner." I reach for the last door, but the knob doesn't turn. I jiggle it again, to no avail. "Anna? Are you in here?" I call out. A keypad rests above the handle, requesting a passcode to get in. "Anna, come on. This isn't funny." I push a couple digits, and the keypad flashes red. I try again, as if I have any chance of getting it right.

"Are we lost?"

I jump out of my skin at the deep sound of his voice. My body jolts, and I fall backwards into Jonathon. His large hands grab at my waist as I stumble.

"Oh my god! You scared me to death. I—I was just trying to get in. Not spy or anything—Anna is hiding. I wasn't sure if she locked herself in this room." I turn with him still holding me. The hallway is barely lit, but I can still see the depths of his blue eyes gazing down at me. "I—"

"My apologies. I didn't mean to scare you."

"Oh...uh, it's okay. I wasn't trying to snoop—"

"It's fine. But she's not in there."

"Oh...okay." We stand there for a beat until his eyes fall on his hands, still holding me. He slowly releases me and steps away. "I guess hide and seek is not one of my strong suits. I swore I heard her down here, but—"

"Anna is too good at that game. I should have warned you to suggest another game if she ever brought it up. She had the last nanny in tears and on the verge of calling the authorities before she finally came out."

My eyes widen. "Oh my God."

"When the house was built, they had secret passages built in to make it easier for their staff to get around without disturbing the owners. Anna likes to lure the sitters down here and take the secret stairs back up, leaving them to fend for themselves. She's actually in her room getting ready for dinner."

What! That little... "Oh, well...okay then. I'm sorry—"

"Do not apologize. She's a bright little girl who doesn't make the best decisions. She's the one who owes you an apology. For the future though, this room is strictly off-limits. Now, come. Let's get settled in for dinner. I've had a hellish day. Some good food and company are just what I need to make it better."

I nod, and he raises his hand for me to go first. Even knowing he's behind me, I can't help but look back, my eyes searching out the lock on the door.

∽

Dinner is pleasant, as always. I really enjoy Jonathon's company. I can't deny he's a very attractive man. His jet-black hair, always perfectly in place. His hard cheek bones and devilish smile. You would have to be blind not to notice or be affected. Our conversation is light and easy. Anna chimes in here and there. The food is out of this world. Alice, their private chef, has been with them since before Anna was born and knows how to serve up a gourmet meal. When my stomach is about to burst, and Anna yawns at the table, I say goodnight to Jonathon and put Anna to bed. When I return, he's nowhere to be found. The curiosity in me wants to sneak back down in the basement to see what was behind that door, but I decide against it.

On the way back to the guesthouse, I reach for my phone. I put it on silent during dinner so I wouldn't be distracted. There's a missed text from Chase.

Chase your boyfriend: Hey, can you relay a message to the donuts you got me? Tell them I miss them and can't stop thinking about licking them clean. Thanks.

Chase your boyfriend: Oh, yeah, sorry. Hope you're doing good too.

I feel like a jerk for blowing him off the last couple of days. My run-in with Jax's mom messed me up. I'm confused and torn. I want something I worry I can't have. Another text pings through—a meme of a dancing donut. I shake my head and chuckle softly. I finally give in and reply.

Me: Sorry to break it to you, but the donuts actually swing the other way. I licked all their icing off and they looooooooved it. They're just bare donuts now.

I smile, waiting for his snarky reply. The three little dots appear then go away. I unlock the door to the guesthouse and slip inside, locking it behind me. I keep checking my phone for a reply, but nothing. Disappointed, I get ready for bed. Why should I even care? Only hours ago, I convinced myself this wasn't going to work and was on the road to breaking it off. Now, I can't manage three whole seconds before checking my phone again.

I grumble while brushing my teeth and slip into a pair of pajamas. I reach for my phone and stop myself. *Get ahold of yourself. You're starting to look pathetic. You were going to dump him anyway. Who cares?* I shouldn't have even engaged in his cute message. It wasn't even that cute. Corny, to be honest.

A small knock sounds against the guesthouse door, and I pause in my step. My skin pebbles with hesitation, and I look at the time. Maybe Anna woke up. Or Jonathon needs to leave. I grab my robe and head toward the door. When I open it, it's not Jonathon I greet.

"Say that to my face. No—show me just how much they enjoyed your tongue licking them clean."

Chase doesn't give me the chance to respond. I don't think he ever planned on it either. He pushes inside and grabs me, his foot kicking the door shut. His mouth crashes over mine, and I don't hesitate to play along. Wrong or not, I need this. I need him. My body sparks to life. The world around me blazes with this bright aura of need, desire…love. I refuse to admit I could love someone this fast. Someone who's not Jax. The way my heart beats wildly for him. My skin tingles every time he touches me. My entire body explodes with desire when he claims my lips and owns my mouth.

I forget all that's wrong in my world. All that will be wrong if I allow this to go too far. Instead, I allow my heart the warmth of his skin against me. His mouth. His hands.

"I would tell you, but I'm not sure you can handle it. It was really, *really* messy."

His growl vibrates against my mouth. He sucks in my bottom lip, pressing his teeth down against my flesh. "How messy? Did you have to clean yourself up afterwards?" His hands skate down my ribs, one disappearing inside my pajama bottoms.

"Yes. God yes."

"Tell me more." He finds my wet center and presses a finger slowly inside me.

"It was so dirty, I ruined my clothes. Had to change my panties. They were soaked with—*Ahh...*" I moan as two large digits thrust into me. He pulls out and serves me with the same glorious torture.

"You are one messy girl. Maybe it's my turn to clean you up." He lifts me, forcing my legs to wrap around his waist. His strength holds me in place with one arm while he continues to fuck me with his other, his fingers becoming more ruthless with each breathless moan. "Not gonna lie, Angel, I'm feeling really jealous of those donuts." In and out. "It's only fair I give you the same treatment so you never think of those donuts again."

He walks us to the bedroom, and before I can manage a breath, tosses me onto the bed. "Now, my little sugar addict, show me exactly where you spilled the icing?"

My gaze fills with mischief. "I'd have to take my clothes off to show you. Specifically, these." I point to my pants.

His devilish smirk is the sexiest thing I've ever seen. "Do what you must."

Sucking in my bottom lip, I shimmy out of my pajama pants.

"The panties are going to need to go too. Better visual." I can barely contain my excitement. The cool air spreads along my pussy as I rid myself of my panties, leaving myself bare for him.

He clears his throat. "I'm gonna need you to show me exactly where the spill was, ma'am."

I fight my own grin as I lower my hand and point to my sex. His eyes light up like the Fourth of July, and he licks his lips. "Well then, I better get to work." His head dips between my legs, his mouth smothering my slick cunt. I arch my back the moment his tongue swipes along my slit. "This is the icing I've been craving." He spreads my thighs wider, sucking every inch of me.

"Chase," I murmur his name, my hands disappearing into his hair. I can't help but close my eyes, sucking in my bottom lip as a finger slides deep inside me. "Yes…" God, I needed this. Craved this. My hips lift from the mattress with each slow thrust, and his slowness becomes torture. "More," I beg, running my fingers through his hair, putting pressure against the back of his head. He sucks me deep into his mouth, inserting two fingers. "Yes. Oh, yes…" I ride his mouth, then grab at his shirt to pull him up, needing more. "Inside me. Now."

"I love it when you get bossy with me." He's out of his pants and pushing my thighs wide open. When I look at his beautiful face, it practically knocks me off my axis. He strokes himself as he stares down at me, wanting me to beg.

"Give me what I want or I'll just finish myself—"

He plunges into me, robbing me of my next breath. "Ask and you shall receive, my little sugar Angel." He grabs at my wrists, pulling them above my head. His face is tight. Determined. He pulls his hips back and powers in, fucking me with an intensity that rocks my entire being. As much as I fight to make it last, my body trembles with my pending orgasm, and a hoarse moan travels up my throat as my body falls apart. "Say it, Angel. Say my fucking name."

His name is like ecstasy falling off my tongue as every nerve-ending in my body detonates. He groans, and his cock jerks inside me as he lets out a grunt then falls next to me.

"Jesus Christ, I will never look at a donut the same," Chase pants, trying to catch his breath.

I sprawl myself over his chest. "I won't tell you what I did with the ice cream cone I had for dessert tonight then."

Chase flips me onto my back, his naked chest in full view

as he hovers over me. "First off, do not tell me. At least wait about three more minutes. And why are you eating ice cream cones with your boss?"

His jealous scowl makes me laugh. "I wasn't eating ice cream with just him. Anna was there."

"I don't care. As boyfriend and owner of this delectable body, I revoke your eating privileges around anyone—especially sweets."

I can't help but snicker. "That sounds a little dramatic, don't you think?"

"Have you ever actually watched yourself eat an ice cream cone? If it's anything like how you claim to eat a donut, I most certainly am. Shit, I bet you looked super-hot. Was it dripping? Did you stroke the cone and lick up the side—*ouch!* Okay, too far."

I lose the battle pretending I'm annoyed at his crude comment and burst out into a fit of giggles. "Has anyone ever told you how ridiculous you are?"

"A time or two. But the girl who keeps telling me is just as crazy—crazy into her boyfriend—so it doesn't matter."

I stare back, happiness in my gaze. I relax under his hold until he lays back down next to me. "Chase, can I ask you a question?"

"Yes, I'll roleplay hot baker and naughty customer any day."

I smack him on his chest. "I'm serious. Why do you think this—us—why do you think we're a good idea? I mean, I get why, but why now? You said the same thing, a relationship wasn't for you. You were hurt and never wanted to put yourself in that vulnerable situation ever again. What makes you think I won't hurt you?"

He turns on his side, props his elbow on the bed, and cups my face. "For starters, you're nothing like the one who did."

"We've only known each other a few weeks. You don't know I won't."

"Let me tell you a little secret. I wasn't always like this."

"Like what?" I ask.

"Amazing. Perfect. A ladies' man—*ow*, okay. I wasn't always so cocky. Jaded. Once upon a time, I was just like my friends. The gentleman who held doors open, paid for dinners, and sent flowers."

"And now you're not? Thanks for the warning."

"You know what I mean. I was naive about the fact that love wasn't messy. I found a girl who took my breath away. We were young, but age doesn't matter when you're in love. I thought she was everything my life needed. We got along. Had similar likes. She stole my heart, and I let her." He takes a deep breath and falls onto his back, raising his arms up and behind his head. "I was so caught up in her bullshit, I didn't see the signs. They were small at first, and then grew. How can anyone who loves you do something to ever hurt you? I always thought that when I'd question her. Ignored the pit in my gut when it told me she was lying. But I trusted her. Because I loved her. I let her run my life. Make choices for me I wouldn't normally make myself. She ran me so ragged emotionally and physically, I wasn't sure what was up or down. But again, what did I know? It was the first time I'd been in love, and I thought my last. I tried putting a ring on it. It had been four years. We were in our sophomore year at school. I was living off school loans and ramen. Thank God for Ben and his parents. They kept us stocked with real food. I may have died of sodium poisoning otherwise."

"Anywho, I took the loans for school and bought a ring. Had this big idea she would say yes and things would magically fall into place. But not only was she sleeping with him, she was pregnant. Claimed they were in love and he was going to leave his wife for her. She told me she never loved me. That I was obsessive and overbearing. Said I had been smothering her our whole relationship."

My mouth hangs open.

"Careful, Angel. You're gonna catch flies. I'm not spilling the beans for you to feel sorry for me. My point is, I'm not that naïve boy anymore. I won't let someone hurt me the way she did. Ever. And I can't ever imagine you would."

I can't believe he told me all that just to make a point. It makes me want to hug him, then find his ex and shank her. We were both wronged by love. The kind that stole your heart, only to rip it apart.

"I'm sorry that happened to you."

"Ew, don't get all mushy on me. I don't want your sympathy. Well...unless it comes with heavy petting—Jesus! When did you get so violent?"

"When you got so sappy. Listen, I wasn't feeling sorry for you."

"That's not nice."

"Chase, for once, please shut up. I just understand. I know what it's like to want something and have it taken away. Feel your life go from reality to fantasy. Have choices taken from you. I've felt lost for so long, I'm not sure if I'll ever know what it feels like to know my place."

"Bridge, you don't—"

"I do." I inhale a breath for strength. "We both lost. Our stories may not be the same, but the outcome is. We've been so damaged by something that should bring us solace. Peace. I loved a boy who left me. It wasn't his choice. He would have stayed and fought for me. But I was selfish. And in the end, he died because of it. He took so much of me with him. I'm not sure I'll ever be enough for someone. And I don't know if I'll ever be able to fully commit to someone. It's too late for me—"

Chase cuts me off, silencing me with his lips.

I've said too much. Confessed too much. I kiss him back, ashamed of the wetness that mingles as our lips touch.

"You're enough, Angel. You're the most beautiful person I've ever met. And yeah, life fucking sucks. But you can't blame yourself. We've both been dealt a shitty hand." He pauses to suck on my lower lip. "But with us, I was dealt a full house. If you ask me, I feel like I fucking won."

Okay, take away his quirkiness, he sure has some words up his sleeve. I pull him to me, deepening our kiss. Pushing him to his back, I climb on top. "You're going to regret this, Steinberg."

"Not a chance, Matthews."

"We're going to break each other's hearts. Broken people like us...we don't ever heal."

His hand lifts to tuck a loose strand of hair behind my ear. "Never say never, Angel." He brushes the rest of my hair away, exposing my hard nipples. Leaning forward, he wraps his mouth around one. "Give us a chance. Let us make our own path." His tongue swirls around my hard bud, and my head dips back. With a pop, he moves to the other. "We get to write this story. No one else." God, he'd convince me to fly to Mars, the way he's teasing my flesh.

"Swallow your pride, Angel. Give in to us." I moan at the feel of his teeth grazing against me. "Say something. Tell me you're in."

Something snaps in my brain. The lights may be low around us, but brightness blares around me. Maybe I *am* ready to let go. Try life again. I never thought I would feel worthy enough. Wrapped in Chase's arms, I feel drunk off his touch. Worthy of so much. Capable of giving.

"Screw it. I'm in."

He pulls his mouth away from my breast. "You're in? Social media official—"

"Just shut up and kiss me before I decide this is a really bad idea—"

Goddammit, does he kiss me.

And yeah...he proves this is a really good idea.

Chapter
Fifteen

Bridget

Two weeks later...

"Oh, goodness. You sure do look like a princess." My smile is strained as I take in Anna. She insisted on dressing herself for her outing today with her dad—in mismatched princess attire.

"Daddy's going to love it."

My brows lift. "I'm sure he will." My phone buzzes and I peek at my phone to see my cousin's number.

"Hey Hannah."

"Hey, just checking in, you got a second?"

I look down at Anna who's twirling in the mirror. "Yeah, what's up?"

"Well! I was *hoping*... you would do me the honor of being my bridesmaid. Please say yes! If you refuse, I may have to tell Levi the wedding's off."

I shake my head, laughing into the phone. "Well, I certainly can't have that on my conscious. Duh, of course I will."

"Yay!" she squeals loud enough to get Anna's attention. "I'm so happy. Obviously, we have the engagement party coming up. I plan on asking everyone else then but wanted you to be my first."

"That's awesome. You know I'd be honored."

"I'm so excited. My mom is going a little nuts over the planning, but it'll be nice. Levi is so swamped at the office that it gives me time to help her. But! If you're free, I'd love to hang out! You can tell me what's *new* in your life."

My lips curl into a cheesy grin. I don't even know where to begin. "Well, actually—"

"Anna? Bridget?"

"Shoot, I gotta go. Mr. Brooks is here to take Anna out for the day. Call you later?"

"You better."

I hang up and peer down at Anna. "Your dad's home. Ready to meet him in the foyer?"

Anna spins one last time in the mirror then races out of her room. I stay close in case she trips on her princess dress as we make our way down the main staircase. When we turn the corner, we find Jonathon waiting at the bottom.

Anna squeals, and I blush. He's in a pristine suit, his hair in place, his devilish smile on his lips.

"Hey there, kiddo. You ready to go on an adventure?"

"Yes, Daddy!"

Jonathon looks up at me as I descend the remainder of the stairs. "Thank you for getting her ready. She looks like a true princess."

I curtsy. "Anything for the queen-to-be."

Jonathon releases a hearty laugh as I straighten. "You two have fun. Did you need me to tell Alice if you'll be home for dinner?"

Jonathon gazes at me for a beat before answering. "You know what, why don't you join us?"

My eyes shoot to Anna as she twirls in her dress.

"I don't want to intrude. It's your—"

"I insist."

"Are you sure?"

"It would make her day. Both of us. Come. You would be a great addition." We hold our gazes for a bit longer, and I force my eyes from his, needing to break the connection.

"I guess I can tag along. As long as it's okay with you, Anna."

"Come! Come! You can eat ice cream with me and play in the park. Daddy is too big to go down the slide."

Jonathon and I chuckle, and I take Anna's hand. "Then it's a date. Lead the way, Princess Anna."

～

Children's museum—check.

Lunch—check.

Ice cream—check.

By the time we make it to the park, I don't know who's more exhausted, me or Anna.

"Bridget, let's go!" She grabs my hand and tugs me down the sidewalk toward the park. I almost lose my footing, and Jonathon reaches out and cups my waist to steady me.

"Easy, kiddo. Let's let Miss Bridget keep her arm." His gaze is heavy on me, his lips turning up into a sensual smile. Warmth spreads across my cheeks. It's a mystery to me why he's still single… If he is. He seems to keep his personal life under lock and key.

"It's fine. I may be just as excited. It's probably frowned upon to go down slides at my age. The little ones get territorial over their playground. I'm using Anna as my excuse to live out my childhood again." I offer a playful smile. "Let's go. I get to go down the big one first!"

I let Anna drag me all over the playground, enjoying every single bit of it. It's been so long since I've felt so carefree. Even as a kid, my time was mostly spent at the church helping my parents. As I push Anna on the swings, I try to calculate how long it's been since I've spoken to them. The day I moved out. Neither of them has tried to contact me. I thought once the dust settled, at least my dad would reach out. He would see he's overreacting and tell me he accepts my choices. But nothing. For a man who preaches forgiveness, he can't find it in his heart to show compassion to his own daughter.

"Bridget, faster."

Anna pulls me out of my thoughts. My eyes find Jonathon in the distance, his phone to his ear, his eyes locked on me. "Wave at your dad." I slap a happy grin on my face, ignoring the ping of lingering curiosity.

"I'm done. Can we go home?"

"Sure thing." I slow her down and help her off the swing. She skips over to her dad and jumps in his arms as he ends his call.

"Swing me, Daddy." Anna grabs each of our hands, and we walk together, swinging her up every third step. Her high-pitched giggles have us both laughing alongside her. "Higher, higher!" she exclaims, and Johnathon and I share in a look and, at the third step, we swing her up. "Yay! I'm flying like a bird."

Her sweet little laugh is contagious. Something out of the corner of my eye catches my attention, and I falter in my step, almost releasing Anna.

"Whoa, are you all right?"

I blink, trying to collect my thoughts. "Yes, yes. Sorry." I bring my eyes away from the woman standing by the tree in the distance, staring directly at us.

A hand presses against my shoulder. "Bridget, what's wrong?"

Why is she here? Is she following me? "It's nothing."

"Daddy, look! A squirrel!"

I excuse myself and walk toward Diane. "Mrs. Taylor, what are you doing here?"

"Just admiring your new perfect life." Her comment irritates me. I look back to find Jonathon and Anna focused on the animal and face back toward her.

"Well…you saw it. Now, leave me alone."

"That was the problem, wasn't it? You wanted my son's money. You were jealous he didn't give you any—that he gave it to me instead?"

"Like I said before, I have no idea what you're talking about."

She takes a step forward and jabs her finger at me. "He wouldn't give you money, so you got him killed. You did this—"

"Shhh…" I snap, hissing at her raised voice.

"Does your new lover know you're a murderer? That you're using him for his money?"

"Will you quiet down? He's not my lover. And I didn't kill—"

"Murderer!"

I step closer, ready to cover her mouth, when Jonathon's deep voice sounds behind me.

"Is there a problem here?" Jonathon asks stepping up beside me.

"No problem," Mrs. Taylor says, wearing a nasty sneer. "Just chatting with an old friend."

Mrs. Taylor stares at me, waiting for my next move. Finally, I force a smile and reply. "She's an old neighbor."

She holds his stare, but her eyes speak a different tune. Hatred. "I'll just leave you two lovebirds to it." Jonathon doesn't correct her, and neither do I. "Always a pleasure seeing you, Bridget." She walks away, disappearing into the busy park. I'm too shaken to say anything, and Jonathon doesn't pry as he escorts us back to the car.

"Are you okay?" he asks as we drive home.

I snap out of my haze. "Yes. Fine."

"You don't seem fine."

I'm not. "I am. I'm sorry. I'm not sure why she was there. Coincidence, I guess."

He turns to me, his gaze sincere. "Bridget, when will you realize you don't have to apologize to me?"

"I know. I'm so—Okay."

Anna starts chattering, and the topic is dropped. When we arrive at his estate, Jonathon excuses himself to take a work call and I help Anna upstairs and give her a bath. The distraction doesn't lessen the tightness in my chest. I clench my hands into fists, willing them to stop shaking. Diane is right. I am a killer. While she's suffering, I'm learning how to fall in love again. One thing I can't keep pretending I'm not doing with Chase. And I'm not sure how that makes me feel. Awful. Hopeful. Guilty.

I should end things with Chase. He doesn't deserve all my baggage. But the thought of never seeing him again. Being with him. It hurts even more.

I go through the nightly routine and wave to Jonathon, who's in his office on a work call, that I'm leaving for the night. Instead of heading to the guesthouse, I order an Uber. I have no idea what I'm doing, but I do know that seeing him will help give me the answers I need.

I bite at my fingernails the entire Uber ride. It feels like eons before I'm raising my fist to Chase's door. A minute or two passes, and I worry he's not home. I knock again, and still nothing. My shoulders slump in defeat. Maybe this is my sign. There's a heaviness in my chest and I try to conceal my disappointment as I turn to leave.

~

Chase

I step out of the shower and dry off. Even after standing under the steaming hot spray, my arms still ache from the long day of work. I toss my towel over the rack when I hear knocking on my door. I lean outside the bathroom door and check the time. "What is Ben doing here now?" This isn't his normal drop-in time. I'm really not feeling like entertaining his ass and was hoping to call Bridget and talk her into some phone sex. Shit, I'll settle for dirty text messages. I've missed her like crazy all day.

Get rid of Ben. Then call my girl.

I slide into a pair of ripped jeans, not bothering to even zip them up. "Dude, coming. Chill out." I open the door, shocked to see Bridget walking away. "Bridge." She stalls in her step and turns around. Her eyes are tight and filled with worry. "Hey, I didn't know you were coming. You okay—"

She runs up to me and I catch her as she jumps into my arms. "I need you to kiss me. Show me this is right."

I don't ask why. Or question. I carry her back into the apartment, kicking the door closed behind us.

I carry her to my bedroom. "What are you doubting, Angel?" I ask, laying her down like she's fragile.

"That I'm not a horrible person for wanting you."

I slowly remove her shoes, then slip off her jeans. "Tell me why you don't think you deserve to be cherished." Tears well up in her eyes as I lift her arms and discard her shirt and bra. "Tell me why you think someone as angelic as you can ever be anything but perfect." My mouth comes down, covering her breast. Her eyes squeeze shut, and I know she's fighting a battle within herself.

"Please, no questions…"

I take her pleading and decide my words are what she needs. "How about I tell you how every single fiber of my being craves you?" I lick her nipple until it hardens in my mouth. "I could eat you alive for every meal. But it's not your milky skin that keeps me wanting more. Or this…" My lips graze down to her navel, and I circle around it. She shivers under my touch. "It's not even the sweetness of your cunt." My finger grazes at her center, and her hips raise for me to touch her. But as much as I want to plunge inside her, it's not what she truly needs.

I work myself back up her little body, until the warmth of my breath heats her cheek. I brush my nose along the side of her face, hating the tears. I would fight all her battles if I could. Protect her from all the darkness that consumes her.

"What makes me break down at night at the thought of you…at this…" I drag my finger gently down her neck to her breastbone, stopping at her heart. "I crave this." I'm a selfish man, so I squeeze her plump breast in my hands. "I'm realizing I need this more than I need the plushness of your body. Your moans. Your taste. I need you for myself. I would fall from the highest pillars to protect you because this heart, it beats for me. I want to claim it. Make it mine. How do I make this completely mine?"

I capture her lips, soaked by her tears. Pain mixes with pleasure as I kiss her deep, her sadness gutting me. "I don't know why you doubt us. What I do know is that I need you. You're making me a better man. Showing me how to love again." I kiss her harder, fighting the sob building in her throat. "I promise I won't let you down. Because I need you. You give me the strength I need to be better. Don't run. Hold onto what this is becoming. It's going to be something amazing."

Her arms wrap around my neck, and she finally kisses me back. A small sense of ease fills me as I kiss her with intent. Need. "Be with me. Ride this crazy wave with me." I slide off my jeans and adjust myself between her thighs, slowly pushing inside her. "I'm falling hard for you, Angel. Don't let go, okay?"

"I won't. I won't." She captures my face and kisses me deeply. I slide my cock out and ease back in. As much as I want to fuck her, I want to cherish her just as much. "I won't let you fall, Bridge. I promise you. I'll always be here to kiss these lips when they're sad. Hold you when you need the comfort. Consume every part of you when you need to feel more loved than you already do."

A sob gets caught in her throat, and I kiss her hard, swallowing her sadness. I spread her lips with my tongue, and we dance around each other, spinning around in this vortex of something too powerful to define.

I make love for the first time, and it's the most mind-blowing experience of my life. We come together, moaning each other's name.

~

Bridget

"Chase, can I ask you something?"

"Anything." He brushes my hair off my shoulder.

"If you knew I did something horrible, would you still feel the way you do about me?"

"Depends on what it is. If you told me you liked a certain guy on a team I despised, I would probably drop you like a bad habit." My chest rumbles against his.

"Good to know."

"Sports are a serious thing."

"I'll keep that in mind."

"I can't think of anything worse. If you killed someone, I'd probably ask if they deserved it, then what you wanted for dinner." I stiffen under his hold. "Oh, shit...did you kill someone? Did he deserve it?"

I sit up. "In a way, yes." He stares up at me, his expression passive. "I want to tell you my full story. When I was young, I met this guy. His name was Jax. He is—was a year older. Came from the wrong side of the tracks, as my father would say. While I lived in the perfect house, with the perfect parents, he was rugged and poor. He had tattoos and smoked. But we worked. He loved me, and I loved him." His beautiful face comes to mind as I talk about him. His devilish smile and luring eyes. The way he used to hold my hand. Play the guitar for me. Loving me.

Chase brushes his fingers down my arm for support.

"One night, under the stars, he proposed to me, and I said yes. We made plans to have this beautiful life together. It was pretty cheesy, your typical two-point-five kids and white picket fence dream, but he made me happy." I pause, taking a deep breath.

"He insisted we do it right. He wanted my father's approval. He came over. Even dressed in some silly blazer to impress him. Asked my father for my hand, and he said no. He would not approve. He would not allow him to ruin my life. When in reality, he was completing mine." I stop to wipe at the tears falling down my cheek. "He wouldn't marry me without my father's consent. I was so mad. I didn't understand. But he refused to put that wall between me and my family. I got mad and took off his ring. Threw it at him and told him to leave. I wouldn't hear anything else he had to say." Chase grabs my hand and squeezes as I struggle to get through my story. "He left. I regretted it instantly and tried to call him, beg him to come back, but he never answered. That night, he was in a head on collision and died. The only reason he was on that road that night was because I made him leave."

The dam breaks, and Chase wraps me in his arms and comforts me as I fall apart. "Shhh…it's not your fault."

"It is. If I hadn't made him leave, he would still be alive."

He pulls back, lifting my chin so his eyes meet mine. "Bridge, you don't know that. Life is mysterious like that. There's no rule book. I'm not a believer, nor do I worship a specific god, but I do believe everything happens for a reason. If it was Jax's time, then you wouldn't have been able to change that. Don't blame yourself. You weren't the one who hit him. You were hurting. There's nothing wrong with that."

"I'm so selfish. He just wanted to do the right thing."

"No, Angel. You're human." He tucks my hair behind my ears. "You're beautiful and thoughtful. You're funny and kind of violent—which I find super hot." A small chuckle escapes my lips while I sniffle. "But most of all, you're giving. You love —and you love hard. Never in a million years would you wish for that to happen or cause it to. Life is ugly sometimes. And painful."

God, it is. It's terrifying.

"But sometimes…" he sits up, taking me with him, "it's beautiful too. Sometimes it leads you to a bar where the most enchanting woman steals your heart the second you see her. And she ends up showing you it's okay to be vulnerable. To love again. That you're worth it."

My mouth finds his. With the salt of my tears tingling on our lips, I pour every ounce of emotion into him. I need him to know how much his words mean. The way they mend the cracks in my heart. The way *he* heals me.

"Thank you," I whisper against his lips.

"For what?" He grabs my ass, pulling me closer.

"For making me feel like it's okay to let go. To love again without guilt."

My back hits the plush bedding, and his mouth clashes over mine. "You're so damn beautiful." He kisses me hard. "You've changed my life. My entire world. Hell, I can't even remember a life before you."

I giggle under him. "Technically it wasn't that long ago—"

He bites down on my bottom lip. "I wouldn't know. You're all I see. All I think about. All I want…" His lips mold to mine, kissing me with such intensity, it sends tingles down to my toes. "Tell me what I've got to do to make you mine. Tell me how to make you let go of your past so you can give me your future. Fuck…Bridget Matthews, I love you. Every single part of you. From your incredibly sexy body to your huge heart, to your beautiful soul." I gasp at his confession. "I love the way I am with you, and God, I love these lips." He kisses me harder. His mouth claiming my lips, his tongue dancing around mine.

He loves me. He just confessed that he loves me.

"Are you sure you want this?" I moan.

"I've never wanted anything more in my life." He grinds his erection into me.

I can't stop kissing him. Feeling him. Loving him. *Gah!* I love him. I pause for a beat, waiting for the panic to set in, the guilt, the rejection that forces me to throw him off me and run far away. But it never happens. My heart continues to beat hard and fast. This is okay. I can let go. I can allow myself to feel like I deserve this.

"You know this might end in disaster, right?" I hum.

"Impossible. Nothing about you will make me run for the hills." I chuckle against his mouth and bite down on his bottom lip, causing him to squirm.

"I didn't mean me. I meant this—us. We're both damaged."

"And I'm making it my mission to put you all back together. Piece by piece."

God, he has a way with words. Not to mention the way he kisses. And smells. And feels. Heck with it. I wrap my legs around him and do some old school gym moves, flipping myself so I'm on top. "Just remember you asked for it."

"God, it's super sexy when you say that."

"Is it going to sound sexy when you realize what a broken mess I am and leave?"

He reaches up and gently pinches my hard nipples, massaging them between his thumb and forefinger. "See, that's the thing. I don't think you're broken. I think you're perfect. Kind. Flawlessly stunning. You're also a little feisty, but baby, that's what I like most about you. If there's anything crazy about either of us, it's me. Because I'm crazy, out of my mind, addicted to you."

Him. And. His. Words.

A smile blasts across my face. "Your funeral, pal."

"That's where you're wrong…"

My brow raises. "How so?"

"For one, you're not my *pal*, and I plan on showing you exactly what you are to me. Second, the things I do plan are nowhere near sad and depressing. More like mind blowing and out of this world, orgasmic." And just like that I'm flipped and tossed like a rag doll, while Chase verbally and physically shows me.

Chapter
Sixteen

Chase

I PRACTICALLY DANCE INTO JIMMY'S BAR TO MEET UP WITH THE guys. I open the door and hug the doorman. He pushes me off, and I come to my senses. *I should probably get my shit together.*

Act cool. Suspiciousness leads to questions. And those are questions I do not have answers to. Nowhere near answers to.

"Hey, Stevoreno!" I wave at the bartender as I walk through. He gives me a strange look, but I don't care. I'm on top of the world. If anyone had told me I'd be head over heels in love a month ago, I would have laughed them out of the room. Fuck, how did my life turn upside down so unexpectedly, but in the most amazing way?

I reach the table, the guys focusing on the game. "What's up, guys? Missed you all. Anyone need a drink?"

Levi turns first. Kip, a solid second after. "What did you just say?" Levi asks.

"Asked if anyone needed a drink."

"Yeah, got that. I'll get back to that one. Before that…"

Why is everyone staring at me? "I said what's up?"

Kip jumps in. "No, no. You said you missed us—"

"I didn't fucking say that."

"Yes you did," Levi backs him up. "Right before you offered to get us drinks."

I throw my hands up. "I'm trying to be a nice guy."

"Yeah, that's the point," they say at the same time.

Kip speaks up. "You okay, man?" He stares me down as if I have two heads. "You've been MIA again, then show up acting all sweet. Something's up."

"Nothing's up."

"Something's up. What is it? Did you lose a bet or something and need money?"

"Did you bang someone's little sister and planning out bail money in advance?" Levi jumps in.

I flip Levi off. "Nice one." Why are my friends being such assholes? "Geez, can't someone be in a good mood?"

I look over at Ben, who hasn't said a word since I walked in. He hasn't bothered to participate in the Chase bashing. Hasn't even looked at me.

"Don't look at Ben for help. He's not gonna bail you out. He has less money than you."

Levi and Kip start laughing, but my mood plummets. And not from their shit talking. Why the hell is Ben mad at me? *You know why, asshole.*

"Or! Have you finally been snatched up by a female? Is that what it is? When a guy goes missing, ninety-nine percent of the time, it means he's got a lady…"

"Maybe he's settling down with someone's mom," Levi starts. "Remember that one time with Tina Wilson's mom? Or was it Becca O'Reilly's mom?"

Kip spits out his beer. "No, it was Jennifer Hallahan's mom."

"Okay, dude. Fess up. Who is it?" They both look at me, waiting for an answer. One I can't give.

I want to scream that I found a girl who makes me absolutely lose my shit because she's so amazing. From the way she snores to the way she looks at me when she's ready to pounce. And boy can that girl pounce. She smells like cherries and forever. I don't know how to process that, but goddamn do I love it. No, I fucking *need* it.

But when I say that, I'll have to follow it up with who she is.

And I don't know how to do that.

So, I dig myself a deeper hole.

"Well, I wasn't gonna say, but it's Ben's mom." Ben is going to hate me. The other two bust out into laughter, and Ben shakes his head, not even giving me the time of day to glance my way.

"Nice cover up. Not that we don't think you've already slept with Ben's mom. Sorry, Benny. Who is she?"

I shrug, the guilt tearing at my bones. "Trust me, no one special. Just my typical weekly fling." *Why, you asshole? Why?*

Kip leans forward, curious. "Okay, you have me intrigued. Do tell. Blonde? Brunette? Married? Underage?"

Jesus. I scoff at him, disgusted, as if I wasn't this person less than a month ago. But I'm too chicken shit to show this new side of me, so I hide behind more lies. "Come on…you know she's ripe and willing." Everyone jumps as Ben's chair skids across the floor as he shoves out of his seat.

"I'm out."

"Dude! Where you going?" Kip yells.

Ben looks my way. "Just not feeling the bullshit." He throws a few bills on the table and walks off.

"What's his problem?" Levi chimes in.

"Who knows? The anniversary of his dad's death and the fire is coming up…"

Fuck. I've been so wrapped up in my own fairytale shit, I forgot about the anniversary. The guilt presses down on me to the point of suffocation.

Kips slaps me on the back. "Don't worry about him. He's probably just jealous. Not everyone can be as carefree as you.

I love my wife, but at times, I envy you. No strings. No commitments. To be able to sleep with women, no feelings or remorse…"

My throat suddenly becomes dry. Even my swagger is ashamed of me. My conscience looks the other way. All because I don't have the balls to admit I'm not that person anymore. That the person who changed my ways is currently knitting my ball sack holder, and I'm gladly approving. That she's Kip's cute-as-a-button, spitfire-in-bed, cousin.

Chapter
Seventeen

Bridget

One week later...

"Oh, boy, these look super yummy!" I boast at the over-decorated sugar cookies drowning in sprinkles. Anna squeals as she shoves a cookie in her mouth.

"These are delicious, Bridget!"

"They sure are, master chef." I eat a small bite, hiding my cringe at the taste of pure flour, too much sugar, and not enough eggs. "You were right. You do know the perfect recipe!" Her infectious smile helps me swallow down the log of ingredients shoved into a bowl, wishing it was cookie mix.

My phone vibrates on the counter. I flip it over to see who's calling. My father. Again. This is the third time he's called today. Like the last two times, I hit decline. I've been so angry that neither of my parents have reached out to see if I'm doing okay, that now, it feels like it's too late. That or maybe it's the guilt. For years, I've harbored this resentment. Every time I looked at my father, it was a reminder of what I lost. What he did. But lately, I've come to the hard realization that it's not all on him. We were both at fault for Jax's death. Him for denying us, me for my selfishness. Maybe part of me fixated on my anger toward my father, so the fact that I was the one who made him leave would hurt less.

For years, I pointed blame. Fed off the hate. Denied myself of my dreams. If Jax didn't get to chase his, I didn't either. It was my burden to carry. And I had accepted my fate. My life would be lived in the shadows of a dream. Feeling hollow, wishing for something that was no longer mine. And I had been slowly accepting that. Until I walked into that bar. Until I made a bold move and gave myself to a stranger. Until he shined this vibrant light into my darkness and forced me out of those shadows. He showed me it was okay to love again. To move on. To accept that fate is sometimes messy. And I still deserve to live. Jax's life was cut way too short, but that doesn't mean I had to die with him.

I lean against the counter, a silly grin forming at the thought of us. How crazy this is. I propositioned him in a bar, and now we're dating and in love. I cover my mouth to conceal my girly giggle. Just thinking about him creates a flutter in my stomach. How hyperaware he is of every little inch of my body. I feel my cheeks warm at the image of him, naked and taking me to an unfathomable level of euphoria.

It hasn't even been a full day, and I already miss him terribly. I don't want to act needy or clingy. It's been so long since I've been in a relationship. Not to mention it's only the second one I've had in my entire existence. I need to play it cool. Hard to get. *He already has you, silly.* True. I unlock my phone, swiping away the missed call, and type out a message.

Me: Made cookies with Anna. Got sugar all over me. In desperate need of a shower.

I quickly snap a picture so Anna won't notice me sucking on my finger and attach it.

He replies almost instantly.

Chase your boyfriend: You're in luck. I have my

PHD in sugar removal. Also, now I'm hard. *insert attachment*

I sport a silly grin when I open the photo of a large construction machine.

Me: Always compensating. Lol. I guess I'll let you get back to work.

Chase your boyfriend: Not sure how I'm going to work with this huge boner. How about I pick you up after you get Anna to bed and prove just how much I'm not compensating?

"What's wrong with your face?" I pull my attention from my phone at Anna's voice.

"Huh? Oh, nothing. Just a friend being funny. Ready to put the last batch in?"

I text Chase back, accepting his offer, add a bunch of kissing emojis, and shove my phone in the back pocket of my jeans. I pick up the cookie sheet and slide it into the oven. "There. How about we start a movie?"

Anna jumps up and down. "Ratatouille!" I smile, repressing my internal groan. I can recite the movie word for word—that's how many times we've watched it.

"You got it, kiddo. Let's clean up first, okay?" By the time the kitchen is back to sparkling, the timer goes off. I take out the cookies and leave them on the cooling rack and follow a bouncing Anna to the entertainment room. At least, if I have to watch a movie to death, I get to do it in style. Plush reclining movie chairs with a gigantic screen is now my only way to watch a show. Jonathon texts, letting me know he has a dinner meeting and not to wait for him. We color while Alice cooks dinner and play I-spy while we eat. Alice leaves for the night, and we head upstairs for bath time.

"Why do you keep looking at your watch?"

"Just wondering what time it is." I can't help but constantly check the time. I check my phone to see if I missed any texts. My shoulders slump every time I see nothing in my inbox. Okay maybe I am needy and clingy. My phone buzzes, startling me, and I look down to see a text from Chase. Back to smiling. I open it.

Chase your boyfriend: Did you know today is the longest day ever? Legit. Looked it up. Also, my boner hasn't gone away. He's craving sugar.

Chase your boyfriend: Shit, sorry. That may have gone too far. What I meant to say is I miss you. My boner has nothing to do with it.

Chase your boyfriend: I feel like that came out wrong too. My boner is all about you. He's in it to win it.

Chase your boyfriend: Again. Foot in mouth. I feel like I'm messing this all up. Don't break up with me. My boner won't survive it.

Chase your boyfriend: Okay, that was corny. Maybe you should... *insert face-palm emoji*

I can't hold in my laughter.

Me: New phone, who dis?

I'm terrible. And giddy. And so freaking in love.

Chase your boyfriend: Oh, good, we're starting over. Hello, my name is Chase and I love to listen. Would you like to touch my boner?

An unrestrained laugh bursts from my lips.

Me: Why yes, I would love to. I just recently became single. Had to get rid of this other guy. Started to get a little creepy. Pick me up at eight? I have to warn you, though, I have small hands. May need to use my mouth too.

Chase your boyfriend: Jesus...you are the devil.

Chase your boyfriend: The sexiest devil. Mine.

I release a long sigh as imaginary hearts blast from my glassy, love-sick eyes.

"The water is cold. Can I get out?" Oh, shoot.

"Yes, of course." I get Anna dressed for bedtime.

"Can I have a cookie before bed? Promise I'll go to sleep right after. Please. Please."

I nod. "Yeah, just one, though." I race her downstairs and into the kitchen. She grabs a chair and pulls it up to the counter while I pull off the top to the cookie container.

A loud crashing noise comes from outside. I stall, my attention focused on the window facing the backyard.

"Can I have the chocolate sprinkle one?" I nod as I look outside the kitchen window. *What the heck was that?* "I'm the best cookie maker in all the land," Anna boasts as I hear it again.

"Anna, why don't you go upstairs and pick out some books to read before bed?"

"Can I bring my cookie?"

I hesitate. "Yeah. Just this one time. I'll be right up."

I wait for her to disappear up the stairs, then grab a flashlight and the large rolling pin. Opening the back door, I peek my head out and listen. "Hello?" I call out, my voice tense. I'm met with silence. Not that a killer would reply with, *"Hey, I'm over here."* I grip my hands around the rolling pin and step outside, pondering what could go wrong here with each step I take. Axed by a murderer. Kidnapped. Attacked by a wild animal— "Okay, too far. We're in the freaking' suburbs for Christ's sake."

"Hello? Anyone there?" I call out as I move farther into the backyard, toward the guesthouse. The flashlight blinks in and out, and my heart beats faster. "Oh no. Don't you— shoot." The flashlight dies, and I'm left in complete darkness. Panic crawls up my spine. Shuffling sounds echo from the side of the guesthouse, and I freeze. Thankfully the motion sensor lights kick in. I start to walk closer and squeal as a plump raccoon jumps out of the garbage. His beady eyes turn in my direction, and I panic, whipping the rolling pin at him, thinking he's about to mistaken me for his next meal. I twist around so fast, I almost sprain both ankles and slam into a hard barrier. I let out a harsh scream when two hands grip my shoulders.

"Relax, it's just me." I take a panicked breath as I look up at Jonathon. "Jesus, you're shaking."

"Well, yeah, you just scared the living hell out of me."

"My apologies. I saw you walk out. What are you doing out here?"

"I heard something. So, I thought I'd be a hero and go investigate."

"No one has entered the property. I would have been notified."

"Yeah, I solved the mystery. Turns out it was a raccoon feasting off the garbage."

"Ahhh..." He releases a low chuckle. "Some things do tend to get past my security." He releases me. "Your safety is most important to me. Next time, don't venture out here. Call me."

Words suddenly escape me, so I nod.

"Good. Let's get you inside." He offers for me to go first, and I trek back up the lawn until we reach the steps to the back of the house.

When we get inside, I grab for my purse. "Well, if you're home, I'm going to get—"

"Sit with me."

"Excuse me?"

"Keep me company while I have a drink. I've had a long day. I'd love for you to fill me in on today."

I quickly glance at the time. It's a quarter to eight. "Uhm..."

"Just one." He walks over to a cabinet and reaches for a bottle of bourbon. "How was Anna's day? She wasn't too upset I couldn't be home for dinner, was she?" He pulls down a crystal glass.

"Uh...it was good. We played a lot. Made cookies. Sang every song she knows a million times. She has no off switch."

Jonathon laughs, pouring the brown liquid into his glass. He turns to face me. "She gets that from her mother. She was always on the go. If you can imagine, I was a lot thinner when she was alive. She kept me going." He occupies a seat at the island, taking a deep sip of his drink. He seems to get lost for a moment. Blinking, he changes the subject. "She loves having you here. She's never been this way with any of the other nannies."

"And what happened to the last one?"

Crap. *Did that just come out of my mouth?* My stupid father and his comment about the missing nanny. And then there's the locked door in the basement he made clear is off limits. I can't deny there's something extremely mysterious about him. As if he's hiding something. Yeah, the nanny chained up in his locked room. *Jesus, shut up, Bridget.* "I—I don't know why I just asked that. You don't have to answer—"

Jonathon shoots back the rest of his drink. His mood darkens, and he slams the glass on the counter. "We had a misunderstanding. It was best she found employment elsewhere."

Okay. His reaction doesn't ease my suspicions.

Could my father be right? I'm about to be stupid and ask what happened to his wife. "What about—?" My phone buzzes. I pull it from my pocket and read the text.

Chase your boyfriend: Your chariot has arrived.

"Never mind. My boyfriend's here. Um, have a good night."

A battle brews behind those eyes as he stares back at me. I feel guilty for asking the question I did. They hit a nerve. He catches himself staring and blinks, pulling at his tie to loosen his collar. "Yes. Have a good night."

I make my getaway, thankful to see Chase's truck. Climbing up, I jump in. "Hey."

"Hey yourself, Angel. Long day? You look stressed." I sigh and lean back, adjusting my seat belt. "What? What happened? Did that douchebag try something? I knew he was—"

"No, it's nothing like that. It's just…"

"Bridge, you're freaking me out. Did that motherfucker do something to you?"

I angle myself so I'm facing him. "No, I promise." Maybe having this conversation with Chase is a bad idea. The last thing I need is for him to go macho man on me and cause trouble. And who's to say this isn't me overthinking? I've had a long day. And the false alarm with the dumpster diving raccoon still has me a little shaken. "Honestly, it's nothing. I've had a long day and just feel bad for Anna. Her father's gone so much. She misses him."

Chase eyes me, giving me the *yeah, right, give me the real reason* look.

"What? I'm telling you the truth. My parents were gone a lot on church missions. I know how it is to feel abandoned in a sense. It takes a toll on a young kid." I can tell I just won the sympathy award by his sullen expression, which was not my intention, but at least he's going to drop it.

"Whatever. I don't believe you, but I'm going to let it slide. If he ever—"

"I know, macho man. If he ever lays a finger on me, you're going to demolish him."

Chase nods like the big bad wolf when he's a cuddly bear who loves talking and chick flicks. "Enough about my day. How was yours?"

"Uncomfortable," he groans, adjusting his crotch.

I burst out in a fit of giggles. "I guess I should say sorry about that. Maybe I can make it up to you." Wiggling my eyebrows, I smirk at him.

"Oh, you're going to make it up to me, but I have something planned first." As if mentioning his plans makes him anxious, he taps his fingertips against the steering wheel. "I mean, it's nothing big." He turns on the heat. Two seconds pass, and he turns it off. "Just something I thought you would like."

"Okay..." I raise my brow, my curiosity piqued, but I don't dig any further for details. We enjoy the rest of the ride back to his place, listening to country music, which isn't as painful as I imagined.

"You hungry? Want me to order us some food?"

"I ate, but thanks." I drop my bag on his couch as he disappears into the kitchen and returns with a bowl of popcorn, boxes of candy, and a variety of drinks.

"I'm going to go out on a limb here and say it's movie night?" His friends weren't lying. He does have a weird obsession with vampires.

"Shhh...you're going to ruin it. Grab the blanket." He nods over to the throw blanket hanging on the side of his couch. I do as I'm told and sit down, leaving space for him. He drops the snacks and snuggles under the blanket, making sure to leave zero space between us. Leaning forward, he grabs the remote and the bowl of popcorn. "Now, before we get started, I want you to know, this wasn't my first pick."

"Let me guess, *Twilight* was?"

He cocks his head and winks at me. "It should always be the first choice." He points the remote at the TV and it turns on. "If you don't like it, we can change it, but I hear you like this kind of stuff."

"This kind of stuff?"

"Shh... It's about to start."

I lean back and get comfortable, tossing a handful of popcorn into my mouth. I wait for the starting credits. A smile builds as realization sinks in. I turn to Chase. "*The Notebook?*"

He fights to make eye contact, keeping his gaze on the television. "Heard it's a fan favorite amongst chicks." He shoves a handful of popcorn into his mouth.

"I love this movie," I say.

Victory beams across his face. "Glad you do. I can't

imagine it's better than *Twilight*, but I'm willing to give it a chance if it makes you happy."

~

The end credits roll as I sigh against Chase. "That movie never gets old." I turn to Chase and blink. "Are you...*crying*?"

"What? No." He swipes at his face. "That ending was dumb. I mean, how could she not remember him? They loved each other their whole life."

I bite the inside of my cheek. "Well, yeah, that's the point. They were so in love, when she loses her memory, he spends the remainder of his days making her remember."

"Why would they even write that in? It's cruel." He shuts the movie off, tossing the remote on the coffee table. "I knew we should have watched *Twilight*."

My handsome, lovesick man. "You're right. Shitty plotline. Would have been better with a shootout and drugs. Maybe throw some vampire action in there. Sparkling isn't just for one genre."

Chase's eyebrows flash up and he looks at me like I just confessed my undying love for him. Leaning forward, he presses his lips to mine. He tastes like buttered popcorn and Sour Patch Kids. Pulling away, he brushes his thumb along my bottom lip. "I've been waiting for someone to say that my entire life." His growing smile is infectious, causing mine to follow.

"You're ridiculous."

"And you're perfect." I adore the way he looks at me. It makes me feel loved. Whole. And the way his eyes shine with happiness, I can tell he sees the same when I look back at him. I laugh to myself at how corny it sounds, but my heart is happy. *I'm* happy. Finding him in that bar has truly changed my life. And I'm so darn grateful for him.

"You know, I'm sitting here realizing I don't know much

about you. Aside from your vampire fetish."

"You love my fetish. And ask away, I'm an open book."

I snuggle up on my side to face him. "Yeah? Nothing's off limits?"

He shrugs and leans against the couch, throwing his arms along the back. "Have at it, Angel."

"Fine. I'll start easy. How old are you?"

His shoulders lift in a carefree shrug. "A man never reveals his true age."

I slap him against the chest. "That's a line a woman would say."

"Well, men and women should be equals. We are in the twenty-first century. Next question."

I roll my eyes. "Favorite color?"

"Don't have one. Oh, wait!" He looks at me. "The color of your eyes. That's my favorite color."

I scoff and roll my eyes again. "That was super corny."

"But did you like it?"

I nudge him in the shoulder. "Not a single bit."

I don't admit a swarm of butterflies just ignited inside my belly. "Okay, next question. What were you going to school for?" This time, he takes a bit to think about the question.

"Don't laugh. I only made it two years, but I was studying to be a doctor."

My eyes go wide. "A *doctor*?" I reply, sounding a bit too surprised. "I mean, not that you couldn't—"

"I know. I get it. No one would look at me now and think I had it in me to do something like that. I've always been intrigued with biology and I'm really good at calculus. Ben and I went to college together, both with the same intentions. We wanted to help people. The short version is—shit got bad for me and I ended up dropping out and coming home. Benny stuck it out longer. He had a partial ride 'cause of football, so he had to, but there was an accident with his dad that had him leaving not too long after me. He ended up taking some local courses and landed a solid job as a firefighter. Sounds super lame, right? Who wants to jump into burning buildings and save cats stuck in trees all day?" He's trying to poke fun, but there's envy in his tone. Ben went on and made something of himself.

"Do you like construction at least?"

Another shrug. "The part where it reminds me of how I ruined my future over something so petty? No. But as we know, I can't take it back. I'm good at it. It's mindless and pays well. Not my dream job, but…"

"Why don't you go back to school then?"

Chase laughs, giving me a side glance. "Angel, I think I'm a little past that opportunity."

"No, you're not. People in their fifties go back to school and get degrees."

He rolls his shoulders back. "I'm not sure it's for me anymore. I feel like that ship has sailed."

I sit up straighter. "Well, tell that ship to come back. Who's out there saying you can't? Oh wait, let me answer that—no one but yourself. Not sure *I* would let you operate on me —*ouch*! I'm kidding. Just don't sell yourself short. I think you'd make a mighty fine doctor."

He sits up, pulling me onto his lap. "And I think you'd make a very, very bad patient." He squeezes my butt. "I bet I'd have to restrain you." One slow thrust, and I already feel the hardness brush against my belly. "I'd probably have to put things in your mouth to keep you quiet." My stomach clenches as he presses his thumb along my bottom lip until my lips part. "But I bet I can reform you into a good little girl." Leaning forward, he captures my lips in a slow, sensual manner that sets my core on fire. Then he stands, lifting me with ease, and walks us down the hall to his bedroom. "All this doctor/patient talk has me eager to practice."

I wet my lips, a slow tingle spreading along my flesh. My sex pulsates at what's to come. "Practice is good. But I'm gonna warn you, I'm a flight risk. Going to have to tie me up so I don't run away."

A low growl vibrates up his throat. He squeezes my butt cheeks, and I fight off a moan at the way his nails dig into my flesh. "Oh, don't you worry, Angel. I plan on doing more than restraining you." He kicks his door open, and before I have a chance to prepare, he tosses me onto his bed. "Jesus, we may have a problem," he says, staring down at me.

"What's that?"

"The way you look right now, so goddamn angelic, I may never let you go."

He doesn't need to tie me up to keep me. His words touch my soul, anchoring me to him. The way he looks at me, I feel cherished. Safe. My protector vowing to guard my heart. The damage left by an old love heals as Chase plants new roots of promise and meaning. The way he shines light into my life, touching my soul...time collapses, and I can't hold in the bursting of my emotions. "I love you."

His intense gaze flares with possessiveness. And it doesn't scare me. His need to own me makes me want to offer myself to him on a platter. I may have fallen once, but I trust he'll never let me fall again. "Well, what are you waiting for?"

"For this moment to never end. To never know a time when you're not laying in my bed. To know you are utterly and completely mine."

I swallow the lump of emotion in my throat. "Well then, get to it, doctor. All this *talking* has me super achy and in need of attention."

He stares down at me, triggering a rush of adrenaline inside my body. My breath quickens. He licks his lips, and I melt. I'm in for it. He covers my body with his, his heat sparking across my flesh. "Baby, the only talking from here on out is going to be you begging and screaming my name. Now, lay back and let the doctor inspect you."

I've never done so much begging in my life.

Chapter
Eighteen

Chase

ONE THING I'VE LEARNED ABOUT MY GIRL—BESIDES HATING green gummy bears, being ticklish behind her thighs, and screaming my name in more than one language—is she sleeps like the dead. That's why I'm not too worried about getting caught staring at her like a creep. Her lips are still swollen from last night, and she's making the cutest damn sound, like a little, purring kitten. God, I want to wake her up with my mouth. Feast on her. Imagine her taut body squirming under me. I told her I was going to keep her here forever—and I've never said anything more true. Every second with her, I fall deeper. Every single inch of her bewitches me.

I may have thought I was in love once, but it was nothing compared to the chaos going on inside my heart. If what I felt for Caroline was love, then this…this is an obsession. A need to own. My heart bangs out of my chest at the sight of her. The feel of her. The sound of her voice has me falling to my knees and offering my soul on a silver platter. Shit. It's officially happened. I should call the guys and let them know

I'd like them to hem my ball sack holder in a lovely shade of silver with tiny specs of blue—the color of my girl's eyes.

One thing is for damn sure: I love her. And I'm going to do whatever it takes to make her happy. Vow to show her every single day how special she is to me. *Pussy alert!* And damn, does it feel good. I should probably apologize to every one of my friends. I get it now. Being pussy whipped is like a drug, and I never want to come down from it.

I disappear under the covers. My tongue finds her center, and I lap at her sex. She stirs, and I slowly suck her into my mouth, loving the taste of her.

"Chase," she calls my name, her voice groggy. I nuzzle my nose into her, the warmth of her arousal soaking my mouth. Damn, I never want to come up for air. My cock is about to rip through my boxers. She finds my scalp and weaves her fingers leisurely through my hair. My tongue plunges into her wet pussy, and I growl at the possessiveness that burns inside my chest. She's mine. I use my tongue to spread her lips as I slide a finger inside her heat and work her until she quivers under me. Her grip tightens. She's about to come. "Give it to me, Angel," I demand, anticipating her orgasm coating my tongue. Her thighs tighten around my head, and she moans, her voice hoarse as she comes. I milk her orgasm, kissing the insides of her thighs.

When she releases her grip on me, I slide up her body and peek out of the sheets, peering at my girl, all glazed over and sweet. "Morning, Angel."

"Morning. I didn't realize it was you down there. I had this crazy sex dream that my doctor came into my room and was doing an exam. I was very dirty, so he had to clean me up. But then I woke up to you..."

She squeals when I pinch her nipple, loving the way it pebbles between my fingers. "Oh, yeah? Tell me more." I graze the side of her neck with my tongue.

"Well, he was big. A lot bigger than you."

"Interesting. What was he going to do with it?" I tease, slowly grinding into her.

Her phones buzzes on my nightstand. "Whoever it is, tell them you're deep into naughty role playing and can't be disturbed." Bridget smirks, and I want to kiss the fuck out of her sexy morning lips. She reaches over to check her phone, and I become territorial over my woman. "If it's your boss, tell him you don't answer to him on your days off—"

"Relax, it's just Hannah. She's asking me if I'm bringing a date to the engagement party."

I bend down and nibble on her earlobe. "Tell her you can't make it. Never letting you out of this bed."

Her perky breasts shake as she laughs, and I ditch the neck for a nipple. "I was thinking we would go together. May be a good time to—ahhh…"

I grind into her, my rock-hard cock silencing her. "We would have to leave this bed, and I'm not going to be anywhere near done with—"

Banging on my front door halts the rest of my reply. I freeze, waiting and hoping I'm hearing things.

It happens again.

"Expecting someone?"

"No. They'll go away—"

More banging, followed by a voice. The one voice I do not want to hear. "I know you're in there. I see your truck. Open up or I'm coming in."

Fuck! Why do my friends all of a sudden feel the need to show up uninvited? And why do I keep giving everyone my key?

"Is that Kipley?"

No, it's my death warrant. "Yeah." Abandoning my plans, I get up and throw on a pair of jeans.

She climbs out of bed, and I watch in horror as she starts

dressing. "Well, this is not the way I figured we would tell him about us, but I guess no better time than—"

"Yeah, about that. Maybe we shouldn't let the cat out of the bag just yet. Kipley is kind of—"

"Protective. I know. But he can't be that mad if he hears my side. It's mutual. Plus, he's not my dad." *No, he's going to be the one to put me six feet under if he finds you here.*

"Listen, I agree. But let's do it when we don't look like we've been doing what we were just about to do. Your face is really flushed. You look like you've been completely ravished by a regal king or something."

Her growing smile gives me hope. "Oh yeah? King?"

"Maybe a Viking. They're savages. Take no prisoners kind of men. You look like you've been through the ringer..." *Please give in and agree to hide. Please, please, please—*

"Fine. I guess I would hate for my cousin to get the wrong idea and beat you up for torturing me." She has no idea how true her words are.

"Great! Okay, so stay in here. My closet is pretty comfy too. Not a peep." *Please don't help sign my death warrant.* I blow her a kiss, because I'm now a certified pussy, and hurry out, shutting the door behind me.

Fuck, this is bad. Why the hell is Kip here? *Maybe you wouldn't be shitting bricks if you just told him.* Like it's that easy. No way I've practiced coming clean had Kip not pummeling me into the ground. He wouldn't believe me if I told him I fell in love and I'm a reformed man. It sounds silly when I say it. But it's the truth. I would never do anything to jeopardize what I have with Bridget. But I don't know how to prove that. Kip only sees me as the playboy who treats women like playthings. No attachments or emotion. I hate myself for ever being that way. I vow never to be again.

The banging sounds again, followed by the jiggling of my lock. The door opens just as I pop out. "Hey! S'up. What are you doing here?"

Kip eyes me. "I texted you to let you know I was stopping by. Are you busy?" He looks over my shoulder, and I about piss myself trying to remember if anything of Bridget's is laying in clear sight.

"No, of course not. Just chillin', man. Long night. Or day. Life's busy." *Shut up, asshole.*

"Yeah?" His brows raise. He's getting curious. Dammit. "You alone?"

No, I have your sweet, innocent cousin naked in my bedroom. "Yeah, of course."

"Wow. Thought you weren't answering 'cause you were treating your recent hookup to breakfast." *Already did that.*

"Nope. Just me."

"Huh. Well, I wanted to stop by and drop off the invitation to Hannah and Levi's engagement party. You're allowed to bring a guest, but not sure how Hannah would feel if you brought a hooker."

I'm praying Bridget is in my closet where she can't hear Kip. "No, man. No hooker. You know me…" *A liar. A horrible friend.*

"Oh, that's right—there's that girl you've been playing around with. You still keeping her on a long leash?" *Like, far inside my closet. Under a pile of clothes.*

"You know me, I like 'em eating out of the palm of my hands." *Why am I sweating?*

"What's up with you? You're acting strange…" He pauses, the wheels in his brain turning. "Wait…" *It's been a nice life. I'm a goner.* "You brought that girl home from the bar, didn't you? I knew it! I knew you just didn't leave that night at Jimmy's. The old sneak-out-the back-with-the-flavor-of-the-night, trick. Or…is there another random back there? Seriously, how many this week?" Okay, maybe I'm going to be the one murdering him. If he doesn't shut up… "Geez, chill out. No reason to get all pissy about it. You worried I offended her? Want me to go back there and fix it?"

I slap my palm against his chest as he takes a step forward. "No, man. It's all good. You know me. I'm not one for chick's feelings. Her time's about to expire anyway." *Like mine is if Bridge isn't suddenly deaf.*

"All right, playboy. Don't ruin her too bad. Again—a date, no hookers. My sister's order."

"Uh...yeah. First off, that was one time and it was a joke. But whatever. Okay. I gotta—"

"Yeah, sure, and don't be late. Or smelling like a strip club. Stacey made a comment last time." Kip hands me the invitation, his eyes scanning the couch where all the stuff from our movie night is still out. He sees himself out, while I stand, staring at the closed door. Did she hear anything Kip and I said? "Fuck," I hiss under my breath. Shoving my hand through my hair, I walk back to my room. A simple explanation should do. I couldn't tell Kip the truth. But I will. After I make up for this. I know exactly how I'm going to ravish—

"Hey. What are you doing?"

As I walk in, she's shoving her legs into her jeans. "What does it look like I'm doing? I'm leaving."

"Why? *Shit.*" I duck when one of my shoes flies at my head.

"If I have to explain, you're a bigger asshole than I thought."

I try to reach for her, but she shrugs me off. "Angel, it's not what you think. What you heard out there—"

"I'm pretty sure bragging to your friends about the flavor of the night you're banging is exactly what I think. Please, don't worry about sparing my feelings."

"I didn't mean—*Jesus!*" I dodge another shoe.

"God! I've been so stupid. You're just like the rest." I make another attempt to stop her, but she jumps out of my reach.

"Angel—"

"Don't call me that!"

"Fuck! Fine. Bridget, just listen to me."

"I'm so done listening to you. What I just heard is enough for me to understand what I've been telling myself this whole time. This is a mistake."

Panic creeps up my neck as she grabs her shirt. "Bridge, please." She can't leave. I reach for her, but she jabs her finger at me. "Don't you dare touch me."

I back off. My hands shake. "I couldn't tell Kip. If he knew—"

"Oh my god, just stop talking!" She looks around, searching for her shoes.

"I was going to tell him. But how was I supposed to tell him? He would have murdered me."

"It's called honesty, Chase. Making me out to be one of your side pieces is not the answer. Making me *feel* like a side piece—not the fucking answer."

"Bridge, you're not a side piece. I love—"

"Don't you dare." I step toward her, and she freaks. "Don't touch me!" She picks up a book from my nightstand and whips it at me, making direct contact with my right pec. My chest tightens, but it's not because of the book. I'm starting to truly fear her walking out on me.

She stares at me. The anguish in her eyes kills me. My stomach bottoms out as everything sinks in. It's final. She's done with me.

She races out of my room, and I rush after her. "This is ridiculous. Hear me out. You can't just leave."

"Watch me. I've heard enough. Or should I remind you, my time is expiring anyway."

I may have gone too far with that comment. I hurry behind her like a lost puppy as she heads to the front door. "You heard what you wanted to hear. You have no idea what it's been like for me. The lying. The—"

She whips around so fast, I stumble back before her hand makes contact with my cheek. "What *you've* been going through? Oh, wow. The lies have been so hard for you. And staying faithful apparently. With all the girls you're picking up at bars. Let me relieve you of all this stress. We are nothing. Do you hear me? Nothing!"

"Bridget!" I call for her as she rips my door open and makes her escape.

Chapter
Nineteen

Bridget

MY EYES ARE SWOLLEN. MY CHEST BURNS. HOW COULD I have been so stupid? So naïve to think I was worthy of a better life? This is fate playing a cruel joke on me. Fooling me into thinking he truly meant all the things he confessed. That he was my salvation. Someone like me doesn't deserve to be saved. I took a life. And this is what happens when I forget my ugly truth.

The Uber ride home is a blur. I barely register the Brooks' estate as the driver pulls up the driveway. Visions of us replay in my head. His gentle touch. His promises. I cover a sob with my fist, biting at my flesh. I trusted him. I opened up to him. I loved him.

And this whole time, I was a conquest.

"Hell with him."

I hurl out of the car and race up the driveway. I just need to make it to the comfort of the guesthouse before I truly break down. My feet slam against the driveway. I run too fast and stumble. My heavy tears restrict my view. I'm unable to steady myself and fall forward. I await the hardness of the concrete below me, needing the pain.

But it never happens.

Two strong arms catch me before I slam against the ground.

"Bridget. My goodness, what's happened?" My gaze peers up at the sound of Jonathon's deep voice. I want to break down and tell him all my deep, dark secrets. Confess the torture that lives inside me. My chest cracks open, and a painful sob erupts up my throat. "Jesus." He gathers me in his arms and carries me into the main house. My tears soak his shirt. Bringing me into his study, he lays me down on his leather couch.

"I'm so sorry. I just—"

"Please. Don't apologize. You're upset."

I sit up, trying to compose myself and failing miserably. "I know, but it's not your problem. I should just go—"

He presses his large hand against my shoulder, keeping me in place. "You will do no such thing. I won't allow you to leave in such distress. Sit here. I'll get you something that will help calm you down." He gets up, and a moment later, he returns with a crystal glass. I take the glass and sling it back, my puffy eyes squinting as the brown liquid burns down my throat. "That should settle you."

I place the glass on the table and wipe at my bottom lip. "I'm not sure anything will help me settle." I hate the sad truth in my tone. "I'm sorry. This is not your problem or anything you need to deal with. I'm going to go." I stand, but sway on my feet.

"Nonsense." His palm rests against my shoulder. The warmth of his hand feels oddly comforting. "As my employee, everything that involves you is my problem."

I know it's wrong. I should leave. But my emotions are in overdrive, and I don't know how to turn them off and walk away.

"Not this problem," I whisper.

"Any problem." I raise my eyes to his. My cheeks flush as he stares down at me. The tightness in my chest is making it hard to breathe. "No one should make a special woman like yourself cry."

My mind is so jumbled, I lose sight of myself. I'm so desperate to numb the pain and need the visions of Chase to go away. His deceit. I want to feel anything but ruined and broken.

Without another thought, I raise onto my tiptoes and fuse my lips to his. I press my body against his, needing him to make this all go away. Just as quickly, his large hands grab at my waist and dig into my flesh, pushing me off him.

"Bridget, whoa. I'm sorry if you've mistaken my kindness, but I'm not interested."

I blink. Shameful tears fill my eyes, and I cover my mouth. What have I just done? "I—I'm so sorry. I don't know—"

I turn on my heel and race out of his office.

I struggle to get into the guesthouse, dropping the key twice. When I finally enter, I run to the bathroom and drop to the floor, expelling the sourness of my humiliation. What is wrong with me? I throw up once more as the image from Jonathon's office plays on a loop in my mind. My legs tremble so bad, I barely make it to my bed before I collapse and fall apart, shedding a lifetime of tears.

I don't know how long I cry for. My eyelids feel like they weigh a million pounds. It's suddenly impossible to hold them open. I hiccup into my pillow, and before I realize, exhaustion takes over and I fall asleep.

～

Jax and I were practically kids when we fell in love. I remember like it was yesterday. Our secret late-night talks. Listening to our favorite songs. Whispers of affection, until those soft murmurs turned into a voice that held a true meaning of love. A love we fought for. Two different worlds. Two young kids, knowing that this was our forever. A darkness that kept us questioning, but the future that held such light in it, that one day, we would be together.

And then one day, we weren't.

My hands shake as I regret the words I spewed out of anger. I dial his number again, praying he answers so I can tell him how sorry I am. To come back so we can talk about it.

Voicemail. Again. "Jax, please. I'm sorry. Please just come back. I know I was wrong. I love you. I don't want anything else. I'll wait. Forever if I need to. I just want you. I won't survive this world without you. Please. Come back. Call me back."

He never called me back. Four voicemails I left. Seven calls unanswered. I never heard his voice again.

So many buried memories.

So many regrets.

I've spent years fighting to bury them deep inside myself. And now, they're resurfacing. I'm falling into the black hole of my past, hitting every jagged edge, the pain tearing open each memory I've fought so hard to repress.

I'm sorry Bridget, he's gone.

He's never coming back...

I sit up, the memory rousing me awake. Chase. His betrayal. Coming home. Throwing myself at my boss. It all comes back like a punch to the gut. I suck in a staggered breath and clench my fists so tight my nails dig into my palms. I'm fighting not to fall apart all over again. I glance over at my clock and swear under my breath when I realize I've been asleep for over five hours.

Raised voices coming from outside grab my attention. I sit up. *Chase and Jonathon.* I hurry out of bed and sneak a peek out the window, keeping myself hidden from view.

"I'm not going to ask you again. Get off my property."

"I'm not leaving until I see Bridget. This has nothing to do

167

with you, man. Just go back inside and check your stocks or something."

Chase takes a step toward my front door, and Jonathon stops him.

"You serious? What is it with you? Pretty territorial over an employee. One might think you want a little piece of your nanny."

I cringe at his comment. More embarrassment floods my system, making me feel sick all over again.

"So, again, why don't you get out of my way and let me speak to my girl?"

Chase gets into Jonathon's face. He doesn't take the bait, but I worry Chase will do something to hurt him.

"I believe she doesn't belong to you anymore. Especially after the way she fell at my doorstep in tears. One I had to tend to because she was so distraught. I think you should take a step back and learn how to treat a woman—especially one as special as her. And you're right. I am territorial of my employee. She deserves to be treated with respect. From the looks of it, you're failing at the job. Now, get off—"

I gasp when Chase shoves him.

"Bridget!" he yells my name. "You can't keep her from me, you motherfucker. Bridget, please. Just come out so we can talk." He tries to fight past Jonathon, but Jonathon grabs him by the neck and wrestles him into a choke hold. Chase struggles to release himself from his strong grip. Jonathon's hold only tightens. "Let me go, asshole."

I want to race out there. Break them up. Make this all stop. But I'm not ready to face Chase. I can't. Sirens blare in the background. A minute later, a police car rolls up the driveway.

"You called the cops?"

Jonathon finally lets him go, and with a hard shove, pushes him away. "I told you to get off my property."

"This isn't over. I'll be back."

Chase looks over Jonathon's shoulder, and I dodge away from the window. Minutes pass before a soft knock sounds on my door.

When I look through the shaded window, I only see Jonathon. I open the door, unsure how to start. Give my resignation so he doesn't have to waste his time with the awkward 'you're so fired' conversation. Apologize for my immature, out-of-line actions earlier. Maybe act like I have no idea what he's talking about and I have a fake twin who's trying to ruin my life and pretending to be me.

"Are you okay?" he starts, his voice surprisingly tender.

"Yeah. I'm sorry. I didn't—"

"When are you going to learn you don't owe me apologies? Can I come in?"

"Yeah, sure." I nod and step aside. He enters the guesthouse and walks over to the island. I'm not sure what to do next, but I'm feeling more confident about the psycho twin story. "I'm sorry about earlier," I spit out.

Apologizing for throwing myself at him seems like a good ice breaker. He turns around and leans against the counter. "You asked me the other day why the other nanny left." I slowly nod. "I run a very lucrative business. I'm forced to travel a lot. With that burden, I'm forced to be away from my daughter. It's something I don't like, but it's the way of my world. So, when I hire someone to look after her care and well-being, I need to make sure their whole focus is on her. If I can't be here to do so, I expect all hands on deck from the people I staff."

"Are you firing me?"

"I'm answering your question. Rebecca was the nanny before you. She had been employed with us since Anna was born. My wife dealt with her mostly, but when she passed, I took on that role. I was so engrossed in work, I didn't pay much attention. But the more time went on, the more it became obvious she had developed unhealthy feelings for me.

I ignored her, and she became more aggressive with getting my attention. One night, I came home and found her naked in my bed. I asked her to leave, and she got upset. Told me I had been leading her on. Started to threaten me—which I did not take lightly to. I am not a man to be threatened."

"So, what happened?" *Please don't tell me you killed her.*

"I fired her. I gave her until noon the next day to get her things and be off my property. Two weeks later, I hired you."

My palms are sweating. "So, you *are* firing me?"

"I'm not firing you. I'm telling you why she no longer works for me. I am a professional in all aspects of my life. Rebecca was a good nanny. She was an attractive girl, but I didn't see her other than an employed staff member of our house. I would never cross the line or breach that employer/employee relationship." He pushes off the island to walk toward me. "I'm sorry if I've given off any wrong impression. I have things going on and I've not been myself."

"I know you haven't and I'm so sorry. I don't know what I was thinking—actually I wasn't."

Jonathon nods in understanding. "The way you showed up earlier this afternoon, I understand you were under some stress. I've made some mistakes in my life, so let's just chalk this up to one of those. Anna loves you. And I love the way you are with her. I don't want to take that away from her because of a misunderstanding, understand?"

I struggle to spit out any words. My hands shake in fear his speech is my swan song. My brain kicks in, and I start to nod. "Yes, of course. Again, I'm so—"

"Bridget…"

"Right. No apologies. It's just…please know I have no intentions of showing up in your bed—Jesus, that also sounded wrong. I'm not interested. You're a good-looking guy, but I love…" I trail off before I confess the awful truth. *I love Chase.*

"Speaking of intentions, it wasn't mine to make things

worse for you two. With how upset you were earlier, I assumed you were not ready to see him. I only did what I thought was best."

I let out a heavy sigh and take a seat on the couch. "I appreciate it. I'm not ready. Who knows if I'll ever be. It's over between us."

Jonathon walks up to me and kneels in front of me. "No man should make a woman feel less than perfect. Cherished. If he hasn't done that, then it's his loss. Never sell yourself short."

How can he be so nice to me? I literally tried to attack him, silently accused him of killing his nanny, and caused a scene with my boyfriend. *Ex*-boyfriend.

"Thank you."

He nods and stands. "I'll leave you be. If you need anything, call up to the house."

"I will."

He doesn't say anything more. The door shuts behind him, and my shoulders feel weighted as I slump farther into the couch. My body suddenly feels cold. I wrap myself in the fur blanket, resting my head against a throw pillow. My mind flashes to the night before. Chase confessing his dreams. Feeling like I could push him to get back on the horse. That I would be around to watch him become someone even more remarkable. I shake my head, wishing away the silly thoughts. Hating myself for clinging to these silly dreams. I should have known better than to believe I could have a fairytale ending. They don't exist for me.

My mind filters back to Jax's death.

The tears didn't stop for months. When they did, it was only because my anger took center stage. I pointed blame at everyone around me. And when I exhausted myself of that, the agony of him being gone settled back in, and the tears came in such rapid waves, it would put me down for days. I don't know when it got easier. Maybe when the doctors told me to eat or they would have to force me. When my parents threatened me to get out of bed or they would force me. When I realized almost two years of my life had gone by without anyone caring someone I loved had died.

It took me too long to realize that life doesn't stop just because someone else's did. It didn't wait for me to heal. It didn't allow me to understand why or come to any form of acceptance. Every time I tried to comprehend, another day went by. I wanted him back. I wanted to pour out all the pain I felt inside. The thoughts that led me to strange places. The solutions that would bring me back to him.

I tried my best to be okay, but I wasn't, and I knew I never would be. I was given my one, and he was ripped from me. Who would want me now? Damaged, flawed, broken... Once upon a time, I was headed down the perfect road. Now, I'm holding my breath, hoping I don't fall apart along the way.

I've worked so hard to be okay. And I thought, with Chase, I'd finally found my way to moving on. But I was just falling in love with a fallacy.

No one can save me.

Certainly not Chase Steinberg.

Chapter
Twenty

Chase

"Eight, nine, ten. Way to finish those reps, bro."

"Keep going," I snap to Cliff my gym partner. The bar drops back down to my chest, and I bench another hundred and fifty pounds.

"Dude, you just did five sets in a row. You're gonna blow your—"

"Keep fucking going," I hiss, pushing the bar up. Beads of sweat drip down my face. Every muscle in my body burns. My arms shake, but I refuse to stop.

"Chase, for real, man. You're overexerting yourself."

I ignore him and fight through another rep. My muscles start to spasm, but I push harder. "Okay, I'm done." Cliff grabs the bar and slams it onto the bench. I shoot forward and stand.

"What the fuck? I told you I wasn't done." I get into his face.

"Yeah, and I told you that you were. Whatever shit you're—"

"What's up, ladies? You two about to kiss or something?" Ben walks up, eyeing us both. "You two good?"

I don't back down. If Cliff has something to say, I'll pummel his ass right here. He stares at me a few more seconds, then backs down. "Nah. All's good. He's all yours." He grabs his towel and walks off.

"What was that all about? Thought you and Cliff were cool."

"Well...now we're not." I grab my towel and wipe my forehead. When I turn around, Ben is still eyeing me. "What? You got somethin' to say? Not in the mood. You can fuck off too."

Ben throws his hands up. "Whoa, chill out, man."

I can't chill. I can't eat, sleep, work. I can't do a goddamn thing. I've been so consumed by her absence. It's been three days of constant phone calls and texts where I've begged her to talk to me. Hear me out. Her rejection is killing me.

"What's up, man? You've been ghosting everyone. Totally blew everyone off on guys' night, and now you're looking like you want to fight the entire gym. Talk to me."

"I can't."

"Why can't you?"

"'Cause you wouldn't understand, okay?"

I try to walk off, but he steps in front of me. "Try me."

Running my fingers through my hair, I let out a huge breath. "Bridget—and don't give me that fucking look. You have no idea."

"You're right. But I'd sure love to finally hear the true story of how Kip's little cousin ended up at your place."

"It's a long story." A very long story.

"Lucky for you, I've got all the time in the world."

I'm sure he does, nosy asshole. "Don't you need to go lift some weights or some shit? And I thought you were mad at me?"

"I got over it. Plus, I've been going through my own shit."

"About that. I'm an asshole. I should've remembered the—"

"Stop changing the subject. Let's go hit up Jimmy's Bar for beer and burgers. Your treat. My advice isn't free." He turns around and walks off without waiting for my answer.

Son of a bitch.

~

"Jesus fucking Christ."

I take a sip of my beer, my throat dry from babbling like a schoolgirl. I just told Ben everything.

"Jesus fucking Christ."

"Is that all you can say?"

"Well…for starters, Jesus fucking—*ouch*! Fine. I think that's a crazy story. Crazier that you're, like, in love and shit. You can't really be mad at Kip for only speaking what he knows. He doesn't know your real situation."

"That every single time I've ever made fun of you guys, it's all coming back to bite me in the ass because now I'm the one who's in love and I'm eating my words."

"Well yeah. There's that." He chuckles. "It's the ones who are the most naïve about love that get it the worst. And you my friend have it bad. I can tell by the way you talk about her. You practically have hearts shooting from your lovesick eyes."

"Fuck off, dude. I do not. Plus, it doesn't matter. She wants nothing to do with me. She won't even hear me out." He just shrugs. "I thought you were here to help me?"

"I am. But not sure you can be helped. I guess I should have asked for more details before offering my therapist services. You sound screwed all around."

"Gee, great. Thanks for telling me what I already know." I swig my beer. "If she would just talk to me. She would know it was a misunderstanding." I wish I could rewind time and take back everything I said. Stood behind my relationship and

Bridget and told Kip the truth. Eating his fist was going to hurt no matter when he fed it to me. It would be worth it. She was worth it.

"Say she talks to you again, which I probably wouldn't if I were her." I give him the *watch it* eye. "*Say* she does. What are you going to do about Kip? Telling him you took his sweet, innocent cousin's virginity in a hotel room without even getting her name is not the way to go."

"Clearly I was planning on leaving that part out."

"Shame. Really adds to the story." Ben finishes his beer and flags down the waitress. "Hey, beautiful. We'll take another round."

"Sure thing. You boys celebrating somethin'?"

Ben slaps on a cheeky smile. "We sure are. My buddy over here is in love."

The waitress sighs. "Aw, that's so sweet."

I roll my eyes and drink. "It sure is." More like absolute hell.

"Yeah, he found the one. But he messed up and now she won't talk to him. Any advice for the poor guy?"

She offers me her puppy dog eyes. Great, now I have the damn waitress feeling sorry for me. "You poor thing. Well, for starters, girls don't want flowers or chocolate. That's *sooo* old school. Make her feel special. Buy her diamonds. Or a purse. My ex-boyfriend bought me heels once, and we made up right away."

Great. Wonderful advice. Ben is holding in a laugh, and I'm about to smash my beer bottle over his head. "Diamonds and shoes. Got it."

"Hope it helps. And you? What's your girlfriend like?" Lamest trick in the book. Anyone who has a brain knows she's fishing for information. Even Ben, who sports his cheeky grin.

"No girlfriend here. Still searching for the right one." I almost gag on my beer. Who does that line actually work on?

A million chicks. You're the one who taught it to Ben. Man, I was pathetic.

The girl hands Ben a napkin and he scribbles his number down, telling her to call him sometime, then she runs off to fetch our beers. "You kidding me? You're supposed to be helping me, not landing dates."

He rolls his shoulders in a carefree shrug. "I just did a nice girl a favor. Plus, these hookup apps are getting stale."

"Fucking the entire subscriber list of Tinder would get stale for me too." Ben laughs and stretches out his arms. "Whatever. I'm not picking up this tab. You didn't help me worth shit."

"Yes you are. Because you owe me. Because I'm going to confess I know for a fact your girl is going to be at Levi's engagement party and you can stalk her then. I've solved all your problems. Now, shots?"

Chapter
Twenty-One

Bridget

"I THINK MY MOM WENT A LITTLE OVERBOARD WITH ALL THESE decorations," Hannah says, looking around her parents' living room.

"I mean, who doesn't want two billion balloons at their party?"

Hannah shakes her head and laughs. "Talk about love being in the air. Literally. I don't even know where all these heart balloons are going to go?"

I gaze around the room, fighting to hold my smile. While love is bringing her such happiness, it's tearing me apart.

"It's going to be a beautiful day," I say, admiring all the beautiful details my aunt has put into her daughter's special day.

I bury my face back into my project of assembling the bridesmaid bags, envious of the Matthews' bond. Hannah has never known what it's felt like to fight for attention. Unlike the unconditional love she's always felt, mine was worked for. I lived in a household based on duty. As the daughter of a pastor, it was embedded in me to love the lord and you shall be loved in return. I turned my back on that belief when Jax died. And in some way, my parents turned their backs on me. How could the daughter of a pastor not believe in God? And it wasn't that I didn't. I just no longer believed he was here to save. He took the only thing that made my heart beat with life.

My parents saw my resentment with God as rebellion, and their disappointment hurt. How could they not understand my disgruntled views? I wanted them to love me for me. See that I was hurting and that my morals had been tested to the point that I struggled to believe. Even when Jax was alive they didn't approve. They couldn't see past the troubled boy from the wrong side of the tracks. It didn't matter that he was good to me. He treated me with respect and even though he didn't follow the word of God, he respected his values. I fought so hard to show them our love was honest, and we deserved to live our life together. We were destined for our very own happily ever after.

But life doesn't work that way.

At least not in the eyes of parents who dedicate their life to the church.

"Bridget, this is nonsense. Is his family even around? Does he have a solid home?" Dad demands.

"Why does that even matter? What matters is he loves me. He treats me with respect."

"I will not allow my daughter to lose herself to someone who does not have good intentions, and in my eyes, he is not what you need."

"You know nothing about what I need."

"Bridget, watch your mouth," my mother interjects.

I turn to her, my disappointment shining. She can't ever take my side. "He's kind. He cares about me. He would never hurt me. How is that against your beliefs?"

"He's not one of us."

"You mean he's not kind and considerate? He doesn't give back to the community? Because he does do that. Or let me point out the real reason.

He's not religious. Because in your eyes it seems that's what makes a real man."

"Bridget—"

"*No! Admit it. Because he comes from a broken home, it makes him unworthy. Because he's not a member of your church, it makes him unworthy. How about he loves me? How about he would lay his life down for me? What will ever be enough for you?"*

"Hey, are you okay?"

I blink away the memory and look up at Hannah. "Yeah. Fine." I peer down at the bag I'm working on and cringe.

"You sure? You've been mutilating that bow for about ten minutes now.

I rub out the tension in my forehead. "I'm sorry. I just have a lot on my mind right now." I attempt to un-mangle the bow when Hannah pulls it from my grip.

"Okay, let's give the poor bow a rest. You know you can talk to me, right?"

Not about this. "I know." I grab some pink tissue paper and start stuffing the bags.

"*Okay.* Not sure what that bag did to you, but maybe ease up?"

I drop it. "Shit."

"And now you're cussing. That's it. Spill. I won't take 'nothing' for an answer."

I've been fighting tooth and nail to keep down the hurt and anger. Pretend Chase Steinberg never walked into my life and stole my heart. Then mended it back together just to shatter it. I gave him a piece of me that didn't belong to him. A piece that should have always been reserved for Jax. But I foolishly handed my heart over and he deceived me, destroying it all over again.

"Oh, Bridget." Hannah wraps her arms around me, and I fall apart, the tears I've been holding back all week coming out in a pained sob. "Please tell me this doesn't have anything to do with a specific someone who coerced me into giving him information?" I cry harder, which answers her question. "I'm going to murder him. I should've known better."

"No, I'm the one to blame." I pull away. "I know guys like him. I'm the one who should have seen the signs."

"He didn't do anything to you that warrants—"

"Like break my heart?"

She looks back at me with sad eyes. "Wow, I didn't realize it was that serious."

I didn't realize it wasn't. "I know. So stupid. Who falls in love with a player? I read the signs all wrong. I truly thought he was the one, ya know? Even after Jax. This guy came into my life, pulled me out of the darkness, brought happiness into my world...and I just don't understand what went wrong. How was I so stupid? How did I believe the things he said? It was all fake, and I just don't understand."

"I'm sorry, Bridget. If I would have known his true intentions, I would have never gone along with it. He seemed so genuine, and different. He was changing, and I assumed it was because of you. I wouldn't have guessed he was playing you. Can I ask what happened?"

I dread reliving that day over. "We were at his place and Kip came over—"

"Wait—Kip knows?"

"No. Chase was too scared to tell him. He asked me to hide in his room. So, I did. Well, his walls are super thin and I heard everything they said. Kipley was saying all these things about Chase. How he took a girl home from the bar just days before. Asking what the update was on another girl he was toying with. The worst thing was, Chase didn't shut it down. He admitted to the girl and how *her* time was almost expired." The tears fall once again.

"Oh, Bridge, I'm so sorry."

"It's not your fault. It's mine."

"You did nothing wrong here. He's the jerk. When I tell Kip—"

I pull back. "Please don't."

"Kip is going to want to know this. What Chase did is not okay. He should know better. When Kip finds out—"

"I know. And that's why you can't tell him—"

"Tell him what?" I silently plead with Hannah as Kipley walks into the room. "Uh oh, why are you crying? Who do I have to murder?"

"It's nothing. Just stupid boy drama." Hannah looks at me, disappointed. She doesn't like to lie, and I'm making her lie to her brother for me.

"Give me a name and address."

"It's nothing," I speak up. "Really. I'll be over it by tomorrow."

Kipley peers down at me, his brows squeezing together. He takes a quick glance at Hannah for intel, before focusing back on me. "You look pretty upset for it to be nothing. You sure? I've got nothing on the books tonight. I could use the exercise of digging a large hole."

I force a smile. "Yes, I'm sure."

"Okay. You tell me if you change your mind. We're family. We fight for one another. Whoever it is, it's his loss. You're still young. You have your entire life ahead of you. Don't waste it shedding tears over a loser guy." He pats me on the back, then turns to ruffle up Hannah's hair.

"Hey!" Hannah gripes, swatting at Kip's hand.

"Going to help Mom with the dishes before taking off. You two girls enjoy." We're both silent until Kip is out of sight. Hannah is the first to speak.

"I don't know why you're protecting him. He doesn't deserve it."

"I know. But doing something I know will hurt him won't make it better. I just want to forget it—forget *him*." The tightness around her eyes tells me she wants to say more, but she slowly nods and drops it.

"Fine. How about we finish wrapping these gifts then have

my mom make us her famous ice cream sundaes and snuggle up and watch a movie? Levi is working late so you get me all night."

"I think it sounds like the perfect remedy."

"Good." Hannah claps her hands together. "We can watch a bunch of funny chick flicks."

"As long as it doesn't have vampires in it, I'm good."

"Oh no, he suckered you into—never mind. Anti-romance movies it is. Let's go fill up on sugar."

The simple word sugar triggers my emotions. A heaviness weighs on my chest and my eyelids fill with tears.

"Oh no, what did I—"

"It's nothing...." He's even ruined sugar for me. "Just sugar... it's a thing—and he—"

"I'm going to murder him!" Hannah tugs me toward the kitchen. "Mom! We need something extremely salty. Pronto!"

Chapter
Twenty-Two

Chase

Hey, you look lovely tonight, spare a moment?

No.

Wow, the best-looking girl in the house, forgive me?

Also no.

Hi, I'm an idiot and don't deserve you but at least hear me out…

Dammit! Any angle leads to me getting slapped. Which I deserve. Maybe I should just wait outside and grab her when she walks out. *Okay, creep.* Yeah, bad idea. I just need her to talk to me. I'm going out of my mind without her. The pit in my stomach has grown to the size of a boulder. If I can't get her to speak to me, I don't know what else to do. *Maybe kidnapping isn't the worst idea.* I'm desperate. So desperate, I have a stupid pair of diamond earrings shoved in my pocket.

I pace my apartment until it's time to leave, fixing my hair a billion times. I rehearse my "please forgive me, I'm begging you" speech the whole way over to the Matthews' house. My body is jittery from the nerves. Like I just drank a dozen energy drinks.

"You're the love of my life. We're meant to be together. I'll do anything for you to forgive me." I slam my palm on the steering wheel. This all sounds so pathetic. But what if she doesn't forgive me? "Go with the begging."

I park on the street and grab the giant bouquet of roses.

"Hey, Chase, why do you have flowers for my cousin? Oh, you two hooked up? What was that? You hurt her. Time to die…"

I drop the flowers.

Giving them to her after we make up sounds like a better idea. Grovel first, come clean to Kip, then shower her with all the things Google said to do to make up with an angry girlfriend.

The party is in full effect. The whole Matthews' crew is in attendance. I sneak through the front door and weave through people in search of her. My first stop, the backyard. I'm halfway across the living room when their aunt catches me.

"Chester, come here."

Fuck. "Uh…hey, Aunt Getty. And it's Chase."

"Whatever. Come here. Let me see you. My William, God rest his soul, used to have muscles like that."

I don't have time for this. "You know, I would, but I'm in a hurry. Enjoy the party." I dodge her grabby hands and head toward the kitchen. Another aunt tries to stop me, but I beeline it through a group of Stacey's friends.

"Look, it's the player of the year. Shocked you're not dead from an STD."

I ignore the jab from Hillary…or Jill—whatever her name is.

"Hey, Chase. Wanna go grab a beer together?"

I dodge more grabby hands and wave them all off. "Sorry, can't. I'm a reformed man." The girl hisses at me, but I keep trekking on. Maybe it was a bad idea to plow through all of Stacey's friends, but that was the old me. The new me only has eyes for one girl.

Stepping outside, I block the sun and scan the backyard. I catch Ben over by the pool talking with some chick, and

Stacey and Kip talking with a neighbor. "Definitely not going that way." I turn the opposite direction and start toward the drink table. Someone grabs the back of my shoulder, and I shriek like a girl.

"Jesus. Chill, man. It's just me." I whip around to Levi. "Damn, what has you so jumpy?"

"Uh...nothing. All good. Just looking to grab a drink. Great party. Oh, and congrats. You two are perfect together."

Levi's brows shoot up into his forehead. What did I say? "Did you just say something nice about Hannah and me?" His hand sticks out, trying to touch my forehead, but I slap it away.

"No. Well...yeah. Maybe. It's just nice to see how happy you two are. When you find the one, it's magical. The smiles meant just for you. The inside jokes. The cute little—"

I cut myself off. What the hell is wrong with me? Levi looks at me as if I've just grown two heads. "Or whatever. I'm only here for the burgers. I'll catch ya later." I walk off, silently smacking myself. What in the utter *fuck* was that? It's settled. Bridget has completely broken me.

I grab a beer, disappointed when I don't find Bridget. A lap around the pool and grill area, and still nothing. I start to panic that she changed her mind and didn't show up when I spot her. She's back by the huge oak tree, swinging on the manmade swing.

"Okay, shit..." Sweat pools on my palms. I move in her direction, my legs weighing a million pounds. Each step, my heart pounds. I fear I'm going to pass out before I even make it to her. "Get it together. You can do this."

She seems to be lost in thought, gazing into the distance. Her shoulders are slightly slumped, and I hate the way her lips aren't formed into that playful smile I'm obsessed with. She doesn't hear me when I reach her.

"Bridget."

Her head pops up, her eyes wide in shock. "Go away. I

have nothing to say to you." She stands, and I move, blocking her exit.

"Please, just talk to me——"

"No. Get out of my way."

I grab her wrist before she can flee. "Bridget, for fuck's sake. Please, I'm begging you. You have no idea how fucked up I've been since you left."

She tears her arm out of my grip. "How fucked up *you've* been? What about me? How about what I've been going through after learning I was just a game for you——"

"You've never been a game——"

"Save it. I learned my lesson with you. And I won't be making that mistake again."

She tries to leave, but I block her once more. "That's not fair. What you heard wasn't true. I wasn't toying with you. I fucking panicked! How about you were supposed to love me? You didn't even give me the chance to explain. You jumped ship the second you could. Believed what you wanted. I did what I had to do for us to work out."

Her laugh is anything but humorous. "Oh, give me a break. Are you seriously turning this on me?"

"No! I know I shouldn't have said what I said, but I did. It's not true, and I'm begging you to just stop being so upset about it."

A fire suddenly explodes in her eyes. A look I've never seen before. *Shit.* I'm messing this all up. "Bridget, listen——"

"No, *you* listen, you heartless asshole. For one——I'm not upset. I'm grateful. You showed me who you really were. And now that I see the real you, I know to run."

"Oh, and who's that? The guy who's shown you nothing but respect? Fucking *loves* you? Maybe you should stop for one second and realize what would have happened if Kip found you in my bed. You think life would have been hunky dory? Wrong, Angel. He would have wiped the floor with me and dragged you out. Probably told your parents, as well as his. I would have been banned from all things Matthews and my friendship with Kip would be done. If you thought for a second this whole sweet, innocent way of yours was going to save us, you were—"

Her tiny palm slaps across my face, and I slowly raise my hand to my cheek. I'm no stranger to being sideswiped by a disgruntled chick, but this time is different. It carried meaning.

"I hate you," she says, her lower lip quivering.

"And I love you—"

"What's going on here?" Hannah storms up, her eyes shooting fire at me. She turns to her cousin. "Bridge, are you okay?"

"Fine."

Her response drips with lies. Hannah turns back to me. "I think you should leave."

"I think you should mind your own business. This has nothing to do with you, Hannah."

She marches up to me and shoves her hands into my chest. "This has everything to do with me. You lied to me. You told me your intentions were innocent—then you did exactly what you do best. You hurt her. How could you? She's family."

"Again, you have no idea what you're talking about."

"You're never going to change. You're always going to be this insecure guy who's too afraid to let someone love you or ever understand how special it is to love someone. You're too conceited and selfish. You'll live your whole life dragging nameless women in and out of your bed and you'll always be lonely. The way you treat people, that's how you should be treated."

I've always had my issues with Hannah. Even though we've become closer the last couple months. But she's never spoken to me like this. Never looked at me with such disgust. She's right, though. I've done things I'm not proud of, but I can't take any of it back. And maybe those mistakes are reason enough not to deserve love. I'll always be someone's one night stand. I look over at Bridget. Tears shed down her cheeks. I want so damn bad to bring her into my arms and make all her pain go away, but I'm the one causing it.

I turn to Hannah. "You're right. I'm exactly the kind of guy you've pinged me to be. I've done a lot of shady shit in my past. And I'm not sorry about it. But people change. They find someone who makes them realize what it's like to be loved. To want to be someone completely different. Better. And it makes them fucking change. Because their life depends on that one person to breathe. I may not deserve happiness, and I sure deserve your hate, but I'm done letting you tell me I don't know how to love. If I didn't, I wouldn't feel so broken right now."

My focus lands on Bridget. "I screwed up. I know that. I thought I was protecting us. I made a mistake."

"A mistake?"

"Yeah! A fucking mistake! I was confused. Scared. Fuck, my lifelong friendship was on the line."

"You call him your friend? All you did was lie to him too—"

I step closer to her, but Hannah throws her hands up, pushing me back. "Stay away from her, Chase."

"I don't want anyone but you. Since the moment you walked into my life, I've wanted nothing but. I'll accept the damage with Kip. I'll come clean and fight for us. But I won't accept the damage with you. I haven't slept since you left. I just need for you to understand—"

This time it's Bridget who shoves me. "I won't fall for your lies anymore. I knew this wouldn't work. I convinced myself you weren't the person I immediately labeled you as—a player." I open my mouth to argue back, but she cuts me off. "I even played along with your game because I enjoyed the attention. I've been so shut off for so long, it felt good. I knew I wouldn't keep it, but I indulged in it. Pretend it was real then move on. But you pushed it. You made me feel more than I wanted to." Her voice rises. "You don't get to act like the hero here. You're the villain. You took something that didn't belong to you and treated it like a toy."

"I never—"

"You did! Let's find the most wounded girl in the room and see how much we can mess with her?"

"Bridget, stop."

"I told you to leave me alone, but you wouldn't. You insisted on pushing me. For what? Just to break me—"

"I'm serious, knock it off." I try to reach for her again, but she swats my hand away.

"No. What was I? A game? A notch on your player's bedpost? Did it feel good to brag to your friends how you fooled me into falling for you? Was I at least good enough to make it memorable—"

"I fucking love you. Stop this!" My voice blasts across the backyard. Kip is at my back, grabbing my shoulder.

"Dude, what the hell's going on? Are you seriously harassing my cousin?" He looks back and forth, his eyes bouncing between us. The wheels start to turn. His hands clench into fists as his laid-back smile disappears. He's figured it out. "No... It's you?" He gets in my face, and I don't move or stop him. "Tell me it's not you messing with my cousin. Fucking tell me, man."

Kip and I met in first grade. The resident bully was about to take my lunch and pummel me into the ground. He stepped in and saved me and my turkey burger. Since that day, we've been best friends. No matter our differences, we've stuck together. I've had the best moments of my life with him by my side. And I know, when I answer, it's going to erase everything.

I glance over at Bridget. But she refuses to look at me. Every particle of my being begs for her to stand by me, by us. I'm willing to fight for us, why won't she?

"Don't look at her man, look at me. Tell me you're not.

Tell me you didn't mess with her after I strictly told you she was off limits."

"Kip, it's not what you think——"

"Are you kidding me? She's my cousin! Do you have no boundaries, man?" He shoves me hard, and I stumble back before catching my balance. "You piece of shit."

"Fuck you. You know nothing."

"I know you're a player and have no business near her."

The worst part is, at no point does Bridget speak up. Fuck this. "Why? Cause I'm such a piece of shit *player?*"

"Well, you are, man. You haven't kept a solid girl since college. You want me to say you're a stellar guy? Tell you it's okay to date her and mess with her like you do every chick? She's too good for you, man." Each insult takes its toll.

I step toward Bridget. "You know how I feel about you. Please, let's just go talk some——"

"I told you to leave her alone."

"Fuck you——"

Kip takes a swing, and my head bounces back, his fist hitting me in the mouth. I wipe the blood from my lip. My gaze falls to Bridget, but there's no emotion. The way she looks back at me with hatred tells me I've lost. That no matter how bad I messed up, whatever we had means nothing to her now. A coldness washes over me, chilling my blood and my heart. "You're right, man. I don't have anything to offer. I don't have time for fairytales and silly girl promises either."

"Get the fuck out of here," Kip snaps, and I turn to him.

"Don't worry, I'm leaving." I shove past him, throwing my shoulder into his. I don't bother taking a last look at Bridget.

"Bro, where you going?"

"I'm out," I spit to Ben.

"Dude, the party just started. Did you even talk to——"

"It's over. I'm good. Enjoy a burger for me." I keep going until I'm in the comfort of my truck. I throw it into drive and speed down the road, their hate still ringing in my ears. "Fuck them," I hiss, swallowing down my emotions. "*Fuck* them." Since when did my friends start criticizing me for the decisions I made? Were my choices that disgusting for them? I knew exactly the person I was. But when did they become so judgmental? Because my priorities were different? "Fuck them!" I slam my fists against my steering wheel.

I don't need friends like them. I don't need a girl like her. I don't need anyone.

Chapter
Twenty-Three

Chase

"Oh, come on! Hit the ball!"

I slam my glass onto the bar, signal for the bartender to refill me, and turn to my buddy beside me. "What a shit play, right, dude? What the fuck!"

"First off, I'm not your dude. Second, your team sucks. He caught it. Get over it."

I back off, grabbing my full beer. "Yeah, all good man." Testy motherfucker. "I'm just waiting for my own friends to show, chill."

Not that they're coming.

I haven't talked to them since Levi's engagement party.

"Better beware. My boys hate your team. There's gonna be some shit talkin'." I take a swig of my beer and wiggle my brows at him, then I face forward toward the bar, grinding my jaw.

"Hey, Chase, maybe it's time to call it quits."

Turning back to the bartender, I smile, my lips stretching across my face. The same bullshit smile I've held up since I walked out of the Matthews'. "I'm good. Why don't you be a sweetheart and give me another. Or even better, a round of shots for me and my friends here."

The guy next to me grunts and rolls his eyes. The bartender brings me the shots, but the assholes decline them. I'm not one to waste alcohol so I take all four. My brows draw together at the burning down my throat. "Man, you guys missed out. Tasty shit."

When did people become such douchebags? We're in a sports bar, watching sports. "Whatever. I'm gonna go take a piss. Keep me posted on what I miss." I get up and sway, taking out a stool. "Sorry, sweetheart, not in the market." I laugh, pushing the stool out of the way and stumble to the men's room. A lengthy moan falls off my tongue as I take the longest piss ever. That's what happens when you drink a dozen beers. "See, this isn't bad. No one's holding me down. I can sit at this bar all day with no one griping at me." I nod, fighting to agree with myself. "Yep, this is so much better. No chains or attachments." No comfort and soft kisses. No cherries and vanilla. No her. "Fuck," I hiss, slamming my fist into the wall. I finish up and wash my hands. The person looking back at me in the mirror disgusts me. Just like it disgusts everyone else. "Fuck off," I tell myself and push off the counter. I stumble into the door. "Damn." Those shots are kicking in. I laugh to myself. "Those assholes missed out. I feel great. Happy Sunday to me." I fall into the door, my large frame pushing it open, and make my way back to my stool. "What'd I miss, guys—?"

I'm either super drunk or Ben is sitting in my seat. "Benny! What a surprise. Told you guys my friends were coming. Hey, pretty lady, a round of shots for my friend here."

"Bro, no shots. It's time to go."

"What? No way! I'm just getting started."

Ben stands, throwing a bunch of money on the bar. "Thanks again for the call." He grabs at my shoulder, and I shove him off.

"Dude, what call? I'm not leaving."

"She called me." He nods to the bartender. "Was worried about you. And she was right to be. Look at you—you're hammered."

I look at the chick and realize it's the waitress from the other day. "Hey! Bad advice by the way—"

"Shut up. Let's go."

"No way. It's Sunday fun day, bro."

He shakes his head. "No, man. It's Monday. You need to get ahold of yourself."

"I'm fine."

"You're not fine. Cliff called me. You've blown off the gym all week. Craig called me, 'cause for some damn reason I'm your emergency contact. You haven't been to work. What are you doing, man?"

"I'm living my best life."

"No, you're ruining it. She broke up with you. I get it. But that's life. You can't destroy your entire life over it."

I hate that he's turning this into a pity thing. It fucking broke me. "Why does it even matter? I'm just a piece of shit to you guys anyway."

"You're not. You fucked up. It happens. And no one thinks that. Kip was angry. Give him some slack. You knew his reaction wasn't going to be upbeat and supportive."

I just hoped it wasn't him totally shutting me out. "Let's get you home. You look like shit and could use some sleep." He rests his hand on my shoulder, and I wobble forward into him.

"Fine. Yeah. Sleep sounds good. And burritos? Can we get burritos?"

Ben chuckles. "Yeah, man. We can get burritos. Let's get outta here."

He drives me home, keeping his promise on burritos. I pass out cradling my burrito, and he wakes me up when we're home, then practically carries me into the elevator and to my door.

He drops me on my bed, and I snuggle into the pillow that still faintly smells like Bridget. "Thanks, man." I sigh, inhaling the scent.

"Yep. Get some sleep. We'll talk tomorrow."

I nod and lay on my side. "Oh, wait." I dig into my pocket. "Here, take these. Give them to some nice girl." I turn back over, and within seconds, I pass out.

Chapter
Twenty-Four

Bridget

"ANNA! TIME FOR DINNER." I WAIT FOR HER TO POP OUT OF her playroom.

"Coming!" she hollers back, and I re-enter the kitchen. Jonathon is standing at the island, firing off emails.

"Are you all set?" I ask, heading over to the oven to check on the lasagna.

"Yes. My car should be pulling up any minute. And you know you don't have to cook. That's what Alice is for."

"I know. I enjoy it."

He stalls a moment, his probing gaze trying to dissect my mood. "Are you sure you're okay?" he asks carefully. It's been impossible to hide my sadness. No matter how busy I keep my days, the loneliness always kicks in at night and my mind always goes to him. Guilt eats away at me. It's not Jax I mourn anymore. His memory is fading. I barely remember what it felt like to love him. Hurt for him. My mind has been so consumed with Chase. I need to move on. Fight past the pain.

"Yes. I'm great actually." I put on my brave face. I don't want him to doubt my abilities to care for his daughter. His wary gaze tells me he's hesitant. "Trust me, we're going to transform the entire house into a princess castle and play dress up and eat cookies for all meals. I've got it covered."

He feeds into my humor, his expression softening. His phone beeps, indicating his car has arrived. "Okay. I'll be home as soon as I can. This deal should go smoothly. Three days max."

"No rush. We'll keep plenty busy. Now, go make fortunes. I'm pretty sure your daughter is expecting a pony farm for her birthday."

Jonathon sighs. "Don't encourage her." He takes another moment to take me in, then nods, and I follow him out and up the driveway to the town car. From the bottom of the driveway, a guy wearing a shirt with the fire department logo on his left chest walks up. "What is this? Is something wrong?"

"Ben?" I ask, confused by his presence.

"Hey, sorry to just show up. You got a second?"

Jonathon steps in, ready to shut it down, but I speak up first. "It's fine. He's a friend. Have a safe flight." He's not sold on my answer, but time is money, so he lets it go. We both wait until his car is out of sight before I speak up. "Whatever you have to say, I don't want to hear it. You're wasting your time."

"And I'm not one for long chats. I just wanted to stop by and drop this off." He reaches into his pocket and pulls out a box.

"What—?"

"Chase gave these to me the other day. He was given some backwards advice and told diamonds were a way to being forgiven. Anyway, when he pulled them out of his pocket, this fell out with it. Not sure he remembers, he's pretty messed up about all this, but I figured the earrings and letter are meant for you."

I hesitate, my eyes falling to the letter.

"I gotta get to work so..." Snapping out of it, I take it.

"See ya around." He walks away, then looks back when I call for him. "Yeah?"

"Thank you."

"I've known Chase a long time. I know exactly the guy he's been since we were five. I also know something changed in him recently. He's been acting different. He was secretive about what, but he looked happy for the first time since I can remember. Like something gave him a reason to be better. Work harder. You can't change a person's past. You can only do right in the present." He doesn't say more before turning and walking back down the driveway.

The letter burns between my fingers. I ache to rip it open and read every word, but Anna pops her head out, derailing that plan. "I'm hungry."

"Yep! On it. Let's gobble up some of that lasagna." I shove the letter and box in my pocket and race inside. We eat dinner while I listen to Anna explain how princesses are born, then we dress up and dance around the entire house. She paints my nails a pretty pink, leaving more polish on my fingers than anything.

We take a field trip to the guesthouse so I can pack a bag since I'm staying in the main house until Jonathon gets back, and we have a cookie eating contest.

I peek at my watch. It's almost bedtime. "Last bite. It's time for bed." I sit forward in my chair, the feel of the box brushing against my jeans pocket. I've fought tooth and nail not to think about it. As Anna settles down and knowing I'll be alone to read his letter, my heart accelerates. What is it going to say? Should I read it? Throw it out? *Read it, dummy. You know you want to.* I'm afraid of what's inside. Will his words hurt me more?

I get Anna ready for bed, and thankfully, she zonks out faster than normal. Shutting off her light, I head back down to the kitchen and make myself a cup of chamomile tea, but even that doesn't calm my nerves. I venture into the library and snuggle into the leather reading chair, releasing a long breath. Pulling out the box, I rub my thumb across the velvet top. I slowly open it, but stall midway. Maybe I don't want to see what's inside. *Yes, you do.* Holding my breath, I open it and my palm covers my mouth. My eyes prickle with tears as I stare down at angel-shaped diamond earrings. A thickness grows in my throat. God, that stupid nickname. I remember the first time he called me that.

"Still trying to decide if I'm the devil?"

"No. I'm realizing you may be an angel."

He was so darn strange, I almost passed on him. But then he kept talking. His nervousness intrigued me. I was the virgin trying to proposition a stranger, and he was the nervous one. I laugh as I wipe at a tear.

"Yeah, that's right, Angel. Remember what these lips feel like all over your body."

He made me feel so alive. I could be on my death bed and still feel the warmth of his mouth all over my skin.

I close the box, my emotions so high, I'm reluctant to open his letter. "Come on, Bridge, just rip off the Band-Aid." I blink away tears, inhale a breath for strength, and unfold the piece of paper.

Angel -

I'm writing this under the assumption you may never read it. Which may not be the worst thing, because it's probably corny as hell and making my case even worse. But I was told it's good to write down my feelings. Don't worry, not by one of my past conquests. I've invested in a lot of advice from Google. I'm hoping this letter does the trick because I'm really not into sacrificing a lamb. I would go as far as wearing a vial of your blood, but that's where I draw the line. Fuck, I'm babbling. Get to the point.

The point is, Kip was right. I was a player. I made choices without thinking of who I hurt. And I didn't give a shit. Until I met you. Seeing you in that bar, it was like an angel coming to save me. Before you, I didn't know what true happiness felt like. I didn't think I would ever be vulnerable enough to love anyone else again—until I found someone just as scared. Love is terrifying. But with the right person, it's beautiful., The good, the bad, and the ugly. (I know, corny line. Please burn this after reading.)

I'm sorry I acted like a coward when the time came to step up. I'm the one who didn't fight for us. I'm the one who ruined the most precious thing I've ever had. I know you hate me, but I hate myself more. Just please know my love is real. It was never fake or a scheme. Everything between us was more real to me than I can ever express. I'm sorry I hurt you. You deserve someone who will never stall when it comes to protecting you. I just wish I hadn't fucked up so I could be that person for you. You'll always be my angel. You'll always own my heart.

Chase

I crumble the piece of paper and wipe at my heavy tears. "Damn him." I clutch it to my chest. I do hate him for not fighting for us. For allowing his insecurities to degrade what we had. But my heart won't let me erase him. Because even though the sharpness of his betrayal stings, my love for him wants to mend every sliver. God, I miss him. His corny jokes. The nervous tick in his jaw. The way he knows every single inch of my body. I should have talked it out with him. I didn't give him a chance to explain, and now, I want nothing more than to hear his voice.

I scramble for my phone, but it's not in my back pocket. "Shoot!" I must have left it in the guesthouse when I went to get my things. I stop at the bottom of the stairs and listen for any noises. Feeling confident Anna's still down, I run out the back door. I push open my door and run in, not even turning on the lights, instantly spotting it on the kitchen island. My hands shake as I dial his number. I don't even know what I'm going to say when he answers. My heart beats against my ribcage with every ring. "Come on. Pick up." Shoot. What if

I'm too late and he's purposely not answering my call? I turn to head back to the main house and trip over a large object, stubbing my toe. "Ouch," I groan. His phone rings one last time and goes to voicemail. "Hey, it's me. Bridget. I...I just read your letter and I'm—" I turn on the light to see what I tripped over. "I really want...to...what the heck...*Chase*—"

It happens so fast, I don't have time to react. I barely register the pain that erupts along my skull as a blurry object appears before me and sharp metal crashes against my temple. My phone drops to the ground as I blink once, twice, then collapse to the ground, losing consciousness.

Chapter
Twenty-Five

Chase

"LATER, CHASE. YOU WORKIN' DOUBLE SHIFT TOMORROW too?"

I wave over to Craig. "Sure am. See ya tomorrow."

"You're overworking yourself, son."

"Never overworked. Plus, it's keeping me out of the bars. Have a good night." I walk over to my truck and remove my work gear, tossing it into the bed. For the third day in a row, I've pulled a double shift, working into the night. It's exhausting, but it's keeping my head on straight. Changes need to be made in my life. If not for anyone but myself. Ben's right. I can't fix myself for others. I need to want to do it. And I do. The drinking needs to stop. Hence why I haven't had a sip of alcohol in three days. It only gets me in trouble. Not that I'm worried about overindulging in women. I have no interest in that shit. At least not for the foreseeable future. And who the hell knows? Maybe working overtime will allow me to save enough money to think about going back to school. It may have been a silly pipe dream when Bridge brought it up, but damn, it feels good to imagine it. It's the path I should have stayed on.

I wave to a few guys and jump into my truck. While starting it, my phone lights up. Kip has ignored all my groveling messages, but I don't blame him. I even sent one to Hannah, but she's giving me the cold shoulder too. Levi's at least talking to me. Not that I enjoy his convos since his new nickname for me is 'dumbass'. I can only hope, in time, they'll learn to forgive me.

I check my phone in hopes Kip is done ignoring me, and almost drop it when I see a missed call from Bridget. "Fuck!" She left a voicemail. My hand trembles as I lift the device to my ear and click play. She's probably gonna remind me how much she hates me, but at this point, just hearing her voice will suffice.

"Hey, it's me. Bridget. I… I just read your letter and I'm— I really want…to…what the heck…*Chase*—" She doesn't finish her sentence. Something stops her. An array of static crackles through the line, then the call goes dead. That didn't sound right. The way she said my name at the end. It may be nothing. Maybe her phone died. But the tone in her voice… like something was wrong? I still don't trust her skeevy boss. What if he tried something on her? Took advantage of her vulnerability? I listen to the recording three times over, my stomach churning. I make out a muffled groan and scuffling. Her phone didn't die. Someone ended the call.

I call her back, and it goes straight to voicemail.

"Fuck." Throwing my truck into drive, I peel out of the parking lot, hitting her number again. Nothing. I look at the time. She left the message two hours ago. I hit redial. It doesn't even ring. "Hey, this is Bridg—" Fuck! *What's going on, Angel?* And why the hell is there so much traffic right now! "Move!" I slam on my horn and swerve around a car. Breaking every traffic law is still not getting me there fast enough. The last time she was with me, something seemed off and it was because of that prick, I know it. I shouldn't have let her go back there. Hating me or not.

I blow through another red light while stabbing in a phone number. "Fucking answer, dammit." It rings three times, and my stomach drops, knowing it's going to go to voicemail again.

"Seriously, stop calling me, Chase. I have nothing to say—"

"Hannah, listen to me. It's about Bridget."

"I'm sure it is, and I told—"

"Shut up for a fucking second! I think something's up. Have you spoken to her in the last couple hours?"

She takes too long to respond. "Hannah!"

"No, I haven't spoken to her since last week."

Dammit. "Has she ever expressed any issues with her boss? Like he's a creep or makes her uncomfortable?"

"Chase, where are you going with—"

"Answer me!"

"Calm down. No, she hasn't. Should I be worried?" I speed up. Something is definitely wrong. If that motherfucker did something to her, he's a dead man. "Chase, you're scaring me. What's going on?"

What's going on is I should have never let her go. "I've got a bad feeling. I'm headed to her now." I hang up on her and dial Bridget again. When it goes straight to voicemail, my nerves shoot from worried to terrified. My pulse races. I weave in and out of traffic, my eyes glancing at the clock. Every second that passes sends a tremor of fear to my gut. *It could be nothing. You're going to show up and she's going to slap you.* I don't care if she kicks my ass, so long as she's okay.

The turn for the estate comes into view, and my truck fishtails as I take a hard right into the driveway. I barely have the truck in park before I jump out and run to the guesthouse. A sharp blast ricochets from inside, and I jolt back. "Bridget!"

Chapter
Twenty-Six

Bridget

"BABY GIRL, WAKE UP."

My eyelids are heavy. "I'm too tired," I whisper, falling deeper into slumber.

"Baby girl, I need you to wake up."

A chill washes over me. I shiver, feeling the coldness in my bones. I just want him to cocoon his affection around me. "I'm cold," I whimper. I just want to warm up.

"I know you are. But you have to wake up and fight."

What am I fighting for? "Wake up, Bridget. Wake—"

"Wake up, you little bitch!"

A blast of cold water slaps at my face. I shoot forward, gasping for air. The sudden movement turns my stomach. My vision clouds. I reach out to touch my head and wince at the pain. When I pull back, my fingers are coated in red. I try to stand, but I sway and fall back to the ground. "What...?" I struggle to comprehend what's happened. How long have I been unconscious? Oh God, Anna. I make another attempt, only to smack back against the floor.

"About time. That's the third glass of water. About thought I killed ya."

My eyes slowly raise in front of me. Pain radiates from my skull. I wipe dripping water away from my eyes, and I suck in a sharp breath. "What are you doing?" Through my blurred vision, standing inside the guesthouse, I stare up at Mrs. Taylor.

"What does it look like I'm doing, you little brat?" She makes a swift move, hurling herself at me, and I skid back, pressing my back against the couch. "I'm finally collecting what's owed to me. And *you* owe me." She's so close, I can smell the stench of booze on her breath.

"What do you think I owe you? I had nothing to do with Jax's death. I loved him—"

"You didn't love him! You used him! You were gonna take him away from me." She raises her hand and points a gun at me.

I flinch, squeezing my eyes shut, and raise my hands up in defense. "No, that's not true. I never would've done that." I open my eyes to plead with her. "Please. I knew he was helping you. He loved you so much."

"Shut up." She cocks her hand back and slaps me across the face.

I clutch my cheek, whimpering at the pain. "He wanted to take care of you. We both did."

"I said shut up!" Her face reddens with anger. Her jittery hand clenches around the trigger. "You didn't love him. You made him leave. You took everything from me."

My voice trembles. "No...no, I didn't. Mrs. Taylor—Diane, it was an accident—"

"You made him leave! Now, it's time for you to pay!" She whips around, storming over to the kitchen island. When her back is to me, I shoot off the ground toward the front door. A gunshot explodes behind me. I scream as the glass in the front window shatters. Dropping to the ground, I cover my head.

"You bitch!"

"Please! You don't want to do this," I cry out, crawling along the floor to find something to shelter myself behind.

"You're right. I don't. I need you to do something for me first—"

The hinges shriek as the front door crashes open, slamming against the wall and bouncing back. I barely register the quick movement, but my throat locks when he comes into sight. My scream is almost silent as I cry out to Chase. His head whips in my direction. His eyes fall on me, wide with confusion. Unaware of the danger, he darts toward me. "Jesus, Bridget." He skids to the ground in front of me. "What—?" Over his shoulder, Mrs. Taylor raises her gun to point at Chase's back, and terror seizes my lungs.

"No!" I shoot forward to block Chase. "Please, don't. He has nothing to do with this. You want me. Your revenge is with me."

"Fuck, Bridget. Get behind—"

"Don't move!" she yells, and we both freeze.

I refuse to move away from Chase. "Okay. Okay... whatever it is you want, tell me."

Chase captures my arm, and I panic, knowing he's trying to put me behind him. Mrs. Taylor sees it too as the vein in her neck protrudes.

"I told you not to move!" She raises her gun, baring her stained teeth. Her hand shakes, and I panic, fearing she may accidentally pull the trigger.

"Okay!" I throw my hands up. "Okay. Just...please, tell me what you want."

She hesitates, her hand still raised. With her free hand, she uses the sleeve of her shirt to wipe at her nose. That's when I notice her dilated pupils. She's high. "I want money."

"I don't have any money—"

"Then get it!" She lunges closer, jabbing the gun at me.

"Your boss. He's rich. There has to be money somewhere in that house. A safe."

Anna.

I can't let her near that house.

I raise my hands in surrender. "Mrs. Taylor, I don't know of a safe being anywhere in that house. I haven't worked here that long."

Chase eases closer to me. I want to melt into the comfort of his body, but not even his warmth can stop the violent tremors that travel through me. I silently beg him to back off. She's unhinged, and without a source of money, I don't know how to talk her down.

"Listen, I have money. I can take you to my bank. We can… work this—" Black spots mar my vision, and I sway to the right.

"Bridget!" Chase calls for me as two hands grip my waist, bringing me upright.

"Don't move!"

"She's fucking bleeding. She needs to sit down. I'm going to move slowly, but I'm bringing her to the couch."

"I'm fine…" My voice is groggy. My head continues to pound. He walks me over to the couch and bends down with me as I sit. Leaning forward, he speaks low. "I'm gonna get us out of this. Don't worry."

I grab his shirt, barely able to squeeze. "Please. She's crazy. She'll hurt you."

"She's not. Trust me, okay?" I can't. I'm too scared.

"Chase, she's on—"

"Stop talking over there! Step away from her or I'll shoot you both." Her movements become jerky. She searches around the room. A bead of sweat forms along her forehead, and she wipes it off. "You're going to take me to the house." She swipes her sleeve across her nose again. She spots her bag and reaches for it. Chase makes a slight movement, and she jerks, raising the gun. "Don't be the hero."

Chase throws his hands up. "Wasn't trying to be. I'll take you up to the house—"

"No," I spit out.

"Bridge, let me take—"

"Both of you shut up." Mrs. Taylor holds her aim as she reaches inside her bag and pulls out a small plastic baggie containing a white powder. She tries to maintain eye contact with us while she opens it and brings it to her nose. She inhales deeply, snorting the drug. "Shit," she hisses. Her eyelids become sluggish. Chase's shoulders tense. He adjusts his footing and I know he's about to make a move. I choke down my panic. He looks down at me with probing eyes, asking for my approval. My chest tightens. Bile churns inside my stomach. I don't know what to do. Mrs. Taylor's arm relaxes, and her eyes shut completely. Before I can give him an answer, his foot pushes off the ground as the front door opens.

Time suddenly stops. I hold my breath and my stomach bottoms out as my eyes focus on the little girl walking into the guesthouse, rubbing her eyes.

Mrs. Taylor's head jerks up, her attention snapping to the door. She raises her arm, not stopping to see that the little girl is not a threat. My mouth parts, but the shrilling scream tearing up my throat doesn't stop the horrid sound of two rounds of bullets that fly into the air. Images of her smiling face in my head cloud my vision. The sound of her boisterous giggles ring in my ears. My chest breaks open as I'm brought back to reality. I cry out to her, but it's no use. The damage is already done. I push off the couch to run to her, but it's not her who's laying on the ground. It's Chase. Two oozing holes soaking through his shirt.

NO!" I stumble to the ground. "Chase!" I cry out when I reach him. "No, no, no, no…" I look up to find Anna crouched in the corner.

"Get away from him."

"He's shot! We need to call nine-one-one!" I cry out. Too

much blood. It's coming out too fast. "Oh god." My hands hang over his wounds. I don't know what to do. How to make it stop. It's not going to stop. He's going to die. "Please, hang on. I'm going to get you help," I plead. I take a moment and gaze up at Anna. "Are you hurt?" She doesn't answer. "Are you hurt! Tell me!" I snap, hysterical.

"No. He pushed me out of the way."

My eyes fall back on Chase. His lids are closed. The color is quickly draining from his face. "Chase, please. Stay with me. Call for help!" I scream at Mrs. Taylor. She just stands there, high out of her mind and partially in shock. I press my shaky hands over his wounds to stop the bleeding, and he lets out a low whimper. I spot a throw pillow and snatch it up, putting it over a bullet wound, forcing his arms to rest on top of it. He groans, and I panic. "Shit. I'm sorry. I have to stop the bleeding—"

"Get away from him."

"Are you kidding me? He's hurt—"

"I said get away from him." My entire body stiffens when she points the gun at Anna, who cowers deeper in the corner. "You're going to take me into the house or she's next."

My voice trembles as I try to talk. "This is not the answer, Mrs. Taylor. I don't know where the safe is—"

"I know where one is."

My head whips in Anna's direction. "No, honey—"

"You heard the little brat. Let's go."

No, no, no.

I can't leave Chase.

She storms up to me, slamming the gun across my cheek. Pain rings in my ear, and I almost tumble over. Heavy tears mixed with blood stream down my face. I hiccup as I plead with her. "I'm not leaving him. Please. He'll die if we don't call for help."

"Have it your—"

"Fine!" My eyes burn, and I retreat. I can barely stand, my legs tremble so bad. "We can't let him die."

"Go!" she yells, and I jump, hurrying over to Anna. I'm trying to be brave for her, but when I reach for her, I realize I have blood coating my hands. His blood. Oh god. I start to hyperventilate. When Anna runs into my arms, I pick her up, holding her tight, murmuring that everything is going to be okay even though I feel far from it.

She wraps her arms around me, putting her lips to my ear. "I know how to make her go away." Her comment confuses me. She continues. "The safe is in my daddy's room. It has something that will make her go away." I glance back at Mrs. Taylor. She's tweaked out of her mind, her body swaying back and forth. She jabs the gun into my back.

"Go. We don't have all day."

I turn forward and fight not to throw up. "I don't understand," I whisper, walking out of the guesthouse.

"Daddy has the same bad toy. He keeps it by his bed. It's in a safe. I know the code."

My eyes widen. "Anna, how do—?"

"Move it. Ask the little brat where the safe is."

I look down at Anna as she gazes up at me. There's no way she would know where, let alone how to access Jonathon's gun. Even if—there has to be another way. Then it hits me. Jonathon walked me through the security system my first day. If anything was ever wrong, I was to enter in the panic code. It's a silent alarm that will alert the security company. I just need to get into the house and enter in the panic code on the security system and then pray they get here in time to save Chase. Save us all.

"Ask her!" Mrs. Taylor yells, and I nod, looking down at Anna.

"Anna, you don't have to do—"

She speaks up so Mrs. Taylor can hear. "In Daddy's room."

I nod, but my gut is screaming at me to find another way. This is not the answer. I try to count the time in my head. If I can just stall long enough—

"Well let's move it."

We head up to the main house and enter through the back door. "I have to press the alarm. It needs to be reset anytime someone goes in and out after nine at night."

"You're lying to me." She points her gun, and I pivot to block Anna.

"I'm not. If I don't reset it within thirty seconds, it alerts the security company. Along with my boss." I hold her gaze, praying she doesn't see through my lie.

Mrs. Taylor looks at me with suspicious eyes, then points the gun to the alarm. "Do it. Hurry. But I'm watching you. Anything funny and I'll shoot you both."

"Fine. I'm just going to punch in the code, okay?" I take two cautious steps toward the control panel, hoping she can't read far enough to tell which buttons I press. Entering the panic code, I press set. The alarm beeps once, and the red light flashes to green. "There."

"Okay. Now, walk."

I nod and pick up Anna. I gaze down at her while we walk. She's being so brave. "It's going to be okay," I tell her, but my voice cracks. Anna smiles up at me, oblivious to the danger we're in. We walk up the stairs and enter Jonathon's room. It's set up for a king, the huge bed tucked away in the back of the room, dark silk blanketing the top with plush pillows and two massive nightstands on either side.

"Which one is it?" Mrs. Taylor bites out, pushing us forward. I stumble, almost dropping Anna. She lifts her finger and points to the one on the left.

Unsure of what to do, I walk toward the nightstand and place Anna on the ground. How long will it take for the police to arrive? My mind goes back to Chase. He's lying there helpless. I need to focus. Keep us both safe until help arrives.

What happens when we open this safe and there's no money in it?

"Have her open it."

I inhale a shaky breath, a tear falling down my cheek. "Honey, can you open the safe?"

Her head bobs up and down. She steps toward the nightstand and opens the bottom door, revealing a large black metal box. Reaching her little hands inside, she fumbles with the keypad. Anna gets it wrong the first time, and the safe beeps once.

It agitates Mrs. Taylor. She raises her gun to Anna, and I step in between them. "She will get it open. Please, put the gun down. She's just a little girl—"

Three beeps echo, and the safe clicks open. I turn and bend down to Anna's level. Nausea swarms in my stomach at the site of the gun. Where are the police? I'm counting numbers in my head, trying to figure out how much time has passed. They get jumbled and I have to start over. Three minutes? Maybe five? I don't know! Mrs. Taylor is going to see there's no money in this safe. My hands shake. The pain in my head is excruciating. Oh god! I'm starting to fall apart. *Pull it together, Bridget.* I squeeze my eyes shut and inhale a deep breath. I look down at Anna. "It's going to be okay. I'm going to just stand up and go talk to her, okay?"

Anna stares back, and I force a smile. Standing, I face Mrs. Taylor. "You don't have to do this—"

"Shut up and give me the money."

I take a careful step toward her to put space between her and the drawer so she cannot see inside the safe. "I will. It's all yours, but I want you to let Anna leave. When she's safely out of the house, you can have the money and we can search for jewelry or—"

A shot rings in my eardrums. I don't acknowledge where the gun shot came from before I jump and tackle Mrs. Taylor, bringing her to the ground. I fight for the gun, but she's stronger. I lose my grip, and she presses the gun into my stomach. I wait for the onslaught of pain to blast through my flesh, but it doesn't come. Wetness soaks my shirt. I look down just as her hand becomes weak and she drops the gun. Blood seeps between us. I shoot up, feeling my chest for bullet holes. When I look down, I realize Mrs. Taylor is the one who's been shot.

My body trembles as I clutch my chest. I whip back to Anna, and my mouth falls open. "Oh Anna…" I whisper in shock. Anna stands there, her doe eyes staring back at me. It wasn't Mrs. Taylor's gun that went off, it was Jonathon's. "Anna," I groan and run toward her. "Honey, give me that, okay?" Her little hands tremble, as her eyes shift to Diane's unmoving body. Oh god, what did she just do? I take the gun and throw it onto the bed. "Hey, don't look. Look at me." I cup her face. "It's okay." I pull her into my arms.

Sirens blare in the distance, and I cry out in relief. *Chase!* "Anna, we need to get out of here, okay?" I stand up and lift her in my arms. Shielding her from Mrs. Taylor's body, I rush out of the room. The throbbing in my head worsens and white spots cloud my vision. My hand whips out to the wall to steady myself.

Taking a few deep breaths, I push off the wall and hurry down the stairs, fighting each wave of dizziness. My tears mix with the dripping of blood from my head wound and my eyes burn. *Keep going, Bridget.* "We're almost there. Just hang on." The fear of what I'm coming back to has me on the verge of breaking down. What if he's dead? What if it's too late… The kitchen lights up with red and blue as I race out the back door.

A man blocks the stairs and I almost trip backwards as he lifts his gun, pointing his weapon at us. "Help us…" I choke out a sob.

"Is there anyone else inside?"

"She's upstairs. She's been shot—I don't know if she's

dead, but she tried to—Chase—I have to get to—get to—"
My voice trembles so bad, I can't make out a full sentence.
The officer slowly lowers his gun. "The guesthouse. He's in
the guesthouse. He's been shot. He needs help—"

A team of police barge through the back doors and
disappear into the house.

"The guesthouse! He's in the guesthouse!" I panic. Every
second that passes is too much time.

"What's your name, Miss?"

"It doesn't matter! He needs help—"

"Paramedics are already working on him. You're bleeding.
Do you need a medic—"

"Some of it's hers… And his. Oh god, he's—you have to
help him!"

A paramedic comes up and gently asks to have Anna. I
don't want to let her go. She has a death grip around my neck.
"Miss, we need to check her out." I'm hesitant to let her go.

"Anna, honey. I'll be right here with you, okay? They're
not going to hurt you."

"No, Bridget, don't let them take me. What if they ask?
What if they know?"

I shake my head, caressing her cheek. "No. Don't you
worry. You're not in trouble, I promise. I won't let anything
happen to you." She slowly releases me and allows the medic
to take her. I bolt down the steps toward the guesthouse when
the door opens, and paramedics rush out towing a gurney.

"Chase!"

"Miss, please, you need to get out of the way." They hurry
past me, and I run alongside them, trying to see him. His skin
is almost translucent. Blood soaks his shirt, the front nearly
covered. My eyes zero in on his chest. To see the rise and fall.
To see any movement. It's there, but barely. "Is he going to be
okay?" I ask the stupid question as they lift him into the
ambulance. "Please, can you tell me anything?"

"Bridget!" I take my eyes off the ambulance for a second.

Just enough time for the doors to shut. A sob tears up my throat and I call out as I stare after the blinking lights until the vehicle turns onto the street and disappears. "Bridget! Jesus, you're covered in blood. What happened?" I barely register the person in front of me. *Blink. Blink. Blink.* This is a bad dream. This isn't real. "Bridget?"

Hannah. She's in front of me. Why is she here? "Oh, honey, what happened?" My throat burns. Each attempt to speak feels like a sliver slicing across my chest. "He...I..." The words won't come. This isn't real. Please wake up. This isn't real.

Levi rushes up behind her. "Bridget, what the hell happened? Is everyone okay? Chase said—"

"He saved her... He saved me... He saved...He..."

"Shit, you're in shock. Someone! She needs a medic." Levi reaches for me, but I slap his hands away.

"It's not my blood. It's his. It's his blood. He saved her. He saved me." A rush of panic surges through me and the dizziness returns. I sway to the right. My chest cracks open, and the pain cripples me. My knees give out, and Levi catches me as I breakdown. Anger and guilt tear at my chest, and I fall apart in Levi's arms.

"Shhh, it's going to be all right," Hannah soothes as she rubs my shoulder. The back door opens, and another gurney is wheeled down the steps. Diane Taylor is handcuffed to the bed as they rush her to another ambulance.

"You—" I fight out of Levi's arms to throw myself at the gurney, ready to kill her if she isn't already breathing her last breath. Levi catches me, and I kick and scream in his arms.

"Bridge, chill."

"She killed him! He's going to die because of me!" Tears rush down my cheeks. I hold my stomach, the pain too much to bear. I look up at Levi, whose expression is somber. "I'm so sorry. I killed him. He's going to die because of me."

He can't even look down at me and tell me it's going to be

okay. That his best friend is probably going to die and he won't hate me for it.

"Everyone I love dies." I shake my head over and over. The dizziness becomes too intense. Bile rises in my throat. I struggle in his grip as I choke.

"Sir, we'd like to step in." A man stands next to us. I don't recognize him. Another paramedic.

"I killed him. I killed him..." I repeat.

"I think she's going into shock. She's trembling really bad."

"We can give her something. Let us take it from here." The heat of Levi's hands disappears, replaced by the paramedic, and I become erratic.

"Don't touch me! I need to be with Anna. Where's Anna?"

"Miss, I'm going to need you to calm down. We're going to give you something to relax."

"Anna!" I call her name over and over, pausing at the pinch in my neck. "Let me go! Anna…" My words slowly start to slur. Before I can call out again, I'm falling.

Chapter
Twenty-Seven

Bridget

"*Anna, where are you? Come out, come out, wherever you are... Anna? Anna—*"

"*Anna.*" I jolt awake and shoot forward. The fogginess in my head causes me to sway. I latch on to the side of the bed.

"Relax." My head whips to the right. Jonathon is sitting in the chair next to my bed. "Anna is fine."

"No, she's not. She's—"

"She's fine. She's with a counselor right now. Your mother and father just stepped out. I wanted to see how you were doing."

My parents are here? I look around. I'm in a hospital bed. Memories flood my brain, each horrid detail punching me in the gut. I grab at my chest as his name tears up my throat.

"Chase!" I throw the sheet off and attempt to stand, but I'm restrained by the IV stuck in my arm.

Jonathon reaches for me. "Slow down. He's in surgery."

"Surgery. What does that mean? Is he going to be okay? What do you know? I have to go see—"

The hysteria hits me like a sledgehammer. My body shakes

violently. Memories of the blood. His pale face. His still body. "I have to go see him."

"Right now, you just have to rest. They shot you up with some pretty heavy sedatives."

The last thing I can fathom is resting while the man I love is fighting for his life. When I almost got Anna killed. "Jonathon—"

"Don't."

"No, I have to tell you what happened—that woman—"

Jonathon leans forward, resting his palm over mine. "That woman will no longer be a problem."

My eyes widen. "Did she…?"

"She was pronounced dead when she arrived."

My head shakes back and forth as hot tears shed down my face. "I did this. I caused all of this. I put your daughter in danger and got Chase—" I cover my mouth as a horrid sob rips up my throat. "I'm so sorry."

Jonathon stands and sits on the bed, pulling me into him. "This isn't your fault, Bridget. The disturbed woman who set out to get revenge is at fault."

"You don't know why. If you did, you would—"

"I do know. I spoke with your father. I know enough that you're not to blame." He pulls back and gazes down at me. "Bridget, I need to know. How did you know the code for my gun safe?"

I blink away the tears. My mouth opens and closes. "Anna. She knew." His body stiffens. "She—she told me she knew where you kept the bad toy and knew how to get to it. I—she knew the code. I wouldn't have let her—I took my eyes off her for a second and—what did she tell the police—?"

"Nothing. She hasn't said a word since she was brought in."

I become completely still. My eyes widen. "What?"

"She hasn't spoken. She won't tell us what happened. There's been an officer outside your room since you arrived.

Two people were shot, and no one knows the story. The only thing they are going on is you screaming you killed him."

An icy chill spreads down my spine. I slowly shake my head. "No, I didn't shoot them. I meant I caused it. I didn't... oh god, they think I did this—"

His demeanor shifts. "No more."

"Jonathon—"

"Miss Matthews, can I have a word?"

We both shift to the man who entered my room. "I'm Detective Schmitt. I was hoping to ask you a few questions about what went on at the Brooks' residence."

Jonathon stands and blocks me. "She is in no shape to answer questions right now. Come back—"

"I'm pretty sure I was insistent you do not speak with her before we did. Your house is a crime scene, Mr. Brooks. There are a lot of questions to be answered here. And tampering with an investigation is illegal."

Jonathon's shoulders tense. He clenches his jaw, taking a threatening step toward the detective. "And she won't be answering any questions until my lawyer gets here."

The detective's brow raises. "I have questions. But you may have just answered a few of them if you feel there's a need to have a lawyer present."

"It's fine. I don't need a lawyer—"

"Bridget, not another word—"

"Please. It's okay. I don't have anything to hide." Jonathon's eyes bore into mine. It's not me who has anything to hide. It's his daughter.

His Adam's apple bobs as he swallows. "I'll be outside if you need anything."

The door shuts behind him, leaving me and the detective alone.

"Miss Matthews, can you walk me through what happened tonight?"

"I shot Diane Taylor..."

221

Chapter
Twenty-Eight

Chase

"Babe, I don't know what you're talking about."

"Caroline, I just caught you and him together. Fucking, for Christ's sake!"

Her cat nails swipe through the air as she turns her back to me. "You saw what you wanted to see. Honestly, Chase, you've been so clingy lately, it's getting to be unbearable—"

"Unbearable? Are you kidding me? I've done nothing but love you. I'd do anything for you. How is that unbearable?"

"You're smothering." She continues to walk away from me.

"Where are you going? We're not done talking about this." Her small sigh scratches at my skin. Her way of avoiding what I already know. "Answer me. How long have you been sleeping with your goddamn professor?"

She finally stops and turns, flipping her bleached blonde hair in the process. "You know what? Yes, I am. And he's more of a man than you'll ever be. He's not needy and whiny. He doesn't smother me. And quite frankly, he's a better lover—"

It feels as if my chest is caving in as I struggle to suck air into my lungs. My hands grab at my throat. It burns. I want to yell out, but my mouth is too dry. *I can't breathe. I can't breathe!*

"Hey, hey, you're all right. You have a breathing tube in. Try not to pull it out."

I squint as I try to open my eyes, the bright light stabbing at my corneas. I close them again and try to catch my breath, but I can't. I try to bring my hands to my mouth, but the wires restrict it.

"Chase, you have a breathing tube in and you're going to pull out your IV. Just relax."

A breathing tube? Why the fuck do I have a breathing tube? My eyes focus on the shadow above me. I can't make out a face. Why can't I see him? I blink rapidly until a face comes into view. A man. I try to speak, but nothing comes out.

"Don't try to talk. You're at Crest Health Hospital. You were shot."

Shot.

Shot.

Shot.

Bridget.

My body convulses. I reach back for the tube to pull it out. I need to speak. *Where's Bridget? Is she okay? Fuck, is she alive?*

"Chase, I'm going to give you more morphine. It's going to help calm you. You're not in a state to move. You're going to end up hurting yourself."

Wires constrict my movement. I tug at them, needing to get free. I need to get to Bridget. The doctor brings a needle to an IV bag. Inside, I scream to not give it to me. I need to be awake. I need to know...what...happ...

❧

Beeping sounds lure me awake. I try to open my eyes, but they're too heavy. Everything feels numb. Like my body is being held down by bricks. The only thing I can do is listen to the beeping.

"Has he shown any improvement?"

That voice. I know that voice. I fight to open my eyes, but they won't obey.

"He's lucky to be alive. The first bullet barely missed the subclavian artery. We were able to repair the damage, but it was touch and go. The good news is he's healing nicely, but he's still very weak. At this point, we just have to wait to see how his body reacts."

I'm fucking fine. *Open your goddamn eyes, asshole.*

"When will he wake up?"

I'm up!

"When he's ready. The body is magnificent. It knows when it needs to heal. I need to make some rounds, but I'll check back. In the meantime, talk to him. He can hear you."

A door shutting mingles with that beeping noise. I wish I could shut it off. I need to fight to wake up. Open my eyes.

"Fuck, man. You need to wake up."

I'm awake, Kip.

"God, I messed up. I should have heard you out. Let you explain the situation. I let my own judgment get in the way." *No, you did what was right. I lied. I betrayed our friendship.* "I asked you so many times what was up with you. Why didn't you just tell me? I should have known. If I were a better friend, I would have seen it. I know what love looks like. I was too wrapped up in my own life to see you." His voice sounds different. Sad. He's crying. "Don't give up on me. On everyone. Fight, man. Fight. I need you in my life. You've been my best friend since we were six. Fuck..." He pauses, and I feel wetness on my hand. Then warmth. He's holding my hand. *I'm not going anywhere. I'm here. I'm trying to come back.* "Remember how I saved your ass that first day? Thought you were about to eat a fist for lunch instead of that nasty turkey burger. You never want to admit it cause you're so damn stubborn, but your heart is bigger than any of ours. You've always watched out for us all. Shit, remember that one time you saved Ben from going home with that chick old enough to be your grandmother?" His laughter is filled with sorrow. "You told me you'd always have my back. You can't fucking leave me. You can't."

I'm not! I never will.

Unconsciously, I fight at my restraints, but my body doesn't move. Why won't my eyes open! The beeping sounds become too frequent. Another voice enters the room.

"I don't know…it just started going crazy."

"It's okay," a soft voice says. "I'm just going to give him something to relax."

No! I don't want anything…to…

~

I feel like I'm floating. Almost at peace. It's been forever since I've felt so at ease. There's no pain here. No sadness. Just calm.

"Hey…"

My world shifts. I'm suddenly falling. I reach out to grab at anything that will catch me, but there's nothing there. "I was praying I'd walk in here and you would be staring back at me with those mischievous eyes. They're always up to something. Thinking something. Craving something…"

Bridget.

Why does she sound so sad? She's never sad.

"Why won't you wake up? At least to tell me you hate me. Resent me for what I did. Anything that allows me to hear your voice again."

I don't hate you. God, I love you so damn much.

I scream her name, but there's no sound. It's just me falling. What happens when I stop?

"I know I keep saying this, but I'm so sorry. For us. For what happened. For everything. I would take back so many things if I could. Maybe even wish I never met you, just so I know you wouldn't end up like this." *No. Don't say that. You're the best thing to ever happen to me. Don't say that!* Beeping sounds radiate in my world. They become so loud, I can no longer hear her voice. *Bridget!* I scream her name over and over.

"What's happening?" There's so much anguish in her voice. Why is she so upset? *Someone help her!*

"This is normal. He may be trying to wake up, but it disturbs him. It's a good sign. But we also don't want him to harm himself. This will help."

No! No more! I need to wake up. I need to be with her! I'm no longer falling. It becomes dark. I fade…into…

∼

"Jesus, you look like shit."

I'm dreaming. I hear voices but this has to be a dream.

"Could you imagine what would happen if he knew people were seeing him in this gown?"

The voices. I know them. Ben and Levi. *What's up, assholes?*

"You think he's gonna pull through? It's been too long."

There's a strange sound to Ben's voice. He's crying.

"Dude, fuck off, he's going to pull through. There's no other way this ends."

I wish I could high-five Levi. He knows I'm no quitter. But his tone doesn't sound convincing. *Why wouldn't I pull through? I'm fine. I'm just tired. I'll be up soon. I'm trying. I'm trying.*

"Come on dude. You can knock it off already. This whole attention thing has gone on long enough. Open your damn eyes." Why do they sound so grim? *I'm fine. I'm going to be—*

Loud noises screech in my ears. I want to cover them. The beeping becomes erratic. I want to make it stop. Ben's voice is loud. Too loud. Why is he screaming?

"Help! Someone help!"

Who needs help? Why are they screaming?

Too many voices. I can't make out my friends anymore. Too…many…

∿

"I'm so angry, Dad. You tell me to have faith, but how can I when God has already taken one man that I loved away. And now him. He saved me. He doesn't deserve to die."

I wake up to the sound of her voice. My angel.

"Honey, God works in mysterious ways. Faith gives you strength to fight for the ones who need help fighting."

Her voice is strained. It guts me to hear her so sad. *I'm right here. I'm fighting to come back to you.* "I'm so scared. He needs to live. I can't have him leave me thinking I don't love him, because I do. The last time we saw each other, it was so ugly."

Stop crying, Angel.

Her tears hurt worse than the pain in my chest.

Wake up, asshole. Wake the hell up.

∿

Time doesn't exist where I am. Just voices that come and go. The beeping lures me awake and then back into the abyss of wherever hell I'm stuck in. I attempt to open my eyes, but like every other time, they refuse to open. My frustration builds and I groan to myself. I want to wake up. I'm ready. I need to see my girl—

"Oh god, Chase?"

Her voice. It sounds closer than it's been. Clearer.

I work harder than I ever have. Slowly, light breaks between my lids.

"Hey, hey…" The first thing I feel is warmth. She's holding my hand. *Open your goddamn eyes,* I growl at myself.

227

"Oh, there they are." My vision is blurry. I blink until she slowly comes into focus. Her hair is up in a messy bun. I want to lift my hand and pull it down. I love when it spills over her shoulders. "Shhh...don't move. Hold on. I need to get a——"

I groan again and squeeze the hand she's holding.

"Okay. But I need to get someone. You're awake." I stare at her, mad at the tears streaming down her face. I want to wipe them away. I open my mouth to speak but my throat is on fire. "They took the tube out yesterday. Here." She grabs a cup of water and brings it to my lips. "Slow sips." I lift my head. It feels like a bowling ball. I take the straw and try to suck down the water but end up choking. "Oh god, I need to get the doctor."

I grab her wrist, stopping her. I need to see her. Look at her.

"I'm so sorry," she cries out, tears continuing to stream down her angelic face. "I did this and I——"

"I—I——"

"Don't talk. Your throat is probably sore from the tube."

Frustrated, I refuse to stop until I get out what I have to say. "I—lo...lo...love...you..."

Fuck, I only made it worse. A sob breaks from her lips, and she cries harder. She grabs my hand, holding it to her mouth, pressing her sweet, soft lips to my palm. "Seriously, you've just been through hell and the first thing you have to say is that? Why are you so good—so caring—so perfect?"

I use every ounce of energy I have and pull her hand to my mouth. I press my lips to the inside of her wrist. "Bec—ause. I'm the—one...who should have—never let you go."

She falls apart, and I coerce her to climb up into my bed. I need to feel her next to me. Smell her sweet cherry and vanilla scent. She hesitates, then lays down, careful not to jostle me. I hate myself when I groan and she tries to retreat.

"No...I—I need you." She nods, soaking my gown, but I don't care. I forget the stabbing pain in my side and shoulder.

There's no pain strong enough to force me to move her. "How…long have I been here?"

She chokes again as she cries out. "Six days." Fuck. "You caught an infection and…you were touch and go the last three."

I grip her tighter, holding back the wince in my shoulder. "I'm sorry. I—I messed up. I didn't sa—save you."

"Stop. Don't you dare." I hiss as she sits forward. Her tears wet her face. "This is all my fault. I did this."

"You didn't ask for—"

"Chase, I should have never walked away. It was selfish of me. I let my fears get in the way." She has to stop to wipe at her tears and take a breath, and it kills me. "I was just so scared at how intense my emotions had become. Even more so at the thought of them being ripped away from me. I think a part of me was sabotaging what we had because I'd convinced myself that it was only inevitable that you would hurt me."

"I never would."

"I know that now. I know I'm the one who ruined everything."

The pain is intense, but I don't care. I grab her and pull her down to me. "You showed me I need to be better. Showed me what love truly is. I would have given my life for you if it helped you live." Dammit, I feel like I'm only making this worse. "Please stop crying."

She inhales a ragged breath. "I can't. I'm so happy you're awake. Sorry for so much. I thought you were never going to—"

"Hey," I lift my palm to her cheek. "I'm a certified stalker. I never go away." God, I love her laugh. Her plump lips. Her glassy eyes. No pain is going to stop me from kissing her. "Fuck," I groan at the agony shooting up my side.

"Please, don't move. I have to get a doctor."

"No, don't leave me." Damn, that sounded needy. "I mean…hang out. It's boring in here."

I earn another cheeky giggle. "Seriously? You've been shot twice, and been on your death bed for six days, and you still have your sense of humor."

"Got a girl to impress. And considering I probably don't look my best and I'm in a fucking gown, I have to work extra hard." Dammit, why more tears? "Shit, I'm sorry, I didn't—"

"You don't have to impress me. There's not a single thing I don't love about you, Chase Steinberg. Well…maybe the whole trying to die for attention thing. I would have just taken a confession of your undying love."

"That would have never been enough for me. There may not be enough time on this earth for me to express how damn much I love you." I grab her hand. "I would never have left you. I heard you. Your voice kept me fighting."

Her voice cracks. A small sob escapes her lips. "The doctor told me you could. I wasn't sure, but I did it anyway. And once I started, I couldn't stop. I needed you to know so many of us were fighting for you. That I love you so much. How sorry I was. If it weren't for me, you would have never been at the house that night—"

"I should have been there sooner."

"No, you shouldn't have been there at all. I put you at risk—"

"No, you put me right where I should have been. Trying to protect you. The only thing I regret is failing you."

"You didn't fail me, Chase. Do you even remember? You saved Anna's life. Those bullets were meant for her. You pushed her away and took them for yourself."

The memory of that night is still foggy. Only bits and pieces are coming back to me. What I don't know is what happened after that. "What happened afterwards? Were you hurt? Did she…?" I scan her for bandages or visible wounds and I cuss when I see a bandage on the side of her head.

"It's not as bad as it looks. Minor concussion. A nice gash in the side of my—"

"I'm going to fucking—"

"She's dead."

There's an ache inside my chest, worse than the bullet holes. God, what did she go through? I cup her cheek again. "Angel, what happened?" It guts me to watch her eyes dull. There's fear, uncertainty, guilt written all over her beautiful face.

"I…can't talk about it right now. It's too—"

"Don't. I don't need to know. Just that you're safe."

"Look who's awake." Bridget shifts to face the man entering the room. "Chase, how are you feeling?"

"Better if I weren't wearing a dress." Bridget turns, giving me the *behave* look. "I feel like I've been shot."

"Well, you have been. You're tough, though."

I look at Bridge and wink. "Hear that? Tough."

"Would you knock it off?" If it gets me that beautiful smile, never.

The doctor approaches, looking at my chart. "It's a great thing to see you awake, but I do have to ask the young lady to step out. I'll need to do a full exam."

I grab at her hand, not wanting her to leave.

She turns and pats mine. "It's okay. I'll be right outside. Plus, I think there's a group of sappy boys out there who would love to know you're awake."

"Maybe wait it out a bit, so they're extra nice to me. Maybe tell them to take care of all my unpaid bar tabs and—"

"Chase."

"Or not. But don't go far. As soon as I get clearance from the doc over here, I'm going to need you to do the real exam."

Her cheeks flush as the doc chuckles. She gets up, trying not to look embarrassed. "He's all yours. Good luck with him. He's a pain." Then she turns to me. "And for the record, when you get cleared, you're playing the bad patient this time." I feel like I haven't smiled in ages. It almost hurts, but damn does she make me happy.

I keep my eye on her until she disappears out of the room.

"Okay, Doc. Let's get to the important stuff. When can you clear me to have sex?"

Chapter
Twenty-Nine

Bridget

"WILL YOU AT LEAST BATHE ME?"

"Chase, knock it off."

"What? If the doc said I can't let you ravish me for two to three weeks, which I find stupid since my dick wasn't shot—"

"Chase!"

"I'm serious, how am I supposed to be near you and keep to myself? I want to bend you over this hospital bed as we speak. Should we try it?" He winks at me, and I'm almost tempted to give in. I miss him so much, there's nothing I want more than him inside me again.

"This whole bad patient thing is going to a whole new level."

"Then make me better."

I roll my eyes. This guy never quits. His hospital room door opens, and we both gaze in that direction. My stomach drops when Jonathon walks in.

"You're looking well," he begins, looking at Chase.

"Yeah, finally getting released today. Don't plan on seeing

this place again anytime soon. Well, unless they add beer and burgers to the menu. That Jell-O shit is for the birds."

Jonathon barely smiles at his banter. His attention turns to me. "How are you?"

I lick my lips, suddenly nervous. I haven't seen or spoken to him since the first day in the hospital. I know Anna is still refusing to speak. I've gone to see her a few times, but she's supervised like a hawk, so it's been hard to talk with her in private. I told her everything was going to be okay. That I would always protect her. But I'm not sure if her little mind comprehends. I'm even less sure the police aren't going to barge through this door and arrest me for tampering with evidence, not to mention lying. But I did what I thought needed to be done. It was self-defense no matter who pulled the trigger. I refuse to put that burden on her. She saved both our lives.

"I'm...good."

He stares at me, trying to break me down. And through the cracks, he knows I'm holding back. But the way his gaze holds mine, he doesn't need a confession to know the truth. Did I do the right thing? Would he want his daughter holding on to such a dark secret? I promised him I would keep her safe, and that's what I'm doing.

He breaks eye contact with me and returns to Chase. Eliminating the space between them, he sticks his hand out. "Thank you. For saving my daughter's life."

"Yeah, no problem." Chase shakes his hand.

When he tries to pull back, Jonathon doesn't allow it. "I mean it. Thank you. I will forever be indebted to you." He looks over at me. "To both of you."

Chase nods, looking my way. His brow is raised.

Jonathon finally releases his hand and turns to me. "May I speak with you in private?"

I want to say no. I'm not ready to have this talk. Jonathon deserves the truth about what happened. But the question is what will he do with the information once he knows? I nod and tell Chase I'll be right back. When we're standing alone in the deserted hallway, he begins.

"Thank you."

"I don't think you owe me a thank you. More like I'm fired for putting your daughter in danger—"

"You know what I'm thanking you for." He stares down at me, his eyes boring into mine.

"I did what was right. She has her whole life ahead of—"

"Stop," he cuts me off. It takes him a moment to gather himself. I've never seen him so stripped bare of his emotions. "She may have saved your life, but you saved hers. I will never forget this."

"If the truth ever comes out, I'll accept the consequence—"

"It won't. I'll make sure of it."

The question is, can Anna keep the truth a secret?

Chapter
Thirty

Chase

I WISH EVERYONE WOULD STOP BABYING ME AND GET THE HELL out of my apartment. I've been home a week and feel like I haven't gotten a single moment alone with Bridge.

The guys suddenly live here. I can't get Ben off my couch, and Levi is acting like my mother, putting groceries in my fridge. I almost punched him when I saw him about to clean my bathroom.

I love my friends, but right now, all I need is Bridget. And she seems to get pulled away every time I try to get her alone. Something's going on with her. She's doing everything she can to hide it, but the first two nights, she woke up screaming. I tried to comfort her, but she refused to talk about it. She's been called into the police station twice and has returned distraught both times. I asked her to talk about it, but she kept deflecting and making it about me. When it became too much to bear, she finally broke down and confessed the burden she's been holding. She wasn't the one who shot that woman—a secret only four people share and will stay that way. I will always and forever lay down my life for her.

When she's not trying to baby me, she spends the days with Anna. The little girl still isn't talking. It guts me to think about what she endured. What she witnessed. Since Bridge feels responsible, she's overworking herself to make it better. Not sure how anyone erases the horror of what that kid went through.

Kip's been over every second, but he keeps his distance. He barely says a word. I guess he's still having a hard time getting over what I did. And I get it. I'm just happy he's here.

I grab a beer out of my ridiculously full fridge, pop off the top, and walk back into my packed living room. "Jesus, now Hannah's here?" I look over at Hannah, who's carrying a gift basket. "No, take that shit right back."

"Shut up. It's not from me, so don't worry. It's from my mom. She thought you would like some of her baked goodies."

Ben gets ready to intercept when I storm across my living room. "Not a fucking chance. Give me that basket." I snatch it from Hannah, and she laughs. You'd have to be insane to turn down a bakery basket from Kip's mom.

"What are you doing? No drinking! How many times do I have to tell you?" Bridget comes out of nowhere and snags the beer out of my hand. "You can't drink on your medication."

I pout while the guys snicker. *Assholes.* "Well, I'm a man. I can drink whenever I want."

"What are you gonna do about it, Chasey-poo?" Ben teases.

I'm gonna punch him, for starters, because he knows I'm not going to do a goddamn thing. I'm absolutely whipped and in love. If Bridget Matthews told me to jump off the building, I'd do it while blowing her kisses. "Angel, give me back my beer."

"No."

Damn, that was stern.

"Fine, I'm just going to get another one." I turn my back

to all the laughing jerkoffs and head into the kitchen. Opening my fridge, I push around protein shakes and fruit. "Who the hell eats fruit—?"

"Hey."

I lift my head. Kip stands in the doorway of my kitchen, his hands shoved in his pockets.

"You hungry? I've got a lifetime supply of yogurt parfait bullshit. Not sure what kind of weird crap your sister has Levi eating. Probably gonna throw it out."

He shakes his head. "Nah, I'm good."

"Yeah, me too." I stand, shutting the door. "So, um... yeah. I know I screwed our friendship up—"

"I'm sorry."

His apology catches me off guard. It should be me asking for his forgiveness. "Man, no. I'm the—"

"Just...let me talk, okay? You should have told me."

"I know. I knew you—"

"Would be mad? Hell yeah, I would have been. She's my cousin. She's a good girl. She's been through so much. The last thing she needed was someone messing with her life." He takes a deep breath and walks closer. "But things with you have changed. You've been so against settling down, I never put two and two together. Missing guys' nights. This sudden pep in your step you never had before. I judged a situation I knew nothing about. Love can change a man. It takes a good girl to turn your life upside down in the best ways. I know that firsthand."

"I love her, man. I've never felt this way. It's fucking thrilling and scary. You called it like it is. She's too good for me. But I'm willing to fight tooth and nail to prove to her I can be worthy of her love."

We stare at each other until Kip takes in another deep breath and wipes his hand down his face. I almost don't catch it, but in the process, he wipes away a tear. "I thought you were going to die, man."

"Not a chance."

"The only thing I could think of is the last time we saw one another. A lifetime of friendship and in our last moment, I took a swing at you."

"Well, you took a swing at Levi too, and you two made it out alive. Still can't believe that guy—"

"Chase."

"Right, stale joke. If it helps, I swear to you, I won't hurt her. There's a likely chance she'll get sick of me and leave, but while I have her, I'm sure as hell going to cherish her. Every fucking second."

Kip walks up to me, placing his hand on my shoulder. "She's lucky to have you. We all are." I nod and grab at his back, bringing him in for a hug. I won't admit my eyes also fill with tears. I love Kip like a brother. "Thank you."

"For what?" We pull away.

"Accepting this."

"Oh, I'm only accepting it under the terms that if you hurt my cousin, I'm going to do more than punch you."

"I'll gladly take it."

We go in for another bro hug. This one with fewer tears.

"We should probably get back out there. They might think you're trying to finish the job that looney woman couldn't." Kipley frowns. "Sorry, bad joke. Let's go."

We head out together, feeling lighter for the first time in weeks. When we get into my living room, I cuss. "Seriously? You're here now too, Stacey?"

Bridget rolls her eyes at me. She knows why I'm pissed. I want to be alone with her so I can get reacquainted with her taut little body. Lick every inch of her and make her beg into the wee hours of the morning.

I also know she's going to say no because of the stupid doctor's orders.

Little does she know, I play dirty and had Levi grab a shit ton of icing and sprinkles.

Chapter
Thirty-One

Bridget

SINCE THE INCIDENT, ENTERING THE BROOKS' ESTATE DOESN'T get easier. Every inch triggers my anxiety. No matter how steady I keep my breathing, I still see him on the floor, covered in his own blood. I still see Anna's face and the terror in her eyes. Blood oozing from an evil woman's chest. Anna's tiny hands trembling. The blast of the gunshots. But none of it matters. Because she needs me.

I walk up to the entrance of the main house and knock. Alice is in the kitchen, and she hurries to open the door. "You know you don't need to knock. Just walk in."

"I know. Is Anna up and about?" I've been making it a priority to spend time with her every day. She's still not talking, and the guilt is almost debilitating. I spend hours with her, playing and doing all the talking, but she doesn't say a peep. Jonathon comforts me by saying it's normal. It's shock. She witnessed a lot. Has been through a lot. But I can't help but feel responsible.

"Yep. She's up in her room. She's been waiting for you."

"She has? Has she said that?"

Alice's smile falls. "No. Not yet. But I can tell. She loves you. You're really helping."

I doubt that. I wave at Alice and make my way upstairs to find Anna in her room playing with her favorite dolls.

"Hey, it's my favorite princess." She stops playing and looks up at me. Her smile is barely noticeable, but the fact that it's there at all gives me hope. "Whatcha doin'?"

She raises her doll, then places it back on the ground. If I thought too much into it, her placement is like it was that night. Two standing, one lying. My chest constricts. I walk in, sitting on my knees next to her. "You feel like talking today?"

She doesn't respond, just picks up another doll and brushes her hair.

"Anna, you know I promised you nothing would happen to you. What you did was very scary, but it was so very brave." She doesn't acknowledge my words, just continues to brush. "Anna, look at me. Please."

She does, but her eyes lack that innocence.

"Nothing bad is going to happen to you. No one is going to take you away, okay? I made you a promise. And I will always keep it."

She stares at me, her eyes dull. Suddenly, she jumps into my lap. Her movement startles me, and I almost fall backwards as I wrap my arms around her. Her little lips press to my ear, and I feel the warmth of her breath as she whispers, "It's just between us, right, Bridget?"

I freeze with her in my arms. Tears well up in my eyes. My arms tighten around her, and I inhale the scent of her strawberry shampoo. I hate myself for what I've done to her. Forcing her to hold on to this horrible secret. But I refuse to ruin her young life over it. Taking a shaky breath, I reply, "Just between us, I promise." I gently pull her away from me. "Thank you for saving us. You will always be my hero. My brave little princess. Always remember that."

She nods. "Does this mean you're staying?"

A question I've been asking myself since the incident. How can I leave Anna after what I've caused her? But how can I stay? I tuck a loose curl behind her ear. "I think it's best for you to heal right now. Your daddy has so many exciting plans for you. Everything is going to be okay."

Her slumped posture and distant frown tell me it's not. She has a long road ahead of her. I desperately want to ask her how she knew the code. How she knew exactly what was in her father's safe. But the damage is already done. And it won't change the past. And now she has a long road ahead of her bearing this dark secret.

"What do we have here?" We both look up at Jonathon, dressed surprisingly in a pair of jeans and a casual polo.

"I was just coming to visit my favorite little princess." Anna slowly climbs off my lap. Her demeanor changes, and she goes back to playing with her dolls.

"How's playtime, baby?" Jonathon asks his daughter, but she doesn't respond. My eyes crease with confusion. She just spoke… "Honey, I'm going to have a word with Miss Bridget, okay? Then we can go eat some dinner." Anna nods, not even looking his way.

My heart breaks for her. I pat her on the thigh and get up, following Jonathon into the hallway.

"Did she speak to you at all?"

I struggle with telling the truth or lying. Then Anna's words ring out in my mind. *Just between us, right?*

"No."

Disappointment shades his dark eyes. I think he hopes I'll be the one to get her to open up. "She needs time to heal. To understand. She's a smart, resilient little girl."

"That she is."

A moment passes, and the silence between us becomes too much. "Well, I'm going to go. I only have a small box in the guesthouse. I'm going to grab it and leave the key with Alice."

"You don't have to leave."

"I know. I don't want to leave Anna. I'll still be here for her. Visit as much as I can. But I think this is best."

Jonathon made it clear he still wished for me to stay as Anna's nanny, but I can't see myself ever feeling confident enough to protect her. I let them both down. Monsters are always lingering. I've already brought one to his front door. I won't do it again.

"We will miss you around here. And, please, don't be a stranger."

"I'll be here for Anna. So long as I'm welcome."

Jonathon nods. "What will you do now?"

The million-dollar question. My life has been such a whirlwind the past few years. I've felt a pain I never knew existed. I've lost and found again something I thought was gone forever. And now, with life and love giving me a second chance, I don't want to take advantage of it. "Not sure. Settle in with Chase. See where we go. I was thinking of applying to college." I offer him a parting smile and head down the stairs when Jonathon calls my name.

"I'll deposit your last paycheck by the end of the week. Take care of yourself."

"Thanks. You too."

Chapter
Thirty-Two

Chase

Three weeks later...

I LOOK AROUND MY PLACE, MENTALLY CHECKING OFF everything on my list. As I'm staring at the coffee table, pleased with my work, I hear the jiggling of the door. *Fuck, play it cool. You still have your stamina. You're a man. You have skill...*

The lock turns, and the door opens. Bridget walks in, her hair in a sexy little bun, wearing a long trench coat and carrying a bag of groceries. I hate that she went back to work at the library, but she says it helps keep her mind busy until she finds something else. When her head lifts and she takes in the apartment, I begin to sweat.

"What... What is this?"

"I just did some redecorating."

I love her suspicious eyes. I've been getting them a lot this past week. And they're warranted. I've tried to get her in bed in the cleverest ways. Damn shame she never gives in.

"I see that." She walks closer, putting the paper bag on the end table by the door. "Chase, we talked about—"

"I had my doctor's appointment today. I got clearance."

Her eyes pop. "You went without me?"

"I had to! You have a way of convincing the doctor I'm not healed enough. And he gives in because you have that look. I wanted to go, have him look at me, and tell me, man to man, without you giving him the *don't clear him* eyes."

"Chase—"

"He cleared me. He said you have to take it easy. No biting or whipping—"

"Chase!"

I step toward her. "Angel, I was shot—not neutered. *Fuck.* You know what hurts more than these bullet wounds? Feeling like you don't want me." That is *not* what I planned on admitting in my *fill the apartment with roses and candles because it's finally time for me to ravish my girl* mission.

She drops her purse on the couch and walks up to me. "Is that what you think? That I don't want you?"

"Fuck, I don't know. I'm not broken. But I can't go a second longer without being inside you. Marking every single part of your body. I'm starting to feel like you're friend-zoning me and this is just a sympathy arrangement."

Her hand lifts to my cheek, and she gently caresses it. I lean into her touch, groaning when she slaps me.

"*Jesus.* What was that for?"

"For being an idiot! You think I'm here because I feel bad I got you shot?"

I shrug. "I don't know? Maybe? Why won't you have sex with me?"

She rolls her eyes. Dammit, even in a serious moment, I love it. "Because I can't risk hurting you any more than I already have. I need to make sure you're okay. Do you know how bad it hurts me to see those scars? Every time I look at them, I'm reminded of that night. How I almost lost you." She lifts her hands and presses her palms against my pecs, slowly working them down my chest. "What happens if we have sex? It could be so explosive, you pop a stitch."

My cock jolts in my jeans. "You know damn well my stitches have dissolved."

"What happens if I ride you too hard? You know I get rough sometimes. I can easily ruin all the progress you've made."

A layer of sweat builds across my forehead. Maybe I'm not ready. Maybe I should have jerked off a few times so I don't perform like an inexperienced kid.

"I let you lick the icing off me, and because I love you, I allowed you to use the sprinkles, which you were too exhausted to finish—"

"That's not fair. I accidentally dumped *waaay* too many, and you were wearing the matching cherry bra and panties. I didn't stand a chance."

The little minx just rolls her shoulders. "Just saying. I don't think you're ready."

"I'm ready. I'm fucking ready. I even had the doc write me up a note in case you didn't believe me."

She steps back and examines the apartment, showing no emotion at the roses placed throughout the apartment. The candles that have about five more minutes until something catches on fire or my smoke alarm goes off. The television is playing *Twilight*—because I know that shit always gets her in the mood. But most importantly—

"Are…?" She bites her bottom lip, hiding her smirk. "Are you wearing a shirt with my face on it?"

I nod. *Have confidence.* "Ben's idea. Said it would seal the deal."

She shakes her head, offering me the tiniest grin. "And all this is for me? To get me to sleep with you?"

"Well, the *Twilight* is more for me."

"Hmmm…." Not sure if that is a good or bad hmmm. Maybe I should have bought her a purse. The candles are a bit overkill and—shit, I think I see a rose petal catching fire. "So then, I guess it's a good thing I dressed for the occasion."

She pulls at the straps of her long coat. It falls to the ground, and I practically come at the sight of her in a white lace bra and panties. "Jesus, did you go grocery shopping in that?" *I'll murder every person in that store.*

"Yes. I went there first. Then I got a call from your doctor. Good thing you made me your point of contact when you were nice and high off the pain meds. Since you keep trying to convince me you're fine, I had him call me with updates. He wanted me to hear for myself you'd been cleared."

"Wait—my doctor called *you?* That traitor."

"Are we going to dwell on that, or are we going to continue to discuss how you're recovered enough?" God, she looks like an angel. The most beautiful girl I've ever seen. My life starts and ends with her.

She bends down to grab the coat, and I immediately put a stop to that nonsense, and go to pick her up, but then smarten up, knowing I'm not healed enough. I snatch her jacket and toss it over the couch.

"What are you—"

"I'm taking control. Sort of." I snatch her hand and drag her toward the bedroom.

"Chase…" I feast off her beautiful laugh and pick up the pace.

"What we're *going* to discuss is how you'll need to call off this whole week because I plan on getting reacquainted with every single inch of your body."

"Just a week?"

"Month, year! Forever. I'll never be done with you."

Chapter
Thirty-Three

Bridget

Two months later...

"THANKS, SUSAN! I'LL SEE YOU TOMORROW!"

She waves back. "Same, and good luck!"

My belly does a double flip. I exit the library and run to Chase's monster truck. He's still on medical leave, so I get the luxury of being escorted to and from work. Not that I have a choice. My jealous boyfriend is too worried I'll fall in love with my Uber driver and never be seen again. That, and he's afraid I'll get kidnapped. My clingy man takes no chances of losing his angel. My eyes dance with humor at our daily argument.

"Are you kidding me? Have you watched the news? The statistics on beautiful women being kidnapped are rising."

I scoff at him. "Seriously? First off, when was the last time you watched the news? And second, I doubt I'm going to get kidnapped during my seven-minute ride."

"I watch nothing but the news while you're gone. And secondly, *you're the perfect candidate. Sexy and snarky. That angelic smile and sharp teeth."*

"Jesus, again? How many times are you going to bring that up? You told me to bite you."

"I also told you to call me Edward. You called me Jacob. It killed the mood for me."

"Whatever. Fine. I'll take your truck. Just hope I don't meet another bad boy truck lover. What if we end up talking truck stuff and fall in love over our trucks—?"

"I'm fucking driving you."

And now, like clockwork, my escort is waiting outside to drive me home every day. And just as expected, he always has something to prove. I open the passenger side door, but he shakes his head. "Sorry, riders sit in the backseat. Company policy."

"This again?" He doesn't even reply. He fiddles with the radio. I roll my eyes, shut the front door, and climb in the back seat.

"Same place?"

"Yep." I try not to engage in his little game. His way of proving Ubers aren't safe.

"Where you coming from?" *Here we go...*

"Oh, work. I'm a librarian. I just love reading books. Especially the naughty ones. When no one is looking, I find the dirtiest book in there and read the explicit parts to myself." I lean forward. "And sometimes...when no one is watching...I touch myself."

He swerves, and I snicker, leaning back in my seat.

"Well, that's inappropriate. What time of the day does that normally occur? I love to read and touch things."

He's so ridiculous.

"It happens *all* the time. I'm so worked up by the time I get off work, even this ride home is uncomfortable. I'm so swollen and wet from being turned on all day."

I watch him swallow through the rearview mirror. "Good thing you have a man at home to take care of that."

I press my index finger to the top of my chest, fondling the top button of my blouse. Popping it open, I run my finger between my breasts. "No, actually. I'm all alone."

He slams on his breaks, almost hitting the guy in front of him. "You're not fucking alone. You probably have a hunk at home. A stallion ready to tear you up and eat you 'til you scream."

I bite the inside of my cheek, fighting back my laughter. He's totally losing at his own game, and I love every second of it.

"I do, but he's too needy. I was hoping…maybe you could help me. There's this ache between my thighs…" I run my hand down past my navel to the top of my thigh, pushing my skirt up. "And it desperately needs to be soothed."

"Okay, knock it off."

"Knock what off? My fetish for Uber drivers? If you don't tell, I won't." I brush my fingers along my slit, my eyelids becoming heavy. I pull my finger out. "Oh, goodness, I'm so wet." I seal the deal with a moan, putting my finger to my lips.

Chase curses under his breath, and I fly to the right when he takes a sharp turn into an empty parking lot.

"Uh oh, is this where I get kidnapped, Mr. Uber driver?"

"No, this is where I punish you for being a bad Uber rider." He finds a secluded spot in the back of the lot and throws his truck in park. "Get up here."

"Wait—here?"

"Now, Angel." The way he says my name has my inner thighs soaked. I love it when he gets this way. Determined. Hungry. Obsessed.

Climbing through the seats and over the center console, I straddle his lap. He already has his zipper down and his thick cock hard and ready. He pushes up my skirt and growls when he realizes I'm not wearing any panties. "You went to fucking work with no panties on?" His glare is murderous. My thighs quiver.

"Well, you're the third Uber driver this week who's made

me do naughty things. I wanted to avoid another pair of ripped panties." His eyes darken with lust. "Oh boy, are you getting jealous of my other secret Uber lovers?" I try to stay in character and not laugh, but it's almost impossible. He's getting jealous of himself.

He digs his fingers into my thighs and raises my hips. "After this, you're no longer able to use our services." He brings my hips down, powering the depth of his cock inside me.

"Is that so?" I moan. "That's too bad. I'm quite enjoying —oh God," I moan as he raises me up and slams me back down.

"Screw Ubers. See? I told you. They do things like this." Up and down, he drives into me, fucking me hard and fast, filling me, showing me exactly who I belong to. "Say it. Say my name. Tell me who owns this pussy."

"Ub—shit! You. I belong to you," I pant, his long, thick cock working me to climax. Neither of us stand a chance. In unison, we both moan out our release.

"Are we done playing this game yet?" I say, catching my breath.

"So fucking done. You will never, ever take an Uber."

My jealous, amazing, insane man.

∼

"You hungry? We can order Chinese or from the Italian place you like."

I toss my purse on the couch as Chase disappears into the kitchen. The envelope sticking out of it has my nerves kicking back in. I brush my palms together, then wipe the building sweat off on my skirt. "Um…whatever you want."

He walks back out, holding a bottle of water. He looks me up and down, the corner of his eyes creasing. "Everything okay?"

"Yeah, fine." *Just come out and say it.* I chicken out and break eye contact. "What's on TV tonight?" I walk toward the couch, but he grabs my bicep.

"Angel, what is it?"

I open and close my mouth. *Just do it, Bridget. Rip off the Band-Aid.* I look up at him, and my cheeks instantly flush. I try to blink away the nervous tension, but the way his eyes darken only makes it worse.

"Okay, now you're starting to worry—"

"I did something…" *Okay, not the best way to start off.*

Chase's brow wrinkles. His gaze sears through me. Taking a deep breath, he drops my arm. "Okay…"

"It's not bad. It's…well, I did something, and I'm not sure how you're going to take it. If you'll be mad or—"

"Angel, spit it out. You're really starting to freak me out here."

Grabbing the envelope, I hand it to him.

"What is this?" His eyes narrow as he turns the envelope over, inspecting it.

"First, I have to tell you something." He takes in a deep breath, preparing. "I've been thinking about this for some time now. I wasn't sure it was what I wanted, but then I got this letter."

He looks up from the envelope, his eyes meeting mine, his jaw clenched. He's trying to brace for something bad. "What is this?"

I lick my lips. God, why am I sweating? "I…I…"

"Bridget—"

"I applied to college and got in." The desire to go to college was there, but I had no way of paying for it. It wasn't until I received my last check from Jonathon. He had deposited over a hundred thousand dollars into my account with a note. *Good luck in college.* I knew it was his way of thanking me.

Chase rears his head back in surprise. He grabs the back

of his neck, staring back down at the letter. "You applied to college. That's what you have to tell me?"

I didn't know how he would take it, but I also didn't expect him not to be happy for me. My shoulders slump. I bite the inside of my cheek to hide my disappointment. "Well...yeah. I think maybe it's time. I think I'm ready. I thought maybe you'd be happy for me. Whatever. It's no big deal." I go to snatch the letter out of his hands, but I'm wrapped up in his arms as he presses me to his chest.

"You have a horrible way of starting things. I was thinking the worst was about to come out of your mouth."

I make steady eye contact with him so he can see my truth. "You'll know when I'm about to tell you something bad. Or if I'm going to leave you. I won't just tell you. I'll do something way cooler and creative like burn all your stuff."

"I love it when you talk dirty to me."

He presses his lips to mine. "I'm proud of you baby. I think you're going to make a hot little college student..." He takes a second to consider his own words. "Any chance this is an online school?"

I chuckle, standing on my tippy toes to kiss him back.

"I have something I—"

I cut him off. "Wait...that's not all. Now, *don't* be mad." His smile falls. "I did something else. Please don't be mad, but I just thought..."

"Jesus, you're horrible at this shit. Spit it out."

"Open the letter."

He glances at me, confused. Tapping his fingers against the manilla envelope, he rips open the top and pulls out the thin stack of papers. I watch as he takes in each sentence. Slowly, he looks up at me. "You said forever. For me, that means us as a team. I know we've talked about it, and you said that ship had sailed, but I say it's just getting ready to board. You don't have to do it, but...I just thought..."

"An application?"

"It's the same college I got in to. It has a great pre-med program. I talked to Ben. I know I went behind your back, but he suggested it. I can take undergrad classes until I figure out what I want to do, and you can finish the two years you have left. We could do it together…"

Oh god, he looks like he's going to be sick. What have I done? I should have asked. He continues to stare at the pages, and I know I messed up.

"I'm sorry. I shouldn't have assumed. I love you for whoever you are and whatever you decide to do. This was silly—"

He drops the papers on the couch and walks off toward his bedroom. I cover my face with my hands to hide the sudden tears. I bite at my trembling lip, mad at myself. Drawing in a deep breath, I pull my hands away. To my surprise, Chase is back, standing in front of me.

"Open this."

"Wh—What?"

"Open it."

Confused, I open the white envelope and pull out the trifold piece of paper. I wipe at my eyes so I can see the words clearer. My lips part at the first sentence. I almost have to read the second sentence over again. I look up, my heart beating erratically. "You…"

"I had a talk with a beautiful girl once. She convinced me it's never too late to follow your dreams. It just took me some time to convince myself I could do it." He cups my cheek. "Angel, I want to be better for you. The man you come home to and respect. I want to provide for you and know you'll want for nothing."

"So, you…"

"I applied to go back to school. Not sure I have it in me to take eight years of schooling to become a doctor anymore, but this way, I can at least work towards becoming a general practitioner or something."

I shake my head. "But how? We applied to the same——"

"Ben, that bastard, played both sides."

"You talked to him about it?"

"He was the one who pushed me to this school. Makes sense why now. Told me it would be a great start for you as well. I have registration paperwork in the kitchen for you. In case you were ready."

Before I met Chase, I was drowning. In sorrow. Regret. I allowed a tragedy to rule my life. I took blame for something that was out of my control and vowed to live the rest of my days paying for those sins. I loved a boy, and because of that, he died. I fell so deep into darkness, I truly believed I didn't deserve to love again. To be loved. My heart was too shattered to ever be mended.

And then Chase came into my life. He was my savior. The road to hope and healing. He pulled me out of the darkness and showed me I deserve to live. To be loved. He brought warmth into my heart, and as it slowly mended, he allowed me to see that life does go on.

I once believed there was only one person in this world you would love. It's taken time to accept Jax's death, but Chase gave me a new perspective on love, and it stuck with me. Maybe everything does happen for a reason. Jax taught me how to love. To see beauty in the smallest things. To have faith. And he allowed me to find Chase.

I never planned on falling in love that night. I never imagined wanting to vow myself to another person for eternity as much as I do the man standing in front of me. He's my forever.

I throw myself in his arms and kiss him, telling him how much I need him, love him, admire him.

"I love you, Chase Steinberg. From your insane jealousy to your horribly cheesy one-liners."

"Hey!" He bites on my bottom lip. "They're not cheesy. And I will be insanely jealous until the day I'm old, my balls are saggy, and I can't even growl at other motherfuckers because I'll probably have no teeth. You, Angel, will always be mine."

"Boy, I love it when you talk dirty to me."

He chuckles against my lips. "Now, I'm going to take you to bed and ravage the hell out of you. Make sure you never have the urge to ride an Uber. Then I'll feed you. Whatever you want. We're going to be stuck living off cafeteria food soon. Dorm food sucks."

I laugh as he picks me up and carries me to the bedroom. "We're obviously not living in dorms. I was thinking maybe we can get a place to—"

"Shhh…I want to roleplay the shit out of this one. Now, you have to be very quiet. My roommate is studying, and I'm not allowed to have girls over past ten. No screaming, okay?"

Absolutely ridiculous.

Absolutely mine.

Epilogue

Bridget

One year later...

"ANOTHER ONE BITES THE DUST," BEN SAYS, AND EVERYONE raises their drink for a cheers, then pulls back to take deep swigs.

"Didn't think you were going to make it there for a second, buddy," Kip says, slapping Levi on the shoulder.

"Isn't it supposed to be the chicks who cry?" Ben chimes in.

"Fuck off. Wait 'til it's your turn and the most beautiful woman is walking toward you."

"I'm still shocked Kip let it happen. I mean, you had all this time to say something. Even the pastor gave you the opportunity to speak now or forever—"

"Shut up," the three jerk-offs say at once.

"Kidding!" I chuckle and raise my beer. "Clearly Kip's over it. I mean, he has to be since Hannah Banana's pregnant."

Kip's eyes glare over at Levi. "You knocked my sister up?"

Levi looks just as shocked, while Ben jabs me in the gut. I bust out laughing. "Fucking kidding. Man, you guys really need to lighten up."

Levi turns to me, firing back. "Okay there, lover boy. Why don't you answer us this one? How many times have you watched *The Notebook* this week?"

"Fuck off." *Twelve.*

"Yeah, right. Look at that face. I bet he can recite it word for word," Kip says.

I give him the *like you can't* look. If anyone is more whipped than me, it's him. "Whatever. Unlike all of you, I have a woman who allows me to be the man of the relationship. My balls are still intact, and I can—"

"Chase? Hey, can you run to the bar and get the bridesmaids a round of champagne?"

"Sure thing!" I call to Bridge. I turn back around to three wide-eyed assholes, all biting their tongues. "*The Notebook* is a wonderful fucking movie. If you truly understood the meaning of it, you would cry too." I walk off, ignoring the explosive laughter behind me because my girl asked me to do something.

"What the hell did you just say?" Levi yells to my back, confused. Clearly, he has no idea how powerful that movie is. I raise my middle finger to them as I make my way to the bar and order a round of champagne for a bunch of squealing bridesmaids. What my Angel wants, my Angel gets.

The bartender is just about done pouring the last one when someone behind me grabs my ass. I smile and turn. "I told you to wait—eh...hey, there Aunt Getty..."

"My, my...just like my William."

Kip's aunt stares up at me, licking her lips. I debate ditching the champagne and running.

"Aunt Getty, my mom is looking for you." Bridget walks up, looking flawless in her pale blue bridesmaid gown, accentuating her tits and her beautiful eyes. Her hair is in a fancy updo, and I can't stop thinking about taking it down the second we get to our hotel room. "You okay over here, handsome?"

"Yes, actually. I was realizing how attractive your Aunt Getty is. Life's too short to hold back, ya know?" Her smile wakes the big guy, and I have to shift myself so no one sees the chub through my dress pants.

"Sorry I ruined your plans. Guess you're stuck with me. But I do see Aunt Sidney eyeing you. Never say never."

I look over her shoulder and cringe. "You know she has a mustache, right?"

Bridge giggles and takes a glass of champagne off the tray. "She prefers the natural look. I could always stop shaving my—"

"I'd recommend not," I quickly spit out. "But I'll find that pussy no matter how bushy you go." If she continues to giggle like that, we're not going to make it through dinner. I barely noticed a wedding was going on while Levi and Hannah recited their vows. All I could do was stare at her. The way her eyes glistened. The softness of her painted pink lips. Her hands cupping over her heart. And all I could do was imagine the day I'd have her walking down that aisle in the purest of white, being the angel she is, vowing to be mine for eternity. Yeah, Levi may have cried like a baby, but I couldn't deny getting choked up.

"Well...shoot. And I just shaved a big ol' C in my crotch. Ya know, just in case I got lost and someone needed to know who I belonged to."

I grab her, pulling her into me. My arm locks around her tight tush, not caring which aunt or grandma sees. I catch her dad eyeing me and quickly let go. "There's no need to do that. I will not be leaving your sight, and tonight, when I search out that C, I'll make sure to spell out the rest with my teeth." Her flushed cheeks turn me on. I'm already apologizing in my head to Levi for not making it through dinner.

"Don't even think about it."

"About what?" I ask.

"You know what. I know that look."

"Honestly, this is my bored look." More like *I'm about to take her into the ladies' bathroom and do nasty things to her* look.

"Today isn't about you, Chase. Your needs can wait."

The need to drag you up to that altar and bind you to me forever can't. "Yeah, totally. Why would you think otherwise? If you're done drooling over me, I need to get back to the guys."

Stay strong. Look confident. Pretend you mean it.

Her slow, seductive smile breaks down every single manly part of me. I just want to pick her up and whisk her away. I open my mouth to ask if I can go with her to hang out with the girls just to stay close to her.

"Yeah, I'm done."

"Okay. Well…enjoy. I've got guys—guys' time…yeah." I turn to walk away with some of my balls intact when she calls my name.

"After dinner, though. It's fair game. I have no panties under this, and I can't imagine how much longer it will be until my excitement starts showing through my dress."

～

Weddings are stupid.

When I get married, I'm skipping the dinner portion. People can eat after. The second the server takes away our plates, I go to grab for Bridget, but she's already being hauled off by Hannah. Since it's rude to tackle the bride, I let it go.

I find the guys at the bar taking shots.

"Look who it is, weeping Romeo. The sad, lovesick little boy look is super cute on you." The imprint of my fist is going to look even better on Ben if he doesn't shut the hell up.

Levi slaps Ben on the shoulder. "Oh, leave him alone. It's about time he found his own ball and chain."

"Who has a ball and chain?" I ask like I don't already know.

Ben laughs so loud, it draws attention. "You kidding me? We thought Kip had it bad. Even Levi. That dude literally had Cupid's arrows sticking out of his ass. But you...you've got it bad. I mean, you practically have hearts shooting from your eyes *and* your balls—oh wait...are your balls heart shaped now? Dude, show us—"

I slap his hand away as he tries to grab my nuts. "Fuck you guys. Unlike Benny here, who probably doesn't have balls since they fell off from some venereal disease, my girl likes my balls."

"Oh, she likes your balls—"

"Hey, cool it, that's my cousin," Kip slurs, slapping Ben in the chest.

"She doesn't need to see my balls hanging from her rear-view mirror like an object to know she has me. We get each other. We know each other. It's a mutual...obsession." Fuck. I give up. I throw my hands up as they laugh and enjoy my pain.

Levi slaps me on the back. "I'm happy for you, man. You deserve this."

"What? The relationship or eating crow?"

Levi laughs. "Both. But mainly Bridge. There was a time, long, long ago, when I didn't know how it felt to be so consumed by someone. I didn't get what Kip saw. Not in Stacey, but the whole settling down thing. Then, one day, someone changed my mind." I watch him as he peers over at Hannah, dancing like an idiot with her friends. "It's not love that does you in...it's the little things. The way they snort when they laugh. How they bite their nails. How they sigh in deep thought..." He trails off as he watches his wife, and I slowly get it.

It's the little things about a person that make you the happiest—the things you never knew you needed. Their smell.

261

The snarky looks and stealing the covers in the middle of the night. The kisses and affection. Even the way she dances while she's naked after a shower, thinking no one is watching...

"Yeah, great speech. I...uh...I gotta go..."

I leave Levi standing there and storm onto the dancefloor. "Excuse me, ladies. I need to steal this one." Bridget gives me the eye, but I don't care. There's no way she's not coming with me.

"Chase, the reception is barely over."

"It's fine." I continue to drag her through the crowd until I find an exit and haul us outside onto the terrace.

"Chase, we can't do it out——"

I turn and stare her down. Her playful smile falls at my expression. "What's wrong?"

"What's fucking wrong is I've spent this entire wedding watching my best friend get married."

Her lips tip up. "Yeah, kind of the purpose of a wedding."

"Yeah, whatever. I've watched it, and all I could think the whole time was us being up there."

Her eyes grow wide. "What?"

"All the things they said. The way they both looked at one another. It felt like..."

"Like what?" she asks.

"They didn't even look comparable to how I look at you. And hopefully how you look at me. And if that's how *they* look, how would *we* look up there?"

Her intake of breath scares me. But for some damn reason, I can't shut up. "I want to see us there. I want to say sappy shit to you to make you cry. Well...you'd probably make me cry—but fuck..." I start to panic.

Bridge grabs my waist and pulls me to her. "Hey..." her voice sooths me. "I think weddings are a beautiful way to let others see how happy someone is, but they don't define their true happiness or love. I think that inside, two people know what they stand for."

"And what do we stand for?"

"Forever. We stand for forever."

Don't fucking cry. Remember, you have a set of balls she actually enjoys.

I breathe in slowly, pulling myself together. It felt like eons ago when I was a complete idiot and didn't have someone so perfect in my life. How crazy is it the way love truly changes a person? I hate to think of my past. The person I was. I can't take it back, but going forward, I'm a one woman show.

"Listen, you don't have to say all this sappy stuff just to get me to dance with you. All you had to do was ask."

Fuck, that smile.

"My bad. How about we save this conversation for another time and you whisk me onto the dance floor?"

I dip down, placing my lips against hers. The most heavenly place in the world. "Lead the way, Angel."

∿

"Damn, I'm a lucky man." Levi, smiling like an idiot, stares at Hannah on the dance floor. It seems like yesterday Hannah was running around with her messy pigtails, annoying the shit out of us while we tried to watch sports. Now, she's a grown woman, making my best friend the happiest guy.

"I'm happy for you, man." I slap him on the shoulder. "Good to see Kip finally okay with you two. Therefore, so am I."

Levi throws his head back and bellows out a laugh. "Phew. I was worried, since I just married her and all..."

I shrug, taking a swig of my beer. "What can I say? I'm a reformed man and in love. I seem to have a different view on things."

Levi pats me on the shoulder, humor in his tone. "Good for you, man. You sure as hell have come a long way. You know, I should actually be thanking you for today."

"Why?"

"If I remember correctly, it was your idea to set me up with a random in the supply closet at Kip's wedding—"

"What are you girls talking about?" Ben walks up.

"When Chase set me up in the closet," Levi replies.

Ben busts out laughing. "Rebecca was so pissed. Didn't she slap you?"

"Hell yeah. But that was the least of my worries." There he goes again, giving his wife googly eyes. Back when I was a shitty guy, I tried setting Levi up with one of Kip's wife's bridesmaids at their wedding. He'd been going through a nasty break up, and I just wanted to do my man right. Little did I know, Kip's little sister tricked us all and ended up in the closet that night instead.

"Well, it all worked out. I mean, maybe not for Rebecca—"

"What are you all laughing about?" Kip walks up.

"Your wedding when Levi—"

Levi cuts Ben off. "When I drank too much and barfed in one of the center pieces."

"Gross, man. You know, Stacey spent a lot of time picking those out."

"And I spent a lot of time vomiting in one."

The DJ switches up the song, and the girls go wild, shaking their asses to the music. Man, how times have changed. We've all come a long way. Well...except for Ben who, like the old me, refuses to settle down. And who also looks plastered.

"Dude, who's *that* chick?"

We all look to where he's pointing.

Ben's eyes light up, and he takes a step forward. Levi presses his hand across his chest. "Uh...not a good idea, man."

"Why not? She looks like a *great* idea to me."

"Seriously, dude. Not a good idea," Kip agrees.

Ben pushes Levi's hand away. "Fuck it, I'm goin' in." He

walks off, swaying through the crowd.

"You think he knows who that is?" Kip asks.

I shrug and drink my beer. "Too late. Let him figure it out."

Hannah walks up, and Levi snakes her into his arms. "There's my beautiful bride." He dips and kisses her nose.

"And there's my drunk groom."

"You say drunk, I say happy." Hannah snickers then looks at the rest of us. "What are you all staring at?" She turns to follow our gaze. "Oh no, what is he doing? He knows who that is, right?"

We shrug.

"He's not making it out alive tonight," Hannah says, looking worried for him.

"He's a big boy. Maybe it's time they play nice and make up."

Hannah doesn't look convinced, and to be honest, neither am I. But instead of pulling my best friend out of the crossfire, I watch as an angel steps off the dance floor and falls into my arms.

"What's that cheesy look for?" she asks, like she doesn't know.

"Just looking at the most beautiful girl in the room, wondering if she's an angel or a devil."

Her flushed cheeks from dancing form into the sexiest grin. "Oh, I'm an angel all right. But later, when it's dark and we're all alone, I have some very, very *bad* things I plan on doing. So, one might say, I'm a bit of both."

Hell with this.

I pick her up and throw her over my shoulder, startling everyone around us. "Great wedding. Congrats to the lovely couple. We have to leave now."

"Chase." Bridget laughs while hanging upside down over my shoulder.

"Don't come looking for us!" I wave everyone off and

storm away. Then I spank her tight little ass. "Feel like a little role playing tonight, Angel?" I ask, carrying her out of the banquet hall toward the elevator leading to our hotel room.

"Oh, goodie, what is it tonight? I was a fan of the naughty college student." I spank her ass again, because damn, so was I.

"Even better." We ride the elevator up with her still over my shoulder. An elderly couple side-eyes us the whole way up. I don't put her down until we're in our room and I'm kicking the door shut behind me.

"Oh boy, you look serious. This must be a good one." I walk toward her. I've done a lot of shit in my life, but I've never felt so confident and scared shitless at the same time.

"That depends," I say, stopping before her.

"On what?" Her voice is laced with lust.

"On how you feel about playing my fiancée." I fish for the small box that's been burning a hole in my pocket all night and bend down on one knee.

The End

Want more of Chase and Bridget? Signed up for my newsletter and get an exclusive bonus scene! Download Here.

About the
Author

Best-selling author, J.D. Hollyfield is a creative designer by day and superhero by night. When she's not cooking, event planning, or spending time with her family, she's relaxing with her nose stuck in a book. With her love for romance, and her head full of book boyfriends, she was inspired to test her creative abilities and bring her own stories to life. Living in the Midwest, she's currently at work on blowing the minds of readers, with the additions of her new books and series, along with her charm, humor and HEA's.

J.D. Hollyfield dabbles in all genres, from romantic comedy, contemporary romance, historical romance, paranormal romance, fantasy and erotica! Want to know more! Follow her on all platforms!
Keep up to date on all things J.D. Hollyfield

More from
J.D. Hollyfield

Dirty Little Secret Duet
Bad Daddy
Sweet Little Lies

Love Not Included Series
Life in a Rut, Love not Included
Life Next Door
My So Called Life
Life as We Know It

Standalones
Faking It
Love Broken
Sundays are for Hangovers
Conheartists
Lake Redstone
Junkie
Celebrity Dirt
Chicks, Man
Holiday Ever After

Paranormal/Fantasy
Sinful Instincts
Unlocking Adeline

#HotCom Series
Passing Peter Parker
Creed's Expectations
Exquisite Taste

2 Lovers Series
Text 2 Lovers
Hate 2 Lovers
Thieves 2 Lovers

Four Father Series
Blackstone

Four Sons Series
Hayden

Elite Seven Series
Pride

Visit My Website To Download

Acknowledgments

To myself. It's not easy having to drink all the wine in the world and sit in front of a computer writing your heart out, drinking your liver off and crying like a buffoon because part of the job is being one with your characters. You truly are amazing and probably the prettiest person in all the land. Keep doing what you're doing.

Second most important, thanks for *nothing* to my toddler who made this book take forever to finish because he's so damn needy. Momma loves you.

Thanks to all my eyes and ears. Having a squad who has your back is the utmost importance when creating a masterpiece. From betas, to proofers, to PA's to my dog, Jackson, who just gets me when I don't get myself, thank you. This success is not a solo mission. It comes with an entourage of awesome people who got my back. So, first and most important, shout out to my homegirl Gina Behrends—you are literally the reason I know what day it is, and for that I love you. Thank you for being the best wingman anyone could ever ask for. To Jenny Hanson, Molly Wittman, Cindy Camp, Brandi Zelenka, Jennifer Kreinbring, Kristi Webster and anyone who I may have forgotten! I appreciate you all!

Thank you to Monica Black at Word Nerd Editing for helping bring this story to where it needed to be.

A warm thank you to Molly at Novel Mechanic for having superb insight.

Thank you All By Designs for creating my amazing cover. A cover is the first representation of a story and she nailed it.

Thank you to Michelle Lancaster and your be ltiful eye for photography, as well as Andy Murray who is a beautiful human.

Thank you to my awesome reader group, Club JD. All your constant support for what I do warms my heart. I appreciate all the time you take in helping my stories come to life within this community.

Big thanks to Wildfire Marketing for help push this novel.

And most importantly every single reader and blogger!

THANK YOU for all that you do. For supporting me, reading my stories, spreading the word. It's because of you that I get to continue in this business. And for that I am forever grateful.

Cheers. This big glass of wine is for you.